ADDLANDS

ADDLANDS

A Novel

Tom Bullough

THE DIAL PRESS · New York

Published in the United States by The Dial Press, an imprint of Random House, a division of Penguin Random House LLC, New York.

THE DIAL PRESS and the HOUSE colophon are registered trademarks of Penguin Random House LLC.

Originally published in the United Kingdom by Granta Books, London.

LIBRARY OF CONGRESS CATALOGING-IN-PUBLICATION DATA
Bullough, Tom, author.
Addlands: a novel/Tom Bullough.
pages; cm
ISBN 978-0-8129-9872-6
ebook ISBN 978-0-8129-9873-3
1. Family secrets—Fiction. 2. Domestic fiction. I. Title.
PR6102.U47A63 2016
823'.92—dc23   2015029000

Printed in the United States of America on acid-free paper

randomhousebooks.com

2 4 6 8 9 7 5 3 1

FIRST U.S. EDITION

Book design by Simon M. Sullivan

For Jenny and Will

"**Addlands** (i.e., headlands):
the border of plough land which is
ploughed last of all."

———

W. H. HOWSE, *Radnorshire*

ADDLANDS

1941

B Y FOUR O'CLOCK, when Idris was devouring his tea, perched between the tall, spoked wheels of the whilcar, the fence no longer straggled around Llanbedr Hill but cut out almost to the heather. Its wires whistled in the searching wind. He appraised the bent grass, the sheep's fescue and deep red fern of his new-claimed ground. He checked for rocks with his quick, black eyes, then, tossing a scrap of cake to the dogs, lowered himself back onto his smarting feet, warming his hands inside his old tweed coat before he gripped the shafts of the Ransome and manhandled it over to the working horse, which was tethered to the first post he had sunk.

"Aw!" he called. "Aw whoop! Aw whoop!"

Buster was a contrary animal. To catch him in the mornings took guile and diligence—hiding the harness, proffering bread or threatening him with Albert's bicycle, which always filled him with a paralysing terror. But a horse was a horse: the highest of all animals, whatever the virtues of the sheepdog. Once Buster was hackled he would nettle to his work, and although Idris held the jo-lines and the handles of the plough, he guided him with his words alone—his voice shrill over the clatter of the tack. Short, round-shouldered, he toiled behind him up the shallow slope, one foot in the reen, the other in the crumpled fern. He watched the mountains emerge from the red-green hilltop, snow in the gullies of their long black body like a skeleton exposed. He paused at his former boundary with the common land to hurl a few stones out of the way, but in time he reached the addlands by the green lane to Painscastle and lumped the plough round to face the wind, the valley and the birds already diving and arguing on the scar he had left in the hillside.

"That's him, Buster! That's a boy!"

On occasion, ploughing, Idris had counted thirteen different species of bird in his field. Even now there were seacrows, and starlings, and lapwings, and rooks from the trees at the church. How anybody could think this work was lonely was more than he could understand. And then there was the pleasure of the ploughing itself—of the line, of the furrow falling clean and firm so the seed would sit in the ridge. The War Ag paid every farmer in the country for ploughing up grazing, for putting down crops, but others left grass between their furrows; others still had refused to comply at all and found themselves thrown off their land. Compulsory war work: that was what it meant. Idris, he would do his bit of usurping the common, same as the next man, but he found his defiance in precision, in a tidy job, and if his neighbours took it for acquiescence, well, there it was.

The plough stopped dead in the black, peaty soil. It threw itself forwards so that the handles kicked out hard as a bullock, and Idris caught such a blow to the chest that it was only by grabbing the plain wire fence that he was able to keep his feet. He gasped and choked on the airless wind. His long, pale face turned dark, almost scarlet. In the naked pain it was as if he had been gassed, as if his lungs were blistering all over again.

The sun was falling now, between Mynydd Troed and the far-away plume of the Beacons. Beneath the colouring clouds Idris stood propped against the nearest fence post, coughing, wheezing, wiping the tears from his face. There were ravens in the larches round the cottage at the Island, wethers out for Llyn y March Pool. The sunlight, in places, revealed old copps and reens: the work of the Denes, so his grandfather Idris had told him.

It took all of the strength in his uninjured arm for Idris to push himself upright, then to hoist the plough handles level with his shoulders to allow the horse to pull it clear. The point of the share was snapped off clean. With his hand he tore at the rhizomes of the fern and peeled back the grass from a flat-faced stone a foot in the width and some six inches deep, which he tried at first to lift himself. He tunnelled beneath it, throwing up earth, but even with his boot he could not work it loose, so he trudged across the bank to the whilcar, fetched the chain and bound it round the stone—looping the hook end back through the tee head on the plough.

"Easy, boy," Idris murmured. "Easy now . . ."

He led the horse slowly down the slope, the Ransome dragging uselessly as the long chain jangled along with the brasses, rose with the share and came tight. The birds lapped back down their single furrow. Buster snorted, shaking his head as if bothered by flies. The muscles showed in his thick white coat. He dug up the soil with one feathered hoof, and with another, and then, with a sucking of mud and a tearing of roots, the skin of the hill at last gave way. The stone reared into the evening light: a slab of darkness, cut, not formed, taller than Idris by a head or more—its long shadow lying coldly on the hilltop for a moment before it fell.

AT THE TABLE in the kitchen the white jug fell from Etty's fingers to shatter on the flagstones: an ink spot of water in the last red light from the east-facing window. A moan broke unbidden from the back of her throat and grew into a lowing, like a beast. Her long eyes clenched, her wide lips trembling, she sank until her face was almost in the basin and her nostrils flooded with the reek of yeast. Pain encircled her back and her belly like a noose. An urge came upon her simply to run—even in this sack of a dress, with nowhere to go and the night coming on—but her body held her as completely as the house. The clocks passed the time across the larder door. Somebody was hurrying down the boards of the landing. She looked again into the fist-shaped valleys and the lakes in the dough, which spilled and shimmered as she tried to stand.

"Mam," Etty managed, then with growing panic, "Mam!"

BY THE TIME that Idris had packed up his tools and lowered the long stone onto the whilcar, the first of the nightly searchlights was scouring the sky above the mountains in the south. It trailed through the cobweb clouds, pointed out Venus, found the first new moon of the New Year high over the Twmpa: a dry moon, longer at the bottom than the top, on account of its holding in the water. Idris removed his old felt hat, joined his hands, bowed to the moon and made a wish. This done, he opened the gate he had hung that morning and—with a second searchlight now sparring with the first, patrolling a land in which he could see not one fire, not one window or headlamp—he allowed Buster to make his way home.

> *There's a long, long trail a-winding*
> *Into the land of my dreams,*
> *Where the nightingales are singing*
> *And a white moon beams.*

Bumping and slithering, the whilcar followed the track back down towards the farm, its iron snout digging up the wet ground, taking the weight from the half-seen horse. Idris sat on the head of the stone, his boots among the unused posts and wire, his bad arm tucked across his aching ribs. He sang along to the wind in the trees: the larches at the Island, the hawthorns on the common and the beeches on the bank above Llangodee, where the dogs were yawling into the darkness. He could have told any place in this valley simply by its sounds, by the movement of the air.

> *There's a long, long night of waiting*
> *Until my dreams all come true;*
> *Till the day when I'll be going down*
> *That long, long trail with you.*

On the near side of the brook he slipped to the ground and, with the moon and the searchlights appearing once more from the hill behind him, led the horse through the ford and into the Bottom Field. In the thin, shifting light, he saw the first signs of a glat in the hedge, a fresh mole tump, a ewe he'd known as Bessie as a lamb, which was rubbing on a gatepost and would need to be checked for the scab. He passed the creatures gathered round the hay cratch and climbed towards the Banky Piece, where the barn for the Funnon rose above him, loud with cattle, the wind on the roof and in the surrounding trees.

The stable lamp flared then sank into a glow as the stocking fell back over the flame. Idris had to lift it just to make out the rabbits hanging in braces, their big shadows stirring on the deep barn walls, the bantams roosting on the fat white beams. In the yard the sheepdogs were wagging and whining for attention. The pig he had spared the previous month returned his look from the door of the sty, while the cattle in the beast-house shouted their hunger and the door of the stable swung and creaked—the cob gone out of his bay.

"Drat that boy . . ." Idris started.

He stood for a moment in the stars in the puddles, beneath the tall and blinded house, then, hawking, spitting, he went to fill a bucket in the stone-lined flem, which ran along the top edge of the yard. He washed the feathering of Buster's legs, unhackled the ropes and rose his supper of swedes and oat straw. He took the hay knife down from its peg, but at the first sound of a motorcycle he returned outside to peer down the track at three lines of light, which came blinking out of Turley Wood, throwing shapes like ghosts onto the trees and the hedgerows.

"Good evening, Mr. Hamer," called the midwife, dismounting at the bridge. She stopped the spluttering engine and took her bag from the pannier. "What's news?"

"Well . . . Well, Mrs. Prosser." Idris was looking some inches to her left. "Well, she were heavy on foot this morning."

"You hanna seen her, then?"

"No no. I've only come back but just."

The midwife hesitated, perhaps out of pity. "Oh!" she said. "There was a bomb fell at Boughrood last night. Did you hear?"

"Oh," he said. "Well!"

"Aiming for the railway bridge, they reckon. Made a heck of a hole in the Dderw!"

"Oh," Idris repeated, as if this woman were a stranger, as if they had not sat within ten yards of one another every Sunday for the past twenty years. He turned his eyes another inch into the darkness and held up the lamp to light the old wooden bridge that led across the flem to the house. "I had best fodder the beasts, I had. Please to go on in, Mrs. Prosser."

ALONE, AS HE always had been, Idris sat in his old pine chair beside the fire in the kitchen. With stiffened fingers he peeled back the hems of his corduroy trousers, fought with his laces and stood his boots together on the hob, their raised toes facing out into the room. He smelt the stink of his stockings join the smells of the oil lamp, the stewpot in the oven, the birch logs drying on the nook. He scratched his chilblains, took a swig of tea, stretched out his legs and turned his paper to the light.

"You are asked to plough more," he read. "Brecon Motors, Ltd., are dealers for David Brown Tractors and ploughs."

"Let the stars guide you during 1941."

"If you're feeling all in after a hard day's work **hop** into a LIFEBUOY TOILET SOAP BATH—it'll soon put new life into you."

From the ceiling came another terrible scream.

"**Rhyscog.** Mr. Philip Griffiths, Pant Farm, officiated at the

Methodist Church here on Sunday. Mrs. Joyce Prosser was organist, and Mr. Idris Hamer, Funnon Farm, was precentor."

Idris dropped the paper and folded over his knees, one hand working in the island of hair that remained on the top of his head. He breathed in gasps, groaning to muffle the sounds from the bedroom—the cries, the footsteps, the urgent women's voices—and, by the case clocks that now stood either side of the larder door, some minutes passed before he raised his eyes again to the failing fire and took another birch log from the stack. He sat with his hands clasped at his chin and watched the flames revive on the log's paper skin, sending flurries of light across the embossed roses on the door of the oven, the underside of the mantelshelf, the mistletoe pinned to the black beam above him. He watched them find the splinters left by the teeth of his crosscut saw, and soon both ends of the log were engulfed, and then the log was the fire and Idris felt a flush of heat among the grizzling stubble and the vertical lines of his face.

"O Lord," he said, quietly. "O Lord, give me patience to bear it and all the rest I will leave in Thy hands."

IN THE NIGHT the pain began to shift, to turn, to find its direction. Its colours deepened in Etty's eyelids, became the blues and violets of some ungodly flower. As if in prayer, she knelt beside the bed, and when the pain came upon her she buried her face in its old feather mattress and barely noticed the shrieks that burst from her lips. The room was thick with a faecal stink. She was naked from the waist. Someone was mopping her, unthinkably, talking in a tight, calm voice. In those moments when she recovered her mind she made weak efforts to tug down her dress, but then again the pain returned, her thoughts dissolved in its burning tide and she knew no more than her mother's hand, which she held with her entire strength.

ETTY LAY WITH her shoulders on the pillows and her head against the heavy oak bedhead. In spite of the pain she dozed, drifted, woke only distantly when her mother took the blind from the tall sash window and the morning effaced the night-time shadows, exposed the faded red of the curtains and the pink and yellow flowers of the wallpaper.

In the kitchen the grandfather clocks chimed sixteen times. In the yard the midwife greeted Albert the labourer, who called an instruction to the farm boy. There was the kick and roar of a motorbike. Etty waited for the breakfast train to come whistling and rumbling up the embankment from Llanstephan Halt, then heard the geese and remembered that she no longer lived at Erwood Station, that there was no railway, no road, no shop, no St. John's Ambulance with its three other nurses and its wide doors open to the world. She moaned in her throat and woke up the baby, which began at once to search for her nipple and suckled again with such terrible strength that she could only think of thunder or of the white-tipped Wye in its full winter spate.

"Keep him down, love," said Molly, her mother. "That's it. Head up, see?"

Etty felt the hot tears on her round, girl's cheeks. She lifted her head an inch from the bedhead and looked past the red hair damp and scattered on her shoulders to her swollen breasts, and still she could not believe this furious creature in his towelling cocoon—his wild black hair, his puckered purple face, the two little teeth in his bottom gum, which had tinted dark the milk around his lips.

On the bedside chair, Molly smiled and murmured meaninglessly, and when the baby relented and fell back to sleep she lifted him carefully into her arms. As Molly stood, Etty felt the breath grow tight in her chest. She watched her mother cross the worn oak floorboards, her head bent, her elbows appearing from the fringe of her shawl. She saw her in the three angled mirrors of the dressing table that they had brought with them in the lorry in the summer—her vein-tangled hands, her dark hair protruding from her crimson headscarf—and when she reached the fireplace at the end of the room Etty felt that, if her baby went another inch further, she might be pulled apart.

She looked away quickly to the window and the last, lost reaches of this cleft-like valley: this unkind farm pushed back into the open hills. In the left of the frame were the bare, rook-flapping sycamores of the abandoned church, which sat not fifty yards from the house, at the top end of the yard. Above the stone-tiled roof of the barn a crowd of fieldfares rose from Quebec Field with glimmering wings, grew, contracted and settled in the Panneys. Above them, on Llanbedr Hill, a few ragged hawthorns and the bare, grey larches at the Island stood exposed by the flaming sky and, as she watched, she saw first a dog, then the horse and the whilcar led by her husband: a hunched little figure in an old tweed coat, plodding, climbing the slanting track onto the common. He crossed the lane to Painscastle and stopped in the bracken of his newly fenced field. He turned, legs parted, a hand to his eyes as if surveying his kingdom. But then the arch of the sun broke free of the hilltop and he was lost to the light of a new day.

1947

IT HAD ONCE come as a surprise to Etty to discover that her husband could sing. Nothing but the shrill of his speaking voice would have suggested to her that he was a tenor who had, as a young man, performed the solo from "Sound the Alarm" at county concerts—and the high *A* too, if Nancy Llanedw were to be believed. In Etty's experience, Idris sang hymns and hymns alone. There was rarely a journey when he would not embark on "O'er Those Gloomy Hills of Darkness" or "There Is a Fountain Filled with Blood," and as they drove through the furious night, although she felt no exultation whatsoever, still she found that she was singing herself—her own voice clear and precise, rising into the harmonies. She sat in the trap beneath the heavy blanket, peering past the lantern at the sniping snow, while Oliver huddled under her arm, on the slight, firm bulge of her belly.

Swift to its close ebbs out life's little day;
Earth's joys grow dim; its glories pass away;

Change and decay in all around I see;
O Thou who changest not, abide with me.

The two tall windows of the Methodist Chapel looked blackly down into the lane. In its stable, others who had been at the public meeting were hackling their own traps, eyeing the weather, starting for home. Shadows skitted from their Tilley lamps. Faintly, out towards Rhosei Cottage, Etty could make out the tractor for Walter Cwmpiban—his family crammed in the box on the back, his headlamps blazing from the snow-heavy hedgerows. They followed his tyre tracks left at the crossroads, into the narrowing valley.

Here was the Pant, where Philip had arrived already and raised a hand as he humped a bucket to the beast-house. Here, half a mile further on, was the track that led to Cwmpiban: the last of the houses before their own, the lights of the tractor showing on its gable wall. Idris reached the end of a hymn; he did not begin another. At Cwmberllan Ford he flicked the reins and the three of them leant to put their weight on the shafts, climbing laboriously through Turley Wood, up the pitch and into the yard, where the ducks were circling their space in the frozen pond. The wheels lurched on the hidden ruts. They had barely stopped before Oliver freed himself and sat, almost quivering, on the edge of the soft, plush seat.

"All right, lad," said Idris. "Down you get."

"How are you, Nip?" The dogs came swarming round the boy, tails up, ears down, yawling with excitement. "Hello, Towser! Blackie, did you miss me?"

Albert was ready with his curry-comb in the stable. Taking the bridle, he spoke to Reuben like a long-lost friend and the cob himself grew so calm in his presence that he seemed not to notice his work on the straps. In the light that spilled from the stable door, Etty led her son and his phalanx of dogs across the sloping yard to the snow-drowned flem, which Oliver insisted on jumping, since there was, he said, a troll beneath the bridge. They kicked their boots against the step and tramped into the kitchen, where Molly looked up from her scratch-patterned spectacles—pulling her needle clear of the pullover her grandson had cagged on a bramble by the spring.

She had thought it better for all of them if she remained behind.

"He got his way, I suppose?" she asked.

Etty nodded, avoiding her eye. She hung their hats and coats from the mantelpiece, swept up the snow and held her hands to the long flames surging up the flue.

"It shan't catch on," Etty said. "That's what they reckon."

"I cannot say I am surprised."

"The man from the Electric Board was there, though goodness knows how he aims to get home. There's a queue across the entire country, that's what he says. Every village gets its chance, and them as votes against, back they go right down to the bottom. It defeats me. Really. Ten more years we could be waiting now—"

"Mam?"

"Oliver, I'm talking."

"But I'm hungry!"

"How much cake did you eat just now?"

"You binna sinking, boy," Idris told him, arriving from the hall in a gasp of freezing air.

Oliver vanished behind the brown chenille tablecloth.

"So much for that, then, is it, Mr. Hamer?" Molly asked.

Idris grunted, arranged the long hairs back across his head

and dusted the snow from the lapels of his suit. Checking his clock, which had almost reached nine, he crossed the flagstones to the windowsill—twisting the knob on the grand wooden wireless.

"Consarn it!" he muttered. "I only changed them batteries Monday."

"Well," said Molly. "There's one problem we might have saved ourselves, anyway."

Through the keening wind in the open chimney, the sound of the Home Service rose momentarily. Beneath the table, Oliver made puffing noises for the wooden train he had been sent for Christmas by his grandfather. Etty looked from her husband's back to her mother in her chair beneath the oil lamp, then turned quickly back to the fireplace, testing the weight of the water in the kettle, the chill draught tugging at her hair.

"Now look you here, Mrs. Evans," said Idris. "I has enough people saying how to run my farm. I takes it off the Ministry and I takes it off the taxman, but I's blasted if I shall take it off you. If you has a hundred pound to go wasting on your precious electric, well, that is something different, that is a conversation. But while the money is mine then I shall be making the decisions in this house, and if you dunna like it you can just take your home in your pocket and get yourself back to your husband."

IT WAS RARELY, in the darkness, a tender kind of business— even now that Etty had at last fallen pregnant. Idris had kissed her on occasion, for the scant congregation at their wedding at the chapel, in the weeks and months after she had first come to the Funnon, but more in the way that the boys had kissed her back in Erwood—suddenly, artlessly, as if searching for a way forwards. She could be sitting at her dressing table, dabbing at her eye-shadow or wiping off her lipstick, when she would find him beside her with his coarse, grey stubble, his breath coming sour and urgent.

It had often been surprise as much as revulsion that had made her turn away.

In the end, inevitably, he had settled on an approach that owed less to the embrace between Edmund Lowe and Rose Hobart in *Wolf of New York,* which she had coaxed him into watching at the pictures one market day in Builth Wells, than to the tiling over at the Hergest: the annual breeding of the valley's mares. It was not unkind or, these days, particularly uncomfortable, but as he tugged up her nightdress with his leather-hard hands, as their bellies pressed together and his pelvis bit into the skin of her thighs, it might even have been useful to have had a third party present: a stallion man with cigarette and waistcoat, to guide his penis as he started aimlessly to push.

WITH THESE DAYS a hen's stride longer, Oliver could see a trace of white between the open curtains as he peeped out of the blankets and tasted the clean, freezing air of the bedroom. The wind had, if anything, grown during the night. The sash windows were battling in their frame. There was a screaming and yelping all round the roof, as if the house were under attack from an army of witches. Lifting his eyes a little further, he made out his grandmother in her cardigan and ankle-length skirt, bent by the washstand at the foot of her four-post bed. She struck a match, which died at once with a glimpse of her eyes and shadows dividing her forehead.

"Rise and shine, Olly," she said, glancing in his direction.

"Is it witches, is it, Nana?"

"What?"

"Witches? Are we going to have to fight them?"

"Up you get now."

Since Molly was shielding another match, Oliver burrowed back beneath the blankets, revolved in the hollow of the old feather mattress, clambered over the cold hot-water bottle and extended an arm to the bedside chair. His shirt, his pullover and his corduroy trousers were all stiff with cold. He had to rub them together just to push his arms into the sleeves and his legs into the legs. He pulled on his stockings and his favourite red braces. He waited to be prompted, to have the bedclothes snatched away, but heard only footsteps leaving for the landing. Surprised, intrigued, he slithered out onto the rug, where his boots stood in line with his Noah's Ark animals, his books and his jigsaw bricks.

He almost laughed when he saw the hall. Beneath the two dim windows that framed the front door, there was a thickness of snow across the entire floor, which rose at the walls and drifted up the staircase almost as far as his feet. There was a run of prints where his parents and Albert had gone outside, so, holding the banister with his spare hand, he slipped down the stairs in a series of thumps.

"Nana!" he called, peering round the kitchen door. "There's snow, Nana! There's snow in the hall!"

"Come in or stay out, Olly, would you, please?"

"What happened?"

Besides her shuddering candle the kitchen was dark. The morning showed only at the topmost corner of the window.

Oliver put his hot-water bottle on the draining board for his mother to empty for the washing. He stood on the flagstones bare of snow, wiggling the loose tooth in his lower jaw as he watched his grandmother clear the moaning flue, rise the ashes and light the chats—an operation he had never seen performed, as his mother always woke an hour before him.

"Nana?" he repeated.

"The wind broke the latch," said Molly. "Be a good boy and rise us some eggs, would you?"

The egg basket appeared to have suffered an explosion. He tilted it, then turned it upside-down.

"Is they froze, Nana?" he asked.

"Don't forget your coat," she said. "And give the door a good old pwning when you're back. I shall have to bolt him behind you."

Arriving on the doorstep, Oliver had to hold onto the jamb just to stop himself from falling. The snow met his cheeks like tiny arrows. The wind hurt his ears, his eyes were watering so that it was all he could do to distinguish the great, grey bulk of the barn, and it was only by doubling over, almost by crawling, that he was able to work his way along the bank of the flem, to give a small, token jump when he seemed to reach the narrow point beneath the parlour window and to set out into the storm.

Oliver knew all the nests of the bantams. He and his friend Griffin had almost as many dens in the hayloft as they did, and he had barely scrambled onto the first of its slopes before he found one of the vicious little birds to bully away from her nest. On the tall gable wall there were scratched words and numbers that had been hidden the previous year, he thought, until March or even April: the scribblings of labourers who had been here before he was born. One was a date:

the word OCTOBER had been chiselled out plainly. Another seemed to be a doleful hymn they would sometimes sing in the chapel. Behind him, Blackie came clattering up the ladder with her keen dog stink and her gold-ringed eyes. She followed him to the top of the stack, where he buried his hands among the warm eggs in his pockets and stood on his toes to peer through the slit. In the yard, beyond the snow cascading from the roof, the pond and its girdle of elm trees had vanished almost completely. In their place were nothing but a few maddened saplings and a trench sunk deep into the white expanse.

It was only by the regularity of her movement that he could make out his mother, who was spooning up the snow in quick, wild flurries, while the wind brought more from the sky and the ground so she might have kept digging forever.

"I WON'T SPEAK ill of Idris," said Molly, as she and Oliver stood among the snow-skithed cattle, which were groaning, stamping, bwnting their mangers. "He's not a bad man and he knows this farm like I never will, but I do wish to goodness as he would have the coal by here in the yard and not way down in the Bottom Field."

Turning away from Rachel, the house cow, she hooked her arms beneath the handle of a pail and hoisted it up onto the lip of the trough.

"Is the beasts drinking milk today, Nana?" asked Oliver.

"Got nothing else, Olly, have they?" Molly emptied the pail and crouched down to look at him, her blue eyes patterned with tiny red lines. "Now look," she said. "You's been a good old boy this morning, but you're much too small to be out in this all day."

"I'm big as half of the Juniors, I am!"

"And that's as maybe. I want you please to go in the house, put a brun on the fire and warm yourself up. Fodder the geese, if you're after a job. I've got to go see about the coal."

"But the coal is my job, that's what the boss says!"

"Olly . . ." Molly sighed and inspected her hands, which, even in their gloves, were doubled inwards like a pair of claws. She looked at him again. "You can come with me to the top of the Banky Piece, see what we're up against, but after that you are going in the kitchen. And I don't want no gapesing. You're to hold my arm, you understand?"

What with the snow in the house, the cattle out of water and the wind so strong that it could sclem the boss's hat and a wad of hay and neither of them to be seen again, Oliver had not had a thought for the sheep. He had worried about the ducks, which might have been buried or else have missed to find another pond. He had worried about the robins, the tits and the wrens, as he had not yet sunk them holes to the ground. But it was only when he, Molly and the three dogs reached the gate beside the beast-house that he had any sense of the valley's transformation—of the monstrous ridges that had risen over hedgerows, burst around trees and swallowed whole fields so that every familiar contour was gone. The church bell was ringing away to his left. Squinting ahead of him, Oliver saw the ghost of the oak that should have marked the gate into the Oak Piece. He edged around the end wall of the barn, clinging to his grandmother, looking west to breathe, and when they came to the corner and the full, unhindered gale that fled from Bryngwyn and the desolate slopes of Glascwm Hill, he felt her coat sleeve plucked out of his hand.

"Nana!"

Several times the bank revolved. It stopped only when Oliver landed in a drift, with the barn almost vanished and the bare-limbed oak tree flailing above him. He tried to stand and sank to his waist. He looked up the slope to see his grandmother crawling backwards towards him, but then Blackie arrived with Nip and Towser, more swimming than walking, and by some means he did not pause or think to explain he realized that there were sheep beneath him, waiting in the frozen darkness, and like the dogs he started madly to dig.

THE CASE CLOCKS in the kitchen had drifted some seconds apart since the previous evening, but for once the pendulums were swinging in time and a handful of their nine o'clock chimes rang out almost together. Standing by the fire, Idris breathed his last fit of coughing from his chest, his hands at his sides, shivering, bleeding. Beside him, the women having finished, the boy was sitting in the murky, soap-stinking water of the galvanized bath—a fold between his chest and his belly, his skin clear and bronze, as others became only in the summer. He was watching Idris fixedly, this son for his wife, his fat lips parted, the lashes tabbering on his big black eyes, and suddenly Idris felt a stab of revulsion, which escaped his throat as a growl.

"Boss?" said Oliver again.

"Do you think I binna thinking on it?"

At last he felt some give in his shoulders and he was able to break the spine of his coat, which he peeled off like a chrysalis and leant against a leg of the mantelshelf.

"Time to get out now, Olly," said Etty quietly, and the boy rose with dimpled knees and penis jutting, his wet hair already recovering its waves.

"It's eight below," Idris muttered. "You canna stand. You canna see. The dankering lantern blows out even in the barn!"

"But, boss—"

"They's best off where they are, boy. They'll be scratting on till Monday."

The sensation was returning to Idris's fingers. They felt lacerated, flayed, and he groaned as he unwound the bandage from his head and tested his temple where the wind had planted a shard off the roof that afternoon. There was no fresh blood on his fingers—at least, no more than oozed from his knuckles—and so he filled the jug from the bath and squeezed past Albert at his table in the corner. He made it to the larder, where the geese were in their cubs and the pig was dangling salt-frosted from the gambrel, but while he managed to work up a lather with the brush, even with two hands he could not keep the razor from shaking.

His chair was a mould of his back and his shoulders. He sat with his head slumped onto the top rail, his eyes on the three black stripes in the mantel where they would pin their home-made candles when he was a child, in the days when paraffin was scarce. "Three in one," his father had called them: the tallow, the wick and the flame, which was the Holy Spirit and could be shared by all who held their candles in readiness. He remembered those nights before the Christmas market— himself and his brothers, Ivor and Oliver, cross-legged among the goose feathers, their father still dark-haired and robust, with their mother beside him, singing as she plucked—and he pressed his hands to his face for several seconds before he spread out the paper on his lap.

"**CHILBLAINS! RADOX** RELIEF AT LAST!"

"It has been reported by Mr. J. Prichard, Dderw Estate, that the rainfall for 1946, by his gauge on the Dderw Estate, was 65.23 inches. This compares with 45.49 inches in 1945 and 49.78 inches in 1944."

"**Rhyscog.** Rev. A. W. Chant, Builth Wells, was the officiating minister at the Methodist Church on Sunday. Mrs. E. Hamer presided at the organ and Mr. I. Hamer was precentor."

ASLEEP, IDRIS LOOKED not so much older than his forty-nine years as ancient beyond human reckoning. Sometimes, before she extinguished the candle at night or when she lay awake in the earliest daylight, Etty would watch him for minutes at a time—his head sunk sideways into the pillow, his mouth ajar, his short breaths gargling deep in his chest. He put her in mind of the Rocks at Aberedw, where they would go wimberry combing when she was a girl: pairs of legs and flapping skirts that would turn into people as they moved between the bushes. They would scramble together across those crumbling slopes, and in the shelter of some shelving rock she would always find a cove of flowers—pink erigeron or biting stonecrop—and pick a few to wreathe her hair, wondering that anything could live up here at all.

With the screen back in the larder, she dragged the bath off the hearthrug and spread out the blankets on the table. She fastened the shield to the nearest of the flat irons, wiped it clean and tested its heat with her cheek; then, with slow, rolling movements of her wrist, she smoothed out the creases in her husband's shirt. Only her son remained awake. He was standing on the stool to reach the face of her grandfather clock, which, like her husband's, he wound every night. Both of the clocks were tall and dark, with narrow doors concealing their weights and pendulums. Both had a second keyhole just beneath the hour hand to give the impression they would run for a week. Etty checked the Sunday joint in the oven. She took two cleats from the fire with the tongs and dropped them into the box iron, but by the time that she was sitting in her chair with the paper she could hardly recall how her own best blouse, the boy's shirt and a pair of stiff, starched collars had found their way onto the pile for the chapel.

"BIRMINGHAM offers well-paid factory work to single women age 21–35; lodgings found, fare paid."

"NURSES needed at BOTLEYS PARK COLONY to nurse and train men, women and children with undeveloped minds. **It's a grand job and a grand life.**"

"**Rhyscog.** Rev. A. W. Chant, Builth Wells, was the officiating minister at the Methodist Church on Sunday. Mrs. E. Hamer presided at the organ and Mr. I. Hamer was precentor."

FROM THE FAR Top Field, Oliver could see all the way back down into the yard, where the few ewes that Albert and the boss had freed the previous day were huddled round the door of the barn. He could see the trail of manure they had finally used to tempt the cattle down the canyon to the pond, the snow-weighted sycamores circling the graveyard, even the heads of one or two stones, but the Bottom Field, the Banky Piece, the track and the Cae Blaidd, all of these were lost beneath one mighty drift, while Turley Wood was reduced to a few black branches, which scrabbled into the eerie still— their shadows tangled with the prints of rabbits.

There was smoke in a pillar above the kitchen chimney, luminous against the great, dark flank of Llanbedr Hill: the fire stoked by Molly, who never came to chapel, who held instead to the church down in Erwood—at least, when she was able to go.

"Looks like the sea, boss, you reckons?" said Albert.

"Has you seen the sea, Albert?" asked Oliver.

"*Have* you seen the sea," Etty corrected him.

"I seen the Channel, boy."

"What's the Channel?"

"That's what keeps us from the Froggies." He rolled his chaw of tobacco in his mouth. "Frenchies, look."

"Is they green?"

"Head to toe, boy."

"Urggh!"

Idris said nothing. Limping along the drift that concealed the boundary fence, he stopped at a point that he judged to be the gate and started to climb towards the common, trying to keep the worst of the snow off his suit. This high up, there was still a little movement in the air. It idled over the colourless hills, silent, as if surveying its destruction, and as Oliver followed his deep-sunk prints it must have carried the same, sharp scent of life that it had found in the Bottom Field the previous morning, since the dogs at his heels began to whimper and shake.

"Boss?" said Oliver.

"I seen the dogs, boy."

"Is it wethers, is it?"

"Wethers for Llanowen, I expect." Idris checked the watch in his high-neck waistcoat. "You come along now."

Oliver remained on the top of the drift where Towser and Nip were throwing up snow in clouds. "He binna so deep, boss," he said, tentatively. "We could have them from there, easy."

"What day is it today, boy?"

"The Sabbath day, boss."

"The Sabbath day."

"But, boss, we always fodders the creatures of a Sunday. We fodders the ewes, and we milks the beast—"

"Oliver!" hissed Etty.

Idris coloured behind his stubble. "By Gar, boy," he said, "you's burning in your shins today!"

Away up the slope was a farm named the Welfrey: a high, hard place alone in the common, where John the Welfrey and Sarah, his wife, were toiling out to meet them on the track. Two dark figures in the glare of the hillside; one raised a hand when Oliver spotted them—in their layers of coats and scarves it was tricky to tell which of them it was, although he recognized Sarah's voice when she called him her two-note greeting. The snow had erased all trace of the Welfrey fields, flooded Pentre Wood and swept over the ridge of their barn, but still in their yard there were sheep by the score; they might have recovered their entire flock. Oliver heard Idris summon him again. He saw his eyes beneath his low-brimmed hat, but in his mind he saw only the ewes in the Oak Piece and the Bottom Field, the wethers in the quarries or pressed against the wall of the Panneys—shivering, imprisoned—and he had made no decision and he had no plan when he turned abruptly, ducked past his mother and set out back as they had come.

THERE WAS LITTLE to be told between Oliver and the dogs, which, like him, were not exactly grown-ups and not exactly animals. They would all of them flinch at Idris's glance, work or vanish, attend on his whims without a thought—and yet, within the lines and limits of the boss's rule, they were a band and Oliver was their leader. As he lugged himself back over the gate from the Plock and hurried past the daggy Radnors crowded in the yard, bald in places where, after only a day beneath the snow, they had started to nibble on one another's wool, he had no need to check that Blackie, Nip and Towser were behind him—bounding through the tracks of the cattle, eager to know what wonders lay next.

"Oliver!"

There were tits and piefinches pecking at crumbs on the trampled path to the house. There were footprints leading from the top of the yard: shadows past the end of the beast-house.

"Oliver!"

Oliver slowed down only at the lychgate, where the prints continued through a crested drift and the rooks, still hunched in the sycamores above him, had dislodged snow into the crystalline whiteness. There was a single snowdrop in the shelter of the wall. Panting, struggling, he climbed into the abandoned churchyard, and since his grandmother had followed the path herself he wound up the tump into the ring of the yew trees, heading for the smothered little cell of the church, whose bell hung exposed against the empty sky.

"Oh!" said Molly. "Oh, you gave me a start!"

"Nana . . ." He was breathing so hard that he could scarcely speak.

"What is it, love? What on earth's happened?"

She was sitting in her usual pew at the front, the smoke from her cigarette twining in the light from the door. She flinched when he tripped on a frozen pile of bat droppings, hidden by the snow that had fallen through the roof, and when he reached the end of the aisle she opened her blanket and gathered him under her arm.

"It's not them blasted ewes again, is it?"

"Nana, can you help me, can you?"

"Olly . . . Olly, I wish I could, love."

"Please!"

"Look at me, boy!" She held up her hands. "I can dig the garden, given a good day, but . . . You heard Idris. Ten foot down or more, he reckons, the most of them, and we don't so much as know where they are—"

"The dogs'll mark them."

"I know—"

"I can mark them too, Nana. I can! With the both of us, and Blackie, and Nip, and Towser . . ."

As the door grated open, the light grew again over the backs of the pews, which were as old and worn as the chairs in the house, over the pulpit keeling above them, the altar under its blanked-out window and the memorials on the dull white walls. Oliver's mother must have fallen on the way down the hill. Snow was clinging to her coat and her best black dress. Behind her the dogs were standing in the porch, turned now at nervous, unrelated angles, and when he lifted his eyes to her face Oliver felt a coldness enter the hot, clear purpose in his belly.

"Come by here, girl," his grandmother murmured.

Etty closed the door and again the church was dark. She stopped in the aisle a few rows back, and for a moment it seemed that she was praying, since Oliver waited for tears or fury and heard no more than the gasps of her breath.

"He should never have dragged you to the chapel today. Not on foot. Not in your condition. It were crazy to try . . ."

"You don't want to see him," said Etty at last.

"I don't suppose I do."

"Oliver . . ."

Oliver shrank inside the blanket.

"I know it's none of my affair, Etty," said Molly. "I know that. You must do what you think right. But you just remember, you're his wife, not some blasted slave—and I know what I'm talking about. I had it for years. If it was up to me, well, it's not up to me. I'm not saying what to think, like, but this is your farm too. You remember that."

THE SHEEP WATCHED impassively as Etty sat the blanket and the saddle on the cob, shortened the stirrups and fastened the girth. They bunched together when she returned from the barn with two fat, wire-bound bundles of hay, but they had no strength to scatter or run, and despite the dogs, which waited with Molly as she packed the bait into the baskets and helped her grandson onto Reuben's back, there was little more to reveal their disquiet than their jingling icicles, their flickering ears, the quickening spurts of their breath.

If Oliver felt his purpose return when his grandmother dragged the top gate open, then Etty felt as if she had torn off her clothes and stood naked before a goggling multitude, as if she had taken a step onto air instead of earth and found that it would hold her weight. As they passed between the old churchyard and the prill beneath Pentre Wood, she looked past her son's blue woollen hat and the nodding head of the small bay horse, and with every step he broke through the smooth-backed snow she seemed to see again the catkins of the hazels and the long, bowing boughs of the sycamores, where a squirrel was darting—red as her hair.

She almost wanted to cover her eyes.

"Are you cold, Mam?" asked Oliver, looking back.

Etty realized she was trembling. She smiled, tightening her arms on his waist. "Oh . . . No. No, Olly, I'm fine."

In the dingle that closed around the climbing track, she slipped from the saddle, held out her arms and took the weight of her oversized boy. With the last of the fields invisible behind them, no trace of a tree, a path or a fence, she could tell only from a flatter passage in the snow that they were on the bank of Conjuror's Pool, by the hidden gully of the shrinking prill. Stroking Reuben's steam-blowing nostrils, she took the reins and waded until she had to crawl. Behind her, the horse sank almost to his shoulders. He reared and snorted, snow rolling from his chest, the poles and the shovels clattering on his hips, but she spoke to him softly and again he plunged forwards, and then he was clambering onto the slope—shaking like the dogs, which were scrambling around them.

It was only on the hills and in the shelter of the Bryngwyn track that the snow had seemed to be in any way navigable. The valley beneath them was like some vast snow river: a full half-mile of razor-headed waves and tapering shadows, its occasional trees like pieces of flotsam. Even if they had found a way among the drifts, still they could never have taken the cob, and they could have dug all day in those lightless depths before they found a single sheep. Here, on Llanbedr Hill, the drifts were like hills themselves, but they were divided by spaces blown almost clean in which there were shallow, sporadic quarries—some of them cut to build the Island, the cottage for Dick the gamekeeper and Dilys, his sister, whose smoke spread faintly from a cluster of larches. Other quarries were so ancient that not even Idris seemed to know their purpose. As his mother tied the cob to the little wittan tree at the corner of the New Field, filled the feedbag and drew another blanket over the horse's buttocks, Oliver set out straight across the unseen lane, shielding his eyes against the ice-bright sun. He knew precisely where the wethers would be, even without the help of the dogs. True, they rarely strayed far from their own patch of common, but still he could picture them, trying to escape the two-day storm, retreating through the wind-scourged fern—like a memory of his own.

At the first pale shadow, the hint of a hollow, he tipped up the pole as his grandmother had shown him and sank it hand over hand. He took two steps and tried again, and again, the six-foot length barely reaching the ground, but beside him Blackie was whimpering softly, and when he tried once more the head of the pole stopped level with his waist.

"Mam!" he called.

His coat made it hard for him to bend his arms. The spade was almost as tall as himself. Mostly he watched as his mother dug, as the hole grew beneath them and the snow begin to shudder and fragment—become a curling horn, the top of a head, a pair of thick-set, vigorous shoulders. She dropped to her knees, seized hold of the fleece and tugged until she was groaning. She tumbled backwards as the wether burst free: a seeming miracle matted with snow, falling, struggling back to his feet—turning light-blinded from the transformed hilltop to the wall of the mountains, which rose to the south like a drift on a new scale again.

"One," counted Oliver. "Two!"

"I said to you they were tough," said Etty. Her cheeks were pink under ginger freckles. "Tough old boys! Policemen of the hills!"

"Three!"

In turn the sheep wallowed out of the hole, each allowing the next to escape, and by the time that the snow was still, thirteen of the animals were gathered before them, between the crouching, spring-wound dogs. They stood with their tails to a fresh, faint wind, which whispered in the hawthorns and carried snowflakes twinkling around them, scratting hopelessly for grass with their hooves in spite of a bundle of hay. Picking up his pole, Oliver laughed excitedly and set out in search of another quarry. Sunk to his knees, swollen by his coat and scarf, he looked shorter, plumper, more purposeful than ever. Etty smiled, then turned at a sound to look through the larches—one of them prone with fumbling roots, two more fallen into their neighbours to lean among the cone-spotted branches where a raven croaked and scattered twigs as he launched from his listing nest.

"Hi!" The call came again.

The Island could never have been much of a farm. A five-room hovel of local stone with a few, mean fields mined out of the common, most such places had long since been left to go down. Struggling through the spinney, lifting each foot almost to her waist, Etty crossed the tracks of a hare—the splaying hind feet dwarfing the fore. She slithered down a bank and came to the foxes and weasels on the gamekeeper's wire, which should have led from the trees to the door of the cottage. But of that, like the fences, the barn, the sheep and the couple of cows, she was able to see nothing at all.

"Dick?" she called. "Dick? Dilys?"

"Ethel! Ethel, is that you, girl?"

"Mam!" shouted Oliver, out beyond the wethers.

"Olly, get yourself here, would you?"

"But I marked another one!"

"We'll rise him in a minute. Can you bring me a shovel?"

Etty walked a complete circle of the snowdrift, which started gradually by the lip of the hill and tailed into a cliff some fifty yards distant with a brink like a breaking wave. Had it not been for the smoke, you might never have suspected that there was anything inside at all. She tried to climb the slopes at the north and east, but the snow was loose, as fine as flour, and it sank and cascaded from her boots.

Oliver stood with the dogs among the trees, holding a blotchy, blue-green egg in the cup of his thick woollen glove. Her shovel lay in the snow beside him. He looked up at the raven's nest, down at the wire of ice-caked animals.

"Where's the Island, Mam?"

"Think you'd get up there, do you, Olly?" Etty asked. "You're a handy little climber."

"I am not little!"

She joined her hands to hold his boot and propel him upwards, floundered after him and tried again until at length he crawled onto the back of the drift, moving slowly towards the tail of smoke now snatched and scattering to the west. Oliver slipped the egg into one of his gloves, his fingers braced to keep it safe. It was warm, that was the main thing; it must have fallen from the nest only moments before he arrived. This weather, so Albert had told him, was all the crueller for coming on a few days that might have been spring. He felt the wind on his neck and turned to the slope beyond the vanished barn, to Bryngwyn Hill, to hills whose names he did not know and the distant plain where clouds were ballooning, blazing white. He glanced at his mother, who had already started digging, then lay and peered into a black-fringed hole and beneath him, in the turbulent smoke, saw a pocket of fire, movement in the darkness, the gleam of eyes in a soot-coloured face.

"Dick?" he said. "Is that you, is it?"

"Young Oliver! Is we ever glad to see you, boy!"

DILYS SAT IN her blanket on the hob, beneath the boy in the square of sky. Snow was falling wet on her face. In the night she had been here, listening to the long, despairing cries of the owls, watching the darkness stretch and tear, the sparks from the fire shrink and mingle with the stars. In the storm she had been here, while her brother smashed another chair for its wood and paced the flagstones, cussing and moithering, and the wind in the chimney made its godless scream.

"We found the coal!" Ethel shouted, on the path outside.

"Good on you, girl!" Dick shouted back, and threw himself again against the door.

The blue became grey. The boy was gone, but the snow kept falling.

He had never once looked at her, Idris—not at school, not even that time when he returned to the Funnon with his hair army-short and the hope extinguished in his face. But then, her hair had been dark and skeiny, and soon flecked with grey, and her breasts had always been hopeless gestures on her chest. Even at twenty she could not have held a candle to that flighty piece, Ethel, with her hair like fire and her morals round her ankles. Dilys had heard the clecking at market. She had done her sums. The girl had arrived at the end of July, which was not six months before her gypsy-looking baby came along. Well, Dick could shrug about it all if he liked—he could burn the last banisters to boil the kettle and welcome these people into their cottage—but she at least had a morsel

37

of pride. She sat in her place by the snow-spitting fire, in the airless, dog-stinking cave of the kitchen, and did not utter a single word.

"OLLY, WE *CANNOT*."

"But, Mam, you said!" Oliver clung to the head of the pole.

"Listen to me now."

"Come you back up the Island, Ethel!" Dick was shouting just to be heard, his face still black from his three-day captivity, his long coat flying from the twine round his waist. "If we canna get the horse in the barn, we shall damn well have him in the kitchen."

"Dick, my mam'll be frantic."

"Mam!"

"Oliver, no!"

The cob and the wittan stood alone in the whiteness, tethered together, vanishing slowly. Four thin drifts covered Reuben's legs, for all that he still made efforts to stamp. With his broad, bare hands Dick replaced the poles and shovels. He took Oliver by the waist, dodging the west-threshing branches as he lifted him high onto the horse's back, while Etty tried to catch the stirrup with her boot and then allowed him to help her too.

The wethers had long since returned to their quarry; the fresh-blown snow lay thick on their backs. Flitting like shades among glimpses of hawthorns and drifts that might have been anywhere at all, the dogs closed on their hiding place— driving the sheep before them, stumbling, pitching and struggling to rise when they fell. Etty kicked the cob into the wind, which seemed to pass through her, not troubling to part. A lazy wind, her mother would have called it. Its long notes howled in the branches of the beech trees, thrilled in Oliver's chest and played on his skin in little tremors. With the ground invisible, they might have been flying. Closing his eyes, burying his face in his scarf, he felt his mother's arms around his chest and her swollen belly in his back. He felt the warm, smooth curve of the egg in his hand. With his tongue he fiddled with his wobbly tooth. He thought of those storms when the dogs hid, terrified, and he was left alone to run in the yard or to stand on the tump by the porch of the church, where you could see from the Red Hill to Llanbadarn-y-Garreg and watch the dark sky shimmer and blink—the thunder that followed like a summons to some mighty purpose.

It was only from the angle and the movement of the horse that Oliver could tell that the ground was falling. Slowing, slipping in spite of the frost nails, Reuben began to walk in a zigzag, bringing the wind between their cheeks. They were somewhere close to the edge of the gully when, at last, they stopped. Etty shouted instructions at the dogs, but such was the gale that channelled down the dingle that Oliver could hardly hear her himself. She swung him clear onto the uphill slope, where his knees simply buckled as hard as he tried to stand. She dragged her right leg over the saddle, fighting her heavy, ice-stiff skirts, then slipped suddenly forwards and grabbed at the reins so that she and the horse fell together.

Oliver only noticed the men as they came plunging down the bank from the Bryngwyn track. Trapped on his back, Reuben was bellocking, thrashing his legs at the desperate wind. He did not relent even with Albert beside him, bent to his ear and caressing his nose. Idris flung a wether out of his way. He cursed and shrieked at the plaguing dogs, which disappeared back into the blizzard, but although Oliver was slithering towards them he did not seem to look at him once, nor even to register his existence. When Albert persuaded the horse to roll, Idris dropped into the hole in the snow. He found a patch of loose red hair. He dug again and found an arm, and then dragged Etty back into the air, holding her to his chest, stroking her face and kissing her lips until she started to convulse. Such was the snow that covered her clothes that some moments passed before Oliver saw the blood that was soaking through his mother's petticoats. She tried to sit and turned in his direction, while the boss fell to his knees in the gully—his back to the boy, his chapel clothes white, grey hairs streaming sideways from his head as he closed his eyes and knitted his hands at his chin.

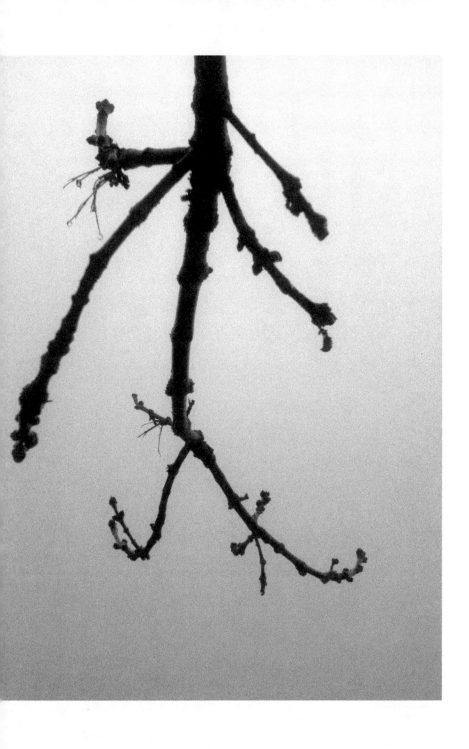

1952

IN THE SILVERY mist the big-bellied ewes flowed out of the yard, squeezed between the gateposts and paused and eddied in the pools of grass and snowdrops on the banks beneath the skeletal hedgerows. Droplets of water clung to their off-white fleeces; they clung to the boy, his cap and the plump black bird on his shoulder, to the dogs, the limping horse and the downy gullies of the pussy willows at Cwmberllan Ford, which sparkled in the glimpsing light as if they were covered in jewels.

"Boss?"

"Boy."

"Boss, is there ravens in heaven, boss?"

Idris paused. "The Lord do look well upon the raven."

"Is they in heaven, then?"

"Well, boy. You tell me. What is immortality?"

"It's an . . . acquired condition, boss," Oliver recited.

"Yes . . ."

"You canna hope for life in the Great Beyond if you hanna converted to the word of the Lord."

"Very good."

Oliver frowned. "How do I convert Maureen, then, boss?"

"The Bible, I is sorry to say, is silent upon that point."

It had, said the wireless, been the wettest February in eighty-two years. Even after a week almost dry, the water continued to roar in the drains; the hooves of the sheep were seething in the puddles. Beneath the oily must of the flock, Idris could smell the cool, damp soil in these more distant reaches of his ninety-one acres—the first, faint song of returning life. His nailed boots clicking on the broken stone, he checked across the shapes of the sheep in the Crooked Slang, in the poochy ground around their cratch. Ahead, he could just make out the heartbeat of a tractor, which he took to be the machine for Cwmpiban. Walter, he supposed, had his morning assignation at the Awlman's Arms, and since the flock was hurrying past the Long Field—some perhaps were already at his neighbour's track—he whistled back the dogs and peered between the hedgerows, into the luminous mist. He ran a hand across the withers of his horse, which always grew nervous at anything mechanical, and as a pair of headlamps appeared, not from Cwmpiban but from the direction of the lane, it struck him that Buster was nuzzling him in return.

"Boss?" said Oliver. "Who's that, boss?"

Ten years must have passed since Idris had last seen Ivor. The man's bald-headed, bloated-looking son, who leapt to the ground to open the gate and drive his sheep from the Cwmpiban turn, had hardly been old enough for school. What they were doing here, five miles from their own farm, with a box full of fence posts, Idris went cold in the imagining. He watched the boy on the far side of the gate glaring at Oliver with cave-like eyes. He watched Ivor drive through the curtains of the air, his face grown creviced beneath his hat, his attention fixed on his steering wheel. For all the words that were boiling in his mind, Idris could not speak; he could not so much as have whistled to Blackie, his dog, which stood high-eared at Oliver's feet, her long teats trembling from her belly, while Oliver's mouth hung ajar in confusion. Idris's breath was choking, seizing the muscles of his jaw and his shoulders. As the gate swung closed and the tractor vanished towards Cwmpiban, he was clinging to the neck of his crippled horse—nothing more than spittle and mucus escaping his gaping lips.

IDRIS DID NOT sing as he followed the valley lane towards Aberedw. He had decided, after long consideration, that he could no longer tolerate spiritual displays. As Solomon had said, there was a time and a place for everything, and there were few sights he found more disagreeable than Joseph Jones the tailor, praying aloud as he made his tour of the farms. Even when he had passed Rhosei Cottage, where Oliver turned right at the crossroads and vanished north into the milk of the morning—the school bell clanking faintly beyond him—there was a chance that Mrs. Price was out in her garden, or that one of the shapes in the neighbouring fields was Bill the Hergest or George Gilfach, and Idris did not so much as hum.

The chapel was the place to proclaim your faith. Outside the sanctuary of its four walls, you had merely, tirelessly to improve yourself, to resist such temptations as were advertised in the newspaper and bend your will to the will of the

Lord. If Idris proclaimed anything as, a mile or so later, he crossed the bridge into Llanbadarn-y-Garreg, where shadows streamed from the wittans and the ash trees, it was only his example. He touched his hat to Blanche Lanmorgan, a cousin of some sort on his mother's side, who was checking her lambs in her one valley field, hard by the little white Church of St. Padarn. He greeted Dorothy, the wife for Albert, who hopped as usual onto her chair to see who was passing their cottage. In the yard of the old forge, Adam Prosser was turning his spokes—the shavings golden in the gathering sunlight—and they swapped a word or two on the weather before Idris continued west, with his work-bowed shoulders, his grand white horse with his crooked hind leg and the two dogs trotting in their wake.

He stopped once more, by the stretch of the Edw known as the Gleision, where a girl named Martha had drowned in his grandparents' time: an aunt for Dorothy, if he remembered correctly, who had missed the lane coming home in the dark. She had been found the next morning, revolving slowly, a tobacco bag swollen in her hand. Idris did emsin, putting his right hand to his chest. Among the strings of light and the catkin-decked hazels, he considered the rocks where he and Ivor had stood as boys with their salmon gaffs and their blackened faces, the banks they had smeared with giant prints to scare off the water bailiffs. He gazed at the glistening surface of the river, listening to the music of a blackbird, but then a large black car appeared on the lane and he hurried to take Buster's bridle.

"Who were that, then, do you suppose?" he asked him, watching the red lights blearing at the corner.

There was no trace of Lewis in the smith shop, although the coals were glowing in the forge and the air was stifling with the sulphur of hoof burn. Idris tethered the horse in the pentis. He waited by the breach of iron and horseshoes, where some rearing animal had punched a pair of holes in the ceiling, but once he had named all the brand-marks on the wall—every farm from Blaenmilo to Pencaenewydd—he returned to the lane with his leg-cocking dogs to glower at the sign for the Awlman's Arms, which showed a man repairing a boot. The valley was tight here, in Aberedw; the sun had yet to emerge from the hilltop and the mist clung thick to the steep, wooded slopes. It dribbled on the bonnet and the mudguards of the tractor stopped on the stones by the inn's front door: the Fordson Major for Walter Cwmpiban, who spent his days on a stool at the bar while his creatures faltered and his hedgerows untangled into trees.

It was, thought Idris, just his luck to have a drunkard for his only direct neighbour: the man who owned every single field between the valley and his hill-framed farm.

"Old Buster, see?" said the blacksmith, when he finally arrived.

He stood in the smith shop: a stout young man with soot on his face and hands like vices.

"Yes yes," said Idris.

"I shouldna thought you'd be working him still."

"He's not out fourteen, that one."

"Tight on sixteen, by the looks of him."

Idris breathed through his ragged teeth.

"He has been worked, like," Lewis continued. He hung his landlord's apron from a peg and pulled on his blacksmith's apron instead, taking the horse's big, feathered foot between his knees. "Had a splinter in there, has he?"

"We had one from there . . . Friday, it was."

"Did you call the vet, did you?"

"Do you know how much that sclem do charge?"

"Poisoned it is, see?" He released the hoof and clicked his tongue, looking back into the wet black eyes half-hidden by Buster's fringe. "If you wants my honest opinion, Funnon, I'll say it's time as he hung up his shoes. Tired, he is. You just got to look at him."

Idris took no chances with Lewis, any more than he had taken with Lewis's mother. A purveyor of drink he might have been—and in Idris's book there were few greater crimes—but he had known a lorry seize when he crossed its path, baffling a mechanic for the rest of the day. He had known men stick a pig on his approach, before the buckets were ready, since everyone knew that he could stem the blood. He had even known him to locate missing sheep in his dreams. Charming was one of those local secrets. Everybody sniffed at it or claimed, if they spoke of it at all, that it was something shameful, consigned to the past—not to be squared with the teachings of the chapel. And yet here was Lewis, a charmer still. To Idris's knowledge, there was barely a farm in the entire valley that did not have one of his plain brown envelopes or little rolls of sign-patterned paper stuffed into a crack behind the mantelshelf or between the stones above the beasthouse door.

He ran his fingers over Blackie's neck, the morning's coughing needling in his chest.

"Well," he said, finally.

"Get yourself a tractor, I would," said Lewis. "Two cows you'll keep on the fodder for a horse, and that is your running costs covered for starters."

"Well," Idris repeated. "If you can keep a horse going. That's what my old man always said."

"It is your farm." The blacksmith shrugged. He dug in the

pocket of his jacket for a pencil. "Well. I can keep you in horses for the time being, like, but this old lad, he shanna be scratting on forever. In't nothing I can do as is going to change that."

FOR ALL OF his size, Oliver had little aptitude for games. His legs were lost beneath the bulk of his body, which had a tendency to overbalance and made his movements awkward and foolish. The entire business upset his poise. He had agreed to play rounders only because he had been picked by Amy Whittal—the pert and fair-haired daughter for the vet—and he was batting first only because he was the eleven-year-old boy on their team. Bent on his mark in the broad, chipping playground, he swung the bat wildly, dropped it with a clatter and ran out of the shadow of the schoolhouse—his raven, Maureen, flapping at his ear. The fielders were turning and shouting in confusion: boys with pens in the pockets of their shirts, girls with bracelets and flying hair. At second base, Ruth, one of the Cwmpiban sisters, seized the tail of his jacket and tried to trip him over, but since no warning came from his team-mates he dragged her almost to the end of the queue.

"Rounder!" he declared, putting back his shoulders. He took out his comb to tidy his parting.

"No rounder!" said Griffin, from the bowler's spot.

"Why the bugger not?"

"We canna bloody rise him, can we?"

The schoolhouse was a long and church-like building, its corners trimmed with yellowish brick. One half contained the single classroom. The other was home to the teacher, Mr. Williams, who might have had only the one hand, having lost the other to the teeth of a thresher, but was still a gardener of the greatest passion, with more rosettes from local shows than the rest of the village put together. Beyond the fence at the end of the playground, where the children now were beginning to gather, his vegetable patches were dark with manure; his blue-chipped path was glinting in the mist-cleansed sunshine. The ball was close to the wall of the potting shed, sunk among rows of daffodils and camellias.

"Well." Oliver shrugged. "You threw him, you rise him."

"You bloody hit him there!"

"I in't getting a stripe to rise your blasted ball!"

"Oh! Chicken, is it? Afeared of old Willie?"

"Oh, and you can talk. Last time I seen you get a stripe you was blubbing like a blasted baby!"

Griffin dipped his head like a cockerel: a rangy boy in too-short trousers, fine hair gleaming along his upper lip, which was red in places from his habit of trying to lick his nose.

"What did you say?"

"Olly!" said Amy.

"You take that back, you bloody gypo!"

"Gypo, is it?"

"Well, it is a gypo you looks like to me. You dunna look like the rest of us now, do you, let's face it?"

The mood in the playground had changed abruptly. The two teams were whispering, forming packs behind each of the boys, while the Infants, who always kept an eye out for fights, gave up picking the skin from their milk and came streaming towards them over the grass. Out on the lane there was the muttering of a tractor. In a moment, Oliver saw through the gate the same machine he had seen that morning—the same hunched driver and his eerie boy, big and bald and scowling back at him—but then the first punch caught him squarely on the ear and, croaking loudly, his raven launched into the air.

Oliver righted himself to find Griffin pink-faced, his eyebrows knotted, his fists shivering one way and the other as if he were trying to catch a fly.

He felt his eyes contract.

"What the bugger were that, then?" he asked.

He was surprised only that his friend was fighting him again. Griffin had, in truth, grown a fair bit lately—he was almost his own height, and his swing had weight—but where Oliver struggled with football or the Sunday School sports day, fighting was something again. Watching his opponent, his feet felt light. A storm seemed to swell in the workings of his belly. His want to win went far beyond the punch, beyond the playground, the watching children and the fact that Amy, the prettiest girl, had joined his group, up into the heights of the cloud-scratched sky, where Maureen had taken herself to circle with fanning tail and fingering wings, to gaze across the neighbouring hills and the lingering mist in the valleys. Oliver felt the sunlight on his burning ear, his cheek and the side of his nose. He felt the breeze that eddied around them. He knew the place of the other boy's boots, the lift of his hands, the turn of his head. When Griffin darted forwards, his right coming back, he dodged to let the blow glance away from his shoulder, and his mind converged on a single instant when he brought down his fist like a hammer on Griffin's temple and sent him crumpling to the ground.

BUCKLING THE FRESH wireless batteries in the panniers, Idris turned the horse to the right—the way of good fortune—and led him back through Aberedw, by the council houses where most of the old labourers now seemed to live, past Bryan the undertaker, Mrs. Weale the seamstress, the smith shop, the inn and the Church of St. Cewydd, which showed grand and grey between the green-black yew trees. The last of the mist was melting with the moving air. On the Mill Pitch he passed the telephone box, which had arrived one morning by the turn to the Court—to the consternation of Mrs. Harley the Post Office, who had always been party to every call into and out of the valley. He crossed the bridge above the turbulent river, but then left the lane for the crushed-stone track to Pentremoel, turning again onto a track thinner and rougher still, which tucked up the bank among the shattered cliffs, the flame-shaped leaves of garlic and bluebells and the bare scrub oaks of Hendre Wood. Curious meadows appeared in places, as if they had been levelled by hand. In one a boy with a brace of rabbits was running in alarm towards the root-twisting outcrop where some old prince had once gone to hide, but otherwise the hill seemed deserted. So Idris gave himself to "All Hail the Power of Jesus' Name"—his voice returning full and rich from the enclosing rocks.

It was only on the ridge that he allowed himself to rest—high above the woods and Pen-y-Garreg Farm, where the mountains rose from the breeze-ruffled feg: precise, close-seeming, promising rain. The encounter with Ivor must have hit him harder than he had realized. Idris took pride in his strength and stamina. He could follow the plough through the span of a day, until the horse himself could hardly stand, and here he was on a lightsome walk home from Aberedw, and he was doubled on a snag by a gaunt little ash tree, panting, wincing with the cramps in his chest. He took out his bottle and drank a little water, listening to the pulsing of the new artillery range on the Epynt; of his household, he alone had not at first taken it for thunder. Below his boots, the stones and the dead fern tumbling into the lowland greens, through the straggling mist of the long Wye Valley, a car passed a lorry on the white-striped road. A train was pulling out of Erwood Station—its steam dissolving from the goods yard, the weighbridge and Michael Evans, the station master, the father for Ethel, who stood plump and alone on the platform.

THERE WAS FROGSPAWN in the weepy ground on Cefn Wylfre: clods like tapioca scattered through the puddles, the dots in their bubbles already extending into commas. Even frogs, it seemed, stopped short of the mawn pools: these spaces of blueness cut out of the hilltop, rippling inside the shade of the banks. They were deep, or depthless, Oliver knew that much. Albert, who remembered them as peat diggings, had seen men tie three ladders together and still not manage to reach the bottom. He had seen them haul up the roots of trees—here, where not so much as a wittan or hawthorn had ever been known to stand. Despite the afternoon sunshine, the flittering reeds and the black-budding cotton grass, there was a darkness about this place: something of the corpse candles which Oliver's mother had seen one night while searching for a sclemming ewe, something of the Lord who dwelt in these hills beyond the walls and the fences. Reversing his cap, murmuring to Maureen, he wove carefully down the thin sheep rack that was the only direct path home from school. He hopped between the tussocks, keeping clear of the soft, grassy banks, which would sink beneath your feet if you took a wrong step and rise to hide any trace of your passing. A couple of plovers lifted from the heather and fled away with flickering wings—dwindling over the isolated fields and the zinc-patched barn and cottage of the Welfrey, where a large black Humber was creeping down the track.

The lambs in the Plock were long-legged, long-tailed—none of them more than three days old—but Jess, Blackie's puppy, was still in her training and bowled up the field as Oliver approached. She sent the lambs in panic back to their mothers. Rolling and growling, she followed him through the gate into the yard, where the other dogs came wagging to greet him, hard as he tried to remain unnoticed.

"Who won?" called Molly from the flowerbed beneath the sitting-room window.

"What's that, Nana?" Oliver kept Maureen close to his head.

"Olly, your ear is purple."

"Oh," he said. "Well."

His mother must have been just inside the hall. He hurried on towards the Banky Piece, but had barely reached the cover of the flowering elms before the front door opened and she appeared on the path with her legs in her skirts and her red hair flooding from her headscarf.

"Oliver," she said. "Were you kept in again?"

"Mam—"

"Show me your hand!" She crossed the long, narrow stone of the bridge.

Reluctantly Oliver took his left hand from his pocket and unfurled his fingers painfully from the palm.

"I'll rise you some ointment," his grandmother murmured.

"Have you got something to say for yourself, have you?" Etty demanded.

"He hit me first, Mam."

"And that makes it fine, does it?"

"He called me a gypo, Mam . . ."

As his mother arrived in the muddy ruts between the pond and the barn's gable wall, she seemed for a moment to pause. She stood above him, blinking quickly, her eyebrows drawn above pinched green eyes, and so he continued in a flurry of words:

"I'll do my jobs. I did come back as soon as I could. I come up-over—"

"It's not the blasted jobs, Oliver!" Etty interrupted, a sharpness at the edge of her voice. Her cheeks were tight beneath the swarming freckles; hollows traced the shape of her lips. "It doesn't matter what anyone calls you. It doesn't even matter that you've done your exam. You go to school to learn, you understand? Not to go mucking about and getting into fights. If you don't learn you are nothing, do you hear me? Nothing!"

OLIVER FOUND ALBERT working in the Bog Field, whistling "I Saw a Lady Walking By," which he always claimed had been written for his wife. He was laying the hedge with his usual, patient attention, cutting the pleachers and weaving the hetherings, but he stopped and turned at the rattle of the gate and watched the boy drop into the grass—his raven, blue and indigo in the sunshine, crossing the field with panting wings to settle on the willow they had pollarded for stakes the previous afternoon.

"How do, how are yer?" he asked, in his best Wilfred Pickles.

He removed his hat to wipe his face—the wispy white hair on the top of his head standing upright like the spines of an urchin.

Oliver grunted, took the spare pair of gloves and pulled one over his bandaged hand.

"You looks like your puppy just grew up a fox!"

"Mam is in a kank."

"I hearkened her, to be honest with you. Kept back again, is it?"

"Six blasted stripes."

"By Gar, boy! What did you do? Punch old Willie?"

"Griffin."

"Griffin." Albert snorted. "Still having a go, then, is he?"

Besides planting a quick or two, no one could have paid any attention to the bog hedge since the war or even before. The old stakes were rotten. There were glats that Oliver could easily have passed through without so much as touching the sides. Hedging took time; that was the main problem. That and the fact that they would none of them lay unless the moon was on-the-grow—in the bare two weeks between the new and the full—or the fresh shoots would go down before they went up and there would be another lot of work in cutting off the rounded pieces.

"Did the boss fettle Buster, did he?" Albert asked.

"I dunno. He is off round the lambs."

"I said to him, I said, it is not worth the trouble. I am a man for horses, like, but the horse in't born as can make these blasted quotas. It is no wonder that old lad's ready to drop. Get a tractor, I said. Three times the work she'll do, and if you dunna buy one today you shall just have to buy one tomorrow. They dunna breed the big horses no more. You canna buy the buggers if you wants to."

Oliver dragged a few blackthorn branches from the ditch, their trailing blossom a cousin for the snow. He tossed the twigs and chippings on the fire, where the billycan was hissing and creaking.

"Albert?" he asked, remembering his question.

"Boy."

"There was this man we seen this morning. Him and this boy. Big lad. No hair on him. Down by Cwmpiban, they were . . ."

Albert paused. He weighed his billhook. "Ivor," he said. "Well. I did wonder when you would rowsel him up."

"Who are they?"

"Mervyn, the lad is. The younger boy. What'll he be now, fifteen, sixteen? Five year older than you, I expect." He moved his tobacco between his cheeks. "I seen them half of the morning and all. I dunna like the looks of it, Olly, to be honest with you. Trouble, it is. You takes it from me. They's been fencing that farm like they owns the damn place . . . Ivor and the boss—I tell you one thing, the two of them is as bad as one another. I'll tell you that for nothing. I said to Idris, I said, you has to give me paid holiday, you do. Paid, mind! And overtime! There is a law now, see? Sixty hour a week I do work for him, and I do stop nights as often as not, and all on ninety-four blasted shillings. The two of us has our history, like. I only wants my due . . . Ivor, see, he'll say as half of the Funnon is his, and Idris, what he says, well, it in't for ears as young as yours. I dunno. I did think Ivor had given it all up. Married that lass up the Vron, didn't he? Up Cregrina way? Got himself a farm of his own, like . . . I tell you, boy, back in the day we used to say as it was Idris and Ivor invented copper wire." He laughed and tapped in a stake with a sledgehammer. "Found a penny in the yard, see? Went to rise him at the same time!"

57

"Yes," said Oliver. "But who is he?"

"Ivor?" Albert frowned. "Well, he's his brother, in't he? Dank me, you can hardly tell the buggers apart!"

IT WAS THE damp that was the problem, not so much the cold. It had, said the paper and the wireless both, been the wettest February since 1870. One day the water had come down the Cae Blaidd in such quantities that it had entered by the back door and left by the front. They had had to leave their boots on the stairs overnight. It had seeped into Molly's bones, as it had seeped into the walls and the flagstones, leaving her ankles little better than pivots and her hands like sockets for her sticks. How she had managed to dig the flowerbed that afternoon she could hardly imagine. Just to hold this needle in her crumpled fist, to tack together the hems of this sheet then slice it down its cobwebby middle, required all the effort that she possessed. She had worked less hard unloading the coal when she was station mistress, a woman of position with clothes that did not hang from her limbs like she was some old bwgan in a field. Side-to-middling. Maid's work. The edge become the centre. There it was, the story of her life.

All sufficient grace!
Never powerless!
It is Christ who lives in me,
In His exhaustlessness.

The prodigal voices of the chapel rehearsal continued in the parlour, Etty's piano chattering beneath them. The bulk of her Sundays, Molly was able still to persuade one of her friends to fetch her down to the service in Erwood Church, but these alternate Wednesdays there was no avoiding the black-hat brigade with their dreary harmonies and joyless heaven, which, so Oliver had informed her that evening, did not so much as permit animals. Levering herself to her feet, she picked her way between the baskets of eggs for the next day's market. The letter from her husband remained on the table, among the files of accounts and tax forms, and despite herself she held it to her nose, smelling its memories of coal and iron before she dropped it into the fire—unopened, the same as the others.

She could hear the swede chopper beneath the music as she crossed the thin, uneven bridge, using her two sticks almost in line.

"Olly?" she said, arriving at the door of the barn.

The boy released the handle and the squealing stopped. He shook out his arm.

"How do, Nana?" he said.

"Olly, have you got a minute, have you, please?"

Oliver held the lantern before them as they steered around the puddles in the yard, passing into the moonlight at the corner of the beast-house, where the visiting tractors for the Pant and Llanedw were stopped next to the mixen. From the moment he could walk at all, or so it seemed to Molly, he had walked in this manner—his shoulders set, his boots falling purposefully on one path or another that she herself could barely perceive. The granary to the stable. The pond to the beast-house. It was not, of course, that she had not seen him, that she did not know his daily routine. It was just that he belonged here so completely—it was a distance between them that grew year on year.

The well was pressed against the graveyard, at the top of

the Funnon Field, surrounded by a sunken wall. Twelve years earlier, before there had been a baby to contend with, it was all that Molly had known about this farm. The holy well. As Penlan water helped the eyes and Ffynnon Gynydd water was said to grant wishes, so the water at the Funnon was good for rheumatics—although the concave steps were so steep and slippery that the healthiest of visitors might easily have fallen and drowned. Coming to the edge of the hole, she allowed her grandson to help her descend, to untie her boots and unroll her stockings so that she could immerse her feet.

"Christ alive!" she said.

"Nesh, is it, Nana?" said Oliver, smiling.

"Bloody froze . . ."

"Do you reckon she'd do my hand any good, do you?"

Molly took out her cigarettes, struck a match and smoked with a moan of relief.

With the lantern's flame on its dribbling walls, the well—the funnon—looked to Oliver like nothing so much as the entrance to an underground world. Beneath the floating scraps of leaves, the reflection of his grandmother's pressed-shut eyes and the sudden angles of her wrists and ankles, the steps continued between bright green plants, which stirred when she moved and dwindled finally into darkness. Sitting beside her, he peeled off the bandage and sank his bad hand into the icy water. The bats from the church passed overhead—their wings catching the moonlight as they turned. Through the faint hymns in the parlour and the cattle calling for their supper in the beast-house, he heard a new lamb wailing down in the Bottom Field and the consoling chuckle of its mother. He heard the grunts of a ewe to her twins, the growls of another defending her grass and the notes of excitement of the sheep at the cratch in the Bog Field. There were more calls to know than animals on the entire farm.

In the kennel Blackie roused and barked: a sound of recognition, not of alarm.

"John the Welfrey," said Oliver, with interest. "What is he upon now, do you suppose?"

IN THE DAMP-HEAVY parlour, Etty sat between the candles in their fresh-polished brackets, her green eyes turning with the faded staves, falling as soon as the tune was established to the brass plaque shining in the open lid. She did not sing when she was playing the piano—at any rate, not with the chapel singers. She sat straight-backed in her Sunday dress, embellishing the hymn with just enough colour to escape her husband's censure, while the candlelight shivered on her tight-tied hair, the skin between her freckles and the line of concentration on her still-smooth forehead. At least on these Wednesdays, when they had guests, she was allowed to light the parlour fire. Sometimes, in her practice, she could hardly feel her fingers at all.

As the door creaked open, her foot slipped from the sustain pedal and her last note ended a moment too soon. She looked over her shoulder to see her son, who was nodding to the black-clad figures.

"What did I say to you, boy?" said Idris.

"I know, boss," said Oliver. "I'm sorry, boss. It is John the Welfrey, it is. He's down by the pond with Duke and Blaze. There is no heed to him."

"Welfrey . . ." sighed Philip the Pant.

"He hanna been the same, look," said Heather Llwyntudor.

"I shall go down, Idris," said Etty, quickly. She got to her feet and turned down the oil lamp, whose wick was just beginning to smoke. "It is for the best. If you would all help yourselves to more tea and cake, I shan't be more than a minute or two."

Oliver led her down the hall and the path. He held the lantern over the bridge but kept his eyes on the ground, then on the pig in her sty, which he usually checked at around this time, since she did like a sense of being cared for. Down by the gate their neighbour stood flanked by his horses—their brasses lit by the high, gibbous moon.

"How is your hand, Olly?" she asked, softly.

"Not so bad, Mam."

"I was hard on you earlier . . ."

Oliver said nothing.

"The auditor had been here, see? It's not been much of a day. It's . . . Of course it's different if someone's hit you first. Of course it is. I . . . I just want to see you get on. That's all."

Chapel secretary though he remained, John the Welfrey could not have seen a bar of soap these past three years. He looked like a space, a hole in the night. Since Sarah's death, Etty had been his only regular visitor—sometimes with her son, sometimes with her mother when the weather was kind—but even Etty was hesitant to enter his kitchen, with its fox-like stench and its windows often so encrusted in filth that they admitted almost no light at all. Her visits now were mostly the same. She worked with the besom, the brush and the pail. He neither helped her nor stood in her way—just sat in his chair in his island of dirt, and now and then shoved the branch on the flagstones another inch into the fire.

"Good night, John," she said.

"Ethel." John gave a little dip of his head.

"Will you have a cup of tea? Slice of cake?" She waited. "What's news?"

"The . . . taxman, he come by today."

"He came to us all, John."

"He did come to me, Ethel."

Etty nodded cautiously. "Will you not come up in the house?"

"You has always been good to me, Ethel," he said. He remained in the horses' shadow. "I am grateful. I did want to say so . . . I brung you the horses, look. I should be glad if you would take them. They is good lads, the both of them. Blaze, he in't out five year old and Duke, he is no more than seven." He paused, seeming to sink into contemplation. "The taxman, he did say to me as I shall have to sell them, but, well, I do have the name of the Welfrey, if not a sight more. It is my place. The way I sees it, if I hanna got no horses I canna sell no horses and the taxman he can blasted whistle."

1957

"And I saw before me," said Philip the Pant, "a grand expanse of land. A grand, golden land it were, with the cattle fat and the wind in the oats and the soil rich and red where it were ploughed. There was houses set with precious stones, all of them with a good plot of ground, and a castle with tall old spindling spires, and the people, they was all of them happy and smiling. Oh, you would have ached to see it. Ached, you would!"

"Get out, dog!" growled John Llanedw.

"But between me and this beautiful land there was this bridge, see? This long, thin bridge across a shining river. No piers he had. To be honest with you, I was afeared as he would not support me. But then I turned to see where I was stood, and around me I saw only a wasteland: a pit of sin lit by livid flames. Infernal, it were! Infernal! There weren't nothing but hunger and intoxication and the very worst of human abasement!" Philip rested his hands on the Bible, casting his eyes meaningfully about the chapel. "The people, they was all of them weeping and moaning, and as I turned again to my little bridge, in that moment I did give myself to the Lord. A wave of faith come upon me and I crossed the bridge in safety!"

On the pews and the benches, the congregation stirred and murmured and waited for this latest account of Philip's famous vision to end. There were muffled sobs from Vera Cwmpiban, whose husband, Walter, the Month's Mind service was intended to remember. There was laughter from boys where once, when the preachers wept and shouted, there might have been cries of "Amen!" As Nancy Llanedw worked the bellows with long, decisive movements, her round face hidden by dark, curling hair, Etty turned on her stool and set her fingers on the manual. The sheet music was open on the stand, but she kept her eyes on the oblong mirror in which Philip was hobbling down the steps from the pulpit and Idris rose from the big seat beneath him—the rest of the chapel following his lead. With the windows at his back, her husband's face was more shadow than light. He struggled a little to breathe between the lines, but still his voice rang over the others: Heather Llwyntudor in her fox-fur stole, Albert in his too-tight collar, Ruth in her lipstick and her shoddy Edwardian coat. The smells of the room were shoe polish, hair oil, coal smoke and mothballs. The colours were black and white, or grey where the one had leached into the other. It could not have been to Etty alone that her son stood apart, taller than Idris by some inches now—his dense black hair slicked back from his forehead, his golden face turned up to the cross on the wall.

And, when the waves of ire
Again the earth shall fill,

The Ark shall ride the sea of fire,
Then rest on Zion's hill.

"Christ, you're a dirty bugger, Griffin," Oliver muttered as the two boys filed back down the aisle.

"Oh? Why's that, then?"

"I seen what you drew."

"Oh! Noah." Griffin laughed, peering up at him sideways. He had ceased to grow some two years earlier, but remained as wiry and restless as ever. "Now, let's face it, boy. He were on that boat for thirteen month. What the hell else were he going to get up to?"

They passed beneath the rickety gallery and wove among the people massing on the steps, spreading into the green-grey graveyard. The day was chill and threatening rain. The smoke of the men was pale against the muckery clouds. As the women gathered round Vera, Ruth and Siân, murmuring memories and commiserations, the two boys leant on the wall by the war memorial—their eyes on a nearby gaggle of girls, their hands in their pockets, since they were not allowed to smoke themselves.

"His boy binna here," said Griffin. "Vivien, like."

"He come to the funeral," said Oliver.

"He shanna come back. You mark my words. What's he gonna want with bloody Cwmpiban? Got himself the good life in Hereford, in't he? Nice job. Nice car. Missus. Kids . . . Christ, if I had a Ford Zephyr you wouldna see me for dust neither!"

"So. You getting soft on old Ruth, then, are you?"

"I'll be soft on the beasts first." Griffin grimaced. "Old Walter . . . Fair play to him, like. He was a good lad, but he wasna no farmer. Cwmpiban's on her uppers, let's face it. They's been leasing fields, what? Five year now? Ruth could be as tidy as you like, and you'd still have to pay me to take the place on . . . I sure as hell in't squabbling with Mervyn for the privilege!"

Oliver's mother emerged from the arch-topped door with her long black coat buttoned up to the neck and her black dress flaring over slim, heeled shoes. Perhaps she had made alterations herself, brought in the waist and lifted the hem. Perhaps it was simply the slant of her eyes, or the colour of her hair, but where others looked awkward in their old-fashioned uniforms, or so it seemed to Oliver, she and her clothes were of a single piece. It was with some pride that he took her arm and followed Idris down the path among the urns and crosses, around the west wall to the back-side of the chapel: the devil's side, as it was known. Here there were no more than half a dozen graves. One belonged to John the Welfrey, who had shot himself as well as his dog. Another belonged to Oliver's brother, as they would call him, who had not lived to be baptized. The three of them stood at his un-marked stone. They prayed in silence. They picked fresh daf-fodils to arrange in the vase.

In the neighbouring field, lambs were calling and jump-ing, chasing wildly between the hedgerows.

"I SAW YOU in the paper," said Amy Whittal.

"Oh," said Oliver. He gave a grunt of amusement and whis-tled up the dog, which was dancing between them, nuzzling him for attention. "Catch us a daisy, Jess! A daisy now. Go on."

"Not a bad likeness, I thought."

"Good girl!" He gave the flower a wipe and handed it over. "A little slobbery, but no worse for that."

"Go on. What's that one, then?"

"That? That's speedwell, that is. And that there is chick-weed. I do not think the dog would know them, mind."

"You aiming to be a florist, are you?"

"It is my mother," said Oliver. "A tremendous one for flow-ers, she is. Stop a day with my mother and you'll know them as well as I do, you can be sure of it."

Amy climbed the stile into the lane, gave a little skip and waited by the hedge as a brown Ford Popular came bowling round the corner, changed gears roughly and turned down the track to the Vron. With his hand on the dog, Oliver found himself for once at the same height as the girl. He saw her bright bay eyes beneath her neat yellow fringe, a patch of powder on the flank of her nose where she appeared to have concealed a blemish. She had not filled much since their primary-school days, but the legs above her gumboots had a new, fluid shape and there was the pressure of breasts in her pale blue pullover. As she started up the slope of Penarth Mount, over the ditch that looped round its base and the sheep racks that made little ditches of their own, he watched her bottom in her pink cotton skirt.

On the summit she waved a stick as a sword—the haw-thorns behind her in the low, dark clouds.

"I saw your uncle Ivor yesterday."

"Oh?"

"He had a calf breach. I went over with Dad."

"Well!"

"I cannot say that I see the resemblance."

"By Thy grace and mercy!" Oliver spread his bag on a fallen tree, lit the two cigarettes he had snaffled from his grandmother and put one of them between her lips.

"Mind you," said Amy, "his boys don't look a lot like him either. It is Vron blood they have, the both of them."

Oliver picked up her stick from the grass and hurled it in the direction of the Edw, here more stream than river, which wove its way south between clustered willows and crowds of purpling alders. On the commons the yearlings were coming to the fences. In the fields where the starlings moved like one amorphous being, a tractor appeared from the barns at the Vron—one man shovelling clumps of muck to be shredded by his brother in the grass. Tapping the ash, he sat down beside her, his jacket open on the ornate birds he had sewn onto his waistcoat with his grandmother's assistance.

"I cannot say," he said, "as I have ever seen their mother."

"Three parts cow, I'd say."

"I know one or two like that."

Amy frowned and punched his arm, which he nursed as if it were broken. She took a shallow pull on her cigarette. "The younger boy, Mervyn. That is her as a man—save for the hair, of course. I've a theory that he cannot speak at all. I've known him since he was, what, four or five, and I cannot say that I have ever . . . No, I tell a lie, I have heard him call his dog, but I've never heard him speak to another human being. Every Saturday night he comes back from Hundred House, driving all over the lane. We found him one morning asleep in the hedge! Honest to God! We figured he must have stopped for a wee and passed out where he was. I don't know. You'd have thought you'd hear him cussing or singing or something."

Oliver slipped an inch or two sideways and felt her hip give minutely as it touched his own. He took the stick from Jess, which was whining, trying to push her nose between them, and as he threw it again he allowed his arm to fall around Amy's shoulders.

"All the boys are bigger than their fathers," she said, reflectively. "You wonder where it will end."

IDRIS COULD REMEMBER the ideal Sunday. His mother had been there, so he could not have been more than eight years old. They had been singing, the two of them. They were always singing. From their blanket in the orchard, among the cornflowers and butterflies, they had been able to see the length of the valley where the fields lay dry and, for all of the dark clouds pressing on the hills, not one farmer was tedding or cocking, loading or humping the hay. That was a Sunday as the Lord intended, a day of rest and holy contemplation. If the other farmers worked he would suffer, of course, but they would see the error of their ways. He would have his reward when the last days came.

The door scraped open and the boy entered the kitchen, his streaming hair almost touching the mistletoe as he took a tiddler from the depths of his coat: a mimmockin thing, all legs and eyes, which he dried on a scrap of towel.

"You're out of bed then, Nana," he said.

His grandmother coughed and managed a smile. "I was needing a change of scene, I was, Olly."

"That's it, little one." Ethel received the lamb. "Lovely and warm it is by the fire, see?"

"You been to see that Amy again, have you?"

"Might have, Nana."

"Pretty girl, she is. You going to bring her by here sometime, are you?"

Oliver shrugged. He removed the sacks from his waist and shoulders and hung them from the mantel, by his mud-spattered suit, allowing his raven to perch on his arm, her wings and her beak stretched open in the heat. Already so much steam was boiling from his sweater and his corduroy trousers that he and the women were enveloped in a dull white cloud.

"Two legs, boss," he said, turning to the table.

Idris sniffed and set down his book. "Has you been smoking again, boy?"

"No no, boss."

"You'll be putting my blasted barn on fire!"

"I never, boss! You couldna light nothing out there, in any case."

"Well," said Idris, after a moment. "Two legs then, is it?"

"Two legs . . . Good size calf by the looks of him. Annie is making some work of it."

"Is it coming the right way?"

Oliver presented two fingers, palm downwards. "Seems OK to me, like."

"You had best rise some rope, boy. Drink up your tea. I shall come out the beast-house presently."

Idris moved his toes in the Radox soak, easing the persistent itching of his chilblains. He lifted Foxe to the rain-muted window and found his place in the story of Romanus, the deacon of the church in Caesarea, who had been condemned by the Roman idolaters on the seventeenth day of November, A.D. 303. The man was scourged, put to the rack, torn with hooks and cut with knives. His face was scarified, his teeth were broken from their sockets and his hair was ripped out by the root. And yet he thanked the governor for what he had done—"for," he said, "every wound is a mouth, to sing the praises of the Lord."

* * *

74

At 7:06 P.M. the following day, Oliver packed his homework into his satchel, rose from his seat and stood with a hand on the luggage grid—inspecting, in the dim evening light, a poster showing an arch of sand where figures lay scattered or played in the waves and a comely girl in a bathing suit was trying to catch hold of a seacrow. It occurred to him briefly that, in a place like this, even Amy might be induced to remove some clothes, but then the wheels juddered on the points, the rails winced and the Edw Valley women came gaggling around him, as they would every Monday, with their flooding skirts and market baskets. As Aberedw Station appeared out of the silhouetted fir trees, the train slowed to a halt and the passengers fed chattering onto the platform, a few Builth boys in the carriage behind them began to bay and stamp their feet.

"Traitors!" one shouted, as the whistle went.

There was a hiss of steam and a clank of steel—red sparks swimming in the blackening sky.

"Get you here and say that!" David and Jeffrey, the two Trevaughan boys, set out after them, dodging round Oliver and Lizzy Glanedw, running alongside the lurching train. One of them reached inside a window, seemed to land a fist, but he jumped away at the end of the platform and came back, cursing, holding his hand.

It was the first of April, the first day of the new moon, but the clouds lay in broad, dark fields above the Wye Valley. With the confusion on the platform and the red oil lamp on the back of the train now shrinking away beneath Aberedw Rocks, it was some moments before Oliver noticed his grandfather, climbing from his Beetle in the car park, weaving among the people of this muddy little station three miles north of his own. He could see little more than the barrel of his body, the glow of his cigarette, the sky's faint gleam on his naked scalp.

"I seen you in the paper," his grandfather said, arriving beside him.

"Famous, I am!" said Oliver.

"Your mother's proud, I should imagine."

"She's read it once or twice, like."

The women squeezed into an Austin Seven, which ground its way up the bank towards the village, its headlamps fanning over Treallt fields.

A Hillman followed a short way behind.

"Did you . . . Did you have a word with your grandmother, did you?"

"I had a go, Grandad. I canna say as I got very far."

"Is she picking up at all, is she?"

"Some," said Oliver. "I don't know. It's still a good day if you see her in the kitchen. It's her rheumatics, that is the problem, see? She'll catch anything going, that's what the doctor says. It is the second time she's had the pneumonia now."

His grandfather shuffled his shoes in the chippings. "There is no aim to it, boy," he said. "I write to her and write to her. I dunno what else I can do, to be honest, save . . . save coming to see her."

"Well. You'll find her in."

"What do you think, like?"

"I think you'd best give Mother a miss."

"Are they doing their singing this week, are they?"

"Wednesday. Pant it is, this week. They was up at ours last."

"Wednesday," he repeated. "You're a good lad, Olly."

As the headlamps faded and the darkness settled, Oliver could see his grandfather a little more clearly—his narrow eyes deep in the folds of his face, his shoulders twisting as he rooted in a pocket of his jacket. He took the cigarettes he offered with a word of thanks. He slipped the clips round the ankles of his uniform trousers, then lifted his bicycle from the wall of the toilet block, flipping the dynamo onto the back wheel, while the new lambs called in the level valley fields and the train's lamp appeared again in the distance— its spark repeated by a curl in the river.

TOWARDS THE END of Turley Wood, the paler clouds above Cefn Wylfre parted to reveal the moon: a hair-thin crescent, long at the top, which the boss would have said meant rain. Slinging his right leg over the saddle, Oliver slowed and hopped to the ground, the headlamp dying into an ember. He removed his cap, put his hands together, bowed his head and made a wish. Beside him in the Middle Ddole, the creatures were calm. The moonlight shone from the puddles in the track, and since it was not fifty yards to the gate he decided to walk the rest of the way—leaning his bicycle in its corner of the stable before he tramped up the path to the house.

"I binna going to no hospital!" Idris exclaimed.

"For crying out loud, Idris," said Etty. "Will you please hold still?"

"I binna—"

"Why on earth do you think we pay taxes?"

"I's blasted if I know!"

Idris appeared to have been flung into his chair. The long grey hairs straggled over his ear, clinging to the clump on the top of his head. His harrowed face was plastered in mud, which continued over the breast of his jacket, covered his hands and stopped abruptly at his gnarled white legs—their hair cut in places by ancient scars, the right calf bloated and twisted in his bunching trousers.

Between the hooks in the kitchen walls hung sheets and pillow cases, shirts and drawers.

"What . . . What happened?" asked Oliver.

"Thank God you're back," said Molly.

"I shall not have the Lord's name used in vain in this house!"

"I said to you that bridge was dangerous," said Etty. "Didn't I, eh? It is too blasted narrow!"

"What do you want me to do, Mam?" Oliver took the heavy, sloshing fountain from his grandmother, who was attempting to lift it with her elbows.

"Have you done your homework, Olly?"

"I done it on the train, Mam."

"Get you round the lambs!" Idris barked.

"Hop back on your bike if you would, please, Olly. You know the doctor's number, don't you? There's pennies in the pot on the mantelpiece."

As Oliver hung the fountain from the swye, Molly sank into a chair by the fire and took the bottle in a thin, crabbed hand to feed one of the tiddlers wailing in the basket.

"Lambs!" Idris repeated, and started to cough.

"Idris!" Etty dropped the flannel in the steaming bowl. Among the shivering shadows of the washing, her hair was loose, her cheeks were pale. "If you do not let me wash you I shall just go off round the lambs myself. I have quite enough to be getting along with until I have found us a boy—"

"Boy?" said Idris. "Boy?"

"You heard me."

"Has you lost your mind, woman? It is lambing, if you had not noticed! In any case, there is a larp of a boy right here!"

"Oliver has his O-levels in a month, as you very well know."

"You squeeze your ears against your head now, woman. This is my farm! I shanna waste one single shilling on no blasted boy, so you can rid yourself of that idea for starters."

"Idris." Etty had still not moved. "The situation is quite simple. I do the books. I know what's what. There is a little money put by for an emergency, and that I shall spend on a boy to work with Albert until you are back on your feet. If you think you're going to wreck my son's education because you cannot be bothered to look where you're going—"

"Are you listening to me, are you?"

"It is that or I sell something."

"Oh! Well! What you going to sell, then?"

"Well, the Welfrey is no blasted use—"

"The Welfrey is mine! That money is mine! You canna do nothing without my say-so!"

"Oliver is going to school. That's my final word."

"And mine and all," said Molly.

"The day I hears your final word, Mrs. Evans—"

"Don't you dare talk to my mother like that!"

Oliver stood uncertainly at the fireplace, still in his school clothes, the penny beginning to sweat in his hand. He watched his grandmother set down the bottle, fixing Idris with her sharp blue eyes.

"Now look you here, Mr. Hamer," she said.

"Mother, I am handling this!"

"That boy goes to school—"

"Or what?"

"Mother!"

"Do you want for me to spell it out, do you? I should like to see you manage without us, I should! You and your broken leg!"

"Oh!" Idris pulled himself almost upright, moaning as his foot dragged over the flagstones. He wiped one hand on the tail of his shirt, pushed the hairs back onto his head and opened his lips on his brown-white teeth, which tapered back to the root. "Well. Where you going to go then, Mrs. Evans? You answer me that, can you?"

IT WAS NORMALLY the geese that heralded a visitor: the geese then the dogs, which refined their cries with calls of greeting or warning. Through the chaos of voices that Wednesday evening, Etty heard the popping and the clatter of a car. She turned down the volume on her little plastic wireless, listening closely, and although the dogs did not seem to know the driver she filled the kettle at the butt in the larder and hung it from its notch above the fire. She emptied the last of the loaves onto the table, piled the next week's sticks in the bread oven, then closed the latch and removed her apron—brushing the flour from her spare, red hands.

"Well," said Idris, through the boards of the ceiling. "If it's not Michael Evans."

Etty froze near the end of the hall, on the mat between the thin, grey windows.

"Good evening, Idris." Her father's voice was low and hesitant. "I didn't . . . Well—"

"What are you upon, boy?"

"I was . . . hoping to see my wife, I was."

"In your cups, is it?"

"I have stopped all that, Idris."

"Oh?"

"Six year now. I've not had a drop."

Second cousins as the two of them were, Etty could see some trace of her husband in her father's face—in his shelving eyebrows, in the verticality of his flushed, heavy cheeks, which had fallen into jowls in the seventeen years since she had last seen him close to. In her old, patched skirt and the lumpish cardigan she had knitted in the winter, she stood on the step beneath the open window where Idris was keeping his invalid's vigil, his electric torch on her father's head. His hair had retreated to a red-grey arch.

"Hello, Etty girl . . ." he said.

He approached the bridge through the darkening drizzle, carrying a pair of cardboard boxes.

"And what do you want?"

"I . . . wanted to see you, girl. You and your mother. I brung presents for the both of you."

"You'll get from here if you know what's good for you!"

"Please, Etty." He held one of the boxes between his knees, opened the other and held up a dress—low-cut, red with a black polka dot. It spread from the belt and shone in the cone of the torchlight. "I did ask Oliver what he thought you would like. I . . . I seen him at the station, down in Aberedw. It was me found him. It is not his fault . . . It is your size, I think, but I can always have it changed?"

"And just what the hell am I supposed to do with that?"

Etty's voice had cracked in spite of her efforts. She turned her head to conceal her eyes, and at the top of the yard she saw her mother: her face like tallow even in the twilight, her walking sticks like additional legs. She was staring back down the slope towards them, tiny-looking beside her grandson and the towering trees that surrounded the churchyard—the knots of their rookery black against the louring sky.

CROSSING THE TACK field on Saturday morning, three days later, Oliver could see a line beside him, extending through the dew all the way to the riverbank: a seam in the air where the light was thin and rainbows blinked and went out of being. It stopped when he stopped, lying motionless as the dogs at his feet, forty-five degrees precisely off his shadow, but the moment he moved it was dancing again—teeming at the far edge of his vision.

It had occurred to Oliver more than once that if Philip was looking for his grand, golden land he had no need to travel further than Llyswen: the tack, where the yearlings had their winter grazing. The house at the Dderw was palatial, pink enough to be bejewelled. The earth was, indeed, red where it was ploughed, and in places, in the banks of the Wye's first meander, you could see its depths, the layers that made the place: not the frail grey shale of Rhyscog but half-inch on half-inch of glorious soil with, far beneath, a firm red sandstone, like the bridge across the flem at the Funnon: the long, old stone which Idris had unearthed once on Llanbedr Hill. Oliver had been to his Geography lessons. He knew about flooding and silt deposition, about river cliffs and slip-off slopes, but the farming he knew was the farming of the hills and this abundance made his eyes swim.

"Get away by, Jess!" he called. "Go round, Blackie! Bring them on now! Bring them on!"

The grass in the valley was greener, brighter. Already the trees were embracing spring: the wych elms were matted with red-purple blossom and the sallies were so thick with yellow-green pussies that from a distance they seemed to be leaves. As he closed the gate and followed the sheep out of their field, back over the railway embankment, he saw cowslips, sheep's sorrel and, among the blackened patches where the sparks from the train had caught, a bulbous flower with sprawling yellow petals, which he did not know and picked and stowed in his pocket.

The railway bridge was grand and ancient: a box of girders that stretched across the river to the bramble-tied cliff and the sun-glinting windows of the school and the houses of Boughrood. Pausing again at the top of the embankment, Oliver watched the sheep crowding into the next field, then whistled at the dogs to lie down. He trod carefully from tie to tie, above the few loose plates not stolen by the wind, and once he could see the water beneath him he straddled one of the glistening rails and let his legs swing loose in the air. His grandfather, by now, would have taken his grandmother off on her day-trip. Where that might lead, what it all might mean, he could hardly bear to think. Its uncertainty hung in him, cold and tremulous. He had three Navy Cut left in his packet. He balanced with his boots as he struck a match, smoking, watching the rocks and the currents until the blood in his ears became so loud that he was forced to close his eyes.

"LLANGODEE," SAID IDRIS. "Black House. Gwarallt. Gilfach. Blaenhow . . . Cloggau?" He lifted his hand. "Cloggau."

He turned to yet another list of farms, with their earmarks cut from the page beside them so that its edge resembled lace. Many of the places he had never even seen—farms out for Eardisley, Rhayader and Kington—but for decades he had been watching their stock, recording here and in the books on the counterpane these hundreds of minutely different slits and notches, the names of sales, buyers and lot numbers. This was the knowledge that allowed you to survive, not the doddle you were told in a classroom. Had he wished, he could have traced the bloodline of almost any sheep within fifteen miles, as like as not through forty generations.

"Fforest Farm. Graig-yr-onen . . . Vron."

With his right leg in plaster, sloping to the ceiling, Idris had to struggle to twist himself sideways, to open the window with the hook of his crook and peer down into the yard. Albert he could see quite plainly from his pillow, sowing the oats in the Sideland Field now that the frost and the old moon were gone, but to see Ethel in the pen by the barn took all of the muscles in his stomach. There she was with a drooling ewe, making an incision in the short head wool, holding the syringe with a nurse's care to draw out the tapeworm and its bladder of eggs.

He had warned her against that beethy hay.

With a sigh Idris fell back onto the bed and looked at the wall above him, its flower-tangled paper, the verse from Galatians embroidered by his mother—fruit trees following its wandering border. In the yard his wife was singing softly; she must have completed the operation. It was a song he remembered clearly from the wireless, back in the war when he still lived alone: something about swallows and choirs and mission bells, which was, in truth, better suited to her voice than the stridency of hymns. Perhaps, he found himself admitting, it would have suited him better as well. The recording he remembered was performed by a quartet, with the lead a fine, slightly quavering tenor, and although Ethel was singing almost to herself she gave the song that same precision and restraint—the delicacy and lightness she brought to the piano and the organ. As she passed beneath the window he murmured himself the long, minor notes of the backing chorus, pausing when she paused, following her timing, until she faded with the corner of the barn and he picked up the book and turned another page.

"Stowe," he said. "Ton Farm. Brilley Court."

THERE WERE SKYLARKS, invisible in the bare, blue air, their wild songs tumbling in conflicting time. There were buzzards flirting, spiralling in the sunlight, and humming cars on the striped main road, which Oliver had been annoying for the long two miles between the bridges at Llanstephan and Erwood. From Glannau Pool, the sheep pressed on through the heather of Llanbedr Hill and, crossing the track from Troesyglowty to Llanbwchllyn Lake, passed the grave of Twm Tobacco: a highwayman, so the story went, who had been hung, drawn and quartered for murdering a farmer, then buried at these crossroads, since none of the local churches would have him. If Oliver had learnt from his mother the birds and animals, the plants and trees, then Idris had at least taught him the places—if only with a word or phrase. He had shown him, by example, that you should always leave a pebble here. Oliver dug one out of his pocket, and stood by the grave for a moment or two, his hand on his chest, while the dogs coused on towards the crumbling cliffs—Garreg Lwyd and Craig-y-Fuddal—where a cousin for Maureen showed his belly to the sky and righted with a satisfied honk.

Yearlings as they were, the sheep knew their patch of the common. They had been here as lambs, the previous summer, and they started to hurry as they sensed its proximity—

spilling over the wether-shorn contours, past occasional wind-shaped hawthorns, until they came to the fences for the Island and began to disperse among the quarries.

"Go back! Go back! Go back!" called a grouse, rising red out of the heather.

Oliver sat against the fence of the New Field and ate his bait, flicking a crust or two to the dogs, which returned, low and wagging, seeking out his hand with their noses. There were Funnon sheep grazing the new grass at the Welfrey. In the valley Albert was working his way across the Sideland Field, the hopper on his shoulder, throwing out arc after arc of grain—as ragged as the bwgan in its old hat and coat, which did nothing discernible to scare off the crows. At Cwmpiban a brown Ford Popular was parked in the yard, by the front door of the house. Mervyn was ploughing a field that, to Oliver's knowledge, he and his father had never ploughed before—the sunlight bright on his big, bald head and the long green bonnet of his tractor. He remembered Griffin's clecking at the chapel. As he watched, he saw Ruth appear with a basket and follow the grass around the lines of the hedgerows until the two of them met among the furrows.

ONCE, AT THE age of five or six, Etty had crept to the privy at Erwood School. The rules among the children were as rigid as the hierarchy. To use the cabs, as they called them, for more than a wee was unthinkable, and yet, without any particular need, she had sat herself on that chill wooden seat—so tense, so alert to voices or footsteps, that she barely allowed herself to breathe. She had that feeling now as she stood in the kitchen, pulled down her skirt, unbuttoned her blouse then peeled off her slip and even her bra and her drawers. The draught from the larder passed over her shoulders, the ingress of her back, her buttocks and close-held legs. The fire mapped her downturned face, her breasts, her stomach rounded only by children, the red hair at the join of her thighs. Although her mother and her son were away, she was trembling as she opened the box—counting to ten once, and again, before she pulled the dress over her head and felt its cool silk arrange itself around her.

"Ethel!" Idris called from the bedroom. "Ethel! How about some dinner, woman?"

Etty heard the rustle as she moved her hips. She looked at the straps on her thin, freckled shoulders and was pleased to see a groove just emerging from the neckline, which, by closing the belt, she was able almost to double in length. She thought about fetching her Sunday heels, which Idris had bought her along with her dress, one improbable day in Builth Wells, but better bare feet than to make any sound. Opening her drawer in the bread-and-cheese cupboard, she dug beneath the books and the photographs, took out the dog tag and tied it round her neck. Then, noiselessly, she glided down the hall to the parlour and stood before the panes of the tall sash window. In the yard there were goslings and filing kittens. Chicks were scurrying after their mothers, yellow in the full, warm sunshine. Etty felt the hardness of her feet and her fingers, the scrawling, uncomfortable veins in her calves, but still, in the reflection, it was a girl she saw: full-haired, straight-backed, with the name of a soldier hanging at her throat as if the father of her son might suddenly appear, begging pardon for these seventeen years.

* * *

THE VW BEETLE had not long returned when a candle appeared in the window of the church—squeezed between the trunks of the sycamores, faint beneath the waxing moon. In the kitchen Oliver completed a long-division exercise, checked his calculations and added it to the pile to be sent to his teachers. He set the next one in the space on the table, but the meaning of the numbers was gone. Years must have passed since his grandmother had last used this signal. There had been a time, when the two of them were allies, when it was usual for him to creep out of the back door and huddle together with her in a blanket. Now, he had been working since six that morning. He was too worn out to go hiding from Idris, and he waited only for Maureen to scale his arm, clicking her beak when she reached his shoulder, before he clumped his way down the hall to the yard and climbed towards the Bryngwyn track—the torch in the window throwing a shadow in front of them.

"How do, Nana?" he said. "Grandad?"

With only the candle, deep in the socket of the window, the half-ruined church was almost as dark as the churchyard. The cross made an elongated shape on the altar, but the bulk of the pews showed only their backs, and the door of the vestry where the bats went to roost was lost in the blackness of its wall.

His grandparents were hunched at the front—each confirming the age of the other.

"How are you, Oliver?" asked his grandfather.

"Where'd you two go, then?" Oliver sat down across the aisle, trying to force some cheer into his voice.

"Llangorse Lake," said Molly.

"Is it?"

"We hired a boat . . . We'd go there a lot, see? Me and Michael."

"I'll have seen you from the hill."

"Keeping up a fair old pace, we were. Blink and you'd miss us!" She smiled momentarily.

"We was wanting to talk to you, boy," said his grandfather.

"What's going on, Olly? Are you working here again next week?"

"Well. I expect."

"What does Etty say?"

"Not a lot she can say, is there?"

"Olly . . ." Molly looked past the collars of her new fur coat at the bats' lozenge droppings and the grass and nettles that were sprouting between the flagstones. She watched Maureen pace on the back of Oliver's pew, then lifted her eyes to his face. "Things has changed, they have. The two of us, we've been talking today and, well, the way I sees it it's been a good long while since I was any sort of use round here. A burden I've become, that's the honest truth—"

Suddenly the two of them were talking at once.

"I've been bad on you, boy," said his grandfather. "I know I have. You and your mother and your grandmother, all of you—"

"You do have a choice, see?"

"Two spare bedrooms there are at the station. You can have your pick. There's a telephone, and running water, and more coal than you'd know what to do with."

"You could hop out of bed and straight onto the eight o'clock. You could be at school Monday, easy as that. And you could go on, like, if you wanted. Do your A-levels . . ."

"Well!" said Oliver.

"You don't have to decide now." Molly ran her fingers up one of her sticks.

"Have you spoken to Mam, have you?"

"She won't have it from us, boy. Perhaps you . . . Well . . ."

Oliver turned and leant on his knees, looking past the light-filled cavity of the window to the bare oak body of the altar. There were dull green lines on the wall behind it, reaching down from the cracks in the roof to grow into moss towards the floor. There were memorials among the flagstones, almost illegible from centuries of feet. When he tipped back his head he saw stars in clusters and the moon on the edges of the broken slates.

"Well," he said. "I cannot leave her on her own, like, can I?"

EVEN AFTER A decade of growth, there remained in the outline of Pentre Wood the long, squint-backed shapes of those terrible snowdrifts where the few starving rabbits that had made it through rationing had gone hopping and creeping, nibbling the bark from the exposed branches. As Oliver left the lychgate for the Bryngwyn track, he remembered their shrivelled, picked-clean bodies revealed by the last of the melting snow. He remembered the sheep that had hung from the trees: fleeces empty of all but their skeletons and the foetal skeletons of their lambs.

"Boy!" shouted Idris.

"Yes, boss?" He climbed into the yard.

"What are you upon, you blasted pwntrel? I opens my window and the first thing I hears . . ."

Once Oliver noticed the keening sheep, he could not believe that he had not heard it before. His mind, it seemed, was in disarray. Thin above the valley, there was the cry of the barn owl in the Oak Piece; the dogs were baying from the Pant to Cwmpiban, joined in moments by Blackie and Jess. Still, under any usual circumstances, the noise of the ewe might have roused him even from his sleep. Fetching the stable lamp from its shelf, he set off into the Banky Piece with Maureen's feet spread wide on his shoulder and Idris's torch-light skidding through the grass. A few lambs ran into the shelter of their mothers, burying themselves with flickering tails. A couple of them fell in behind him, their voices raised, as if in accusation. When he came to the brook he lifted the lantern to throw its ring across the chunnering water. He jumped and landed on the muddy pebble beach at the head of the wash-pool, where the ewe was tucked among the flood-striped roots and the long, limp catkins of the alders. In her lee was a lamb in an afterbirth slick—its eyes red pits, its chin so bloody that it might have been feasting on flesh. It fell and managed to stand again. It opened its jaws in a voiceless gar-gle as Oliver grabbed it by the hind legs and climbed the bank to swing it hard against a rock.

The twitching stopped. The lamb hung still, dribbling blood into the hoof-pocked grass. There was nothing, Oliver knew, that he could have done—the crow would have been here some hours earlier, if it had not been a raven, which he tried not to think about—but it always went bad on him, kill-ing a creature. Laying down the body, he felt in his pocket for the last of his grandfather's cigarettes. He stood among the trees at the foot of the Panneys, trying to conjure up an image of Amy, while the first sheep to yean, on the hillside before him, watched him with the lantern in their eyes. From here, looking eastwards, he could see no trace of the dingle between Cefn Wylfre and Llanbedr Hill. The hills formed a single, moon-trimmed blackness—as if they had joined. As if they had sealed the valley.

IT WAS A wonder, really, how the procedures came back. Moving the washstand to the side of the bed, Etty folded the flannel round her hand and dipped it in the basin. She rubbed up a lather on the carbolic soap and turned to her husband, who was watching her warily, as the soldiers would, from the white towel that covered the pillows and the bolster.

"I shall wash myself," he repeated.

"You will just get the bed wet."

She started with his face, working outwards from his eyes to the grey hair slewing over his head. She washed round his ears and continued down his neck, with each stroke using a different part of the flannel, and once she had passed the nub of his larynx she pulled tight the strop on the window catch and started to sharpen the razor. By the door of the barn her father's car fired and spluttered into life. Its headlamps strafed her face as it turned. For a moment both she and Idris listened to the dwindling engine, and listened for the clatter of the front door latch, then she worried the brush in the shaving soap and painted his cheeks and his chin.

Idris muttered but did not dare to move. He watched Etty sideways as she wiped down the blade, untied the rope from the foot of the bed and fed it through the pulley until his plastered leg was flat on the blanket.

"Oh, he itches!" he said. "Oh, dank me!"

In a mere five days, the sinew of his body had started to soften. As she helped him to sit, to move the towel, a fold appeared among the stone-hard ripples of his belly. There was the slightest slack to the skin of his arm, a little give to the muscles of his chest, where the bullet scar shone white beneath the clavicle.

"No," said Etty, firmly.

"Now—"

"No."

"You're my wife, you are!"

"Idris," she snapped. She did not look at the swelling in his drawers. "I have not slept more than three hours a night all week. I'm the nurse, the cook, the cleaner and the blasted farmer. I'm damned if I'm going to do that as well!" She took his shoulder roughly and rolled him on his side. "Now then. Oliver. Next week."

"It is lambing, woman, for dank's sake!"

"We will be done by the weekend as you know full well."

"The beasts is kindling. The Sideland wants rolling. It is high time the boy paid his way . . . He can go to his exams. I said to you."

Etty soaped the flannel for the nape of his neck, making quick, broad sweeps across his back and the pale, tangled place where the bullet had left.

"If you want a rag," she said, "there is one on the chair, but I'd be glad if you would wait until I'm gone."

"FED UP WITH SLAVING IN AN OLD-FASHIONED KITCHEN?"

"Payments made to Radnorshire for the financial year ended 31st March, 1956, were £15,440 15s."

"Out with the. . . . **OLD**. In with the. . . . **NEW**."

"Sixteen-years-old Oliver Hamer (son of Mr. and Mrs. Idris Hamer, Funnon Farm, Rhyscog) still continues to be very successful in the Three Counties Boxing Tournament. A pupil at the Builth Wells Grammar School, he was the winner in his age group in the recent Scott-Paine Boxing Tournament, and later won his fight against the Worcester Amateur Boxing Club. He is now middle-weight champion of Hereford and holds the Builth Shield for the middle-weight class."

The boy in the photograph wore shorts and a vest. There was a fix to his eyes, a vigour to his proud, strong face. His fists were brought up close to his chest, revealing shadows in his bicep muscles. For a minute or more Etty looked at her son, then she set down the paper and, pulling on her oven gloves, lifted the fountain from its notch above the fire, her boots spread squarely, her thin arms trembling. She sat it on the stool, turned the tap to fill the teapot and ran the rest into the long zinc bath.

The clocks continued.

The bull at Cwmpiban proclaimed his virility.

Finally Oliver arrived in the hall, his hobnails hollow on the flagstones. He ducked for the lintel of the kitchen door, his raven sitting low on his shoulder, having learnt the new dangers of perching on his head. He slumped among his revision at the table, pale as she had seen him, the oil lamp playing on his dishevelled hair.

"You all right, Olly?" she asked.

"Lost a lamb," he said.

"It happens." She put her hands on the back of his chair. "Is Mam—"

"She's gone."

It seemed extraordinary suddenly that Etty was able to stand at all, with just two legs and so much to carry. The sensation that came over her was such an unholy tangle that she could hardly tell her exhaustion from her relief from her old, redoubling anger. She and Molly had long ago agreed. There was no going back. Oliver was one thing; he had not been there. He had known her father only cowed and sober. But her mother, she had seen him throw Etty out of her home and hurl her bag down the platform after her. He had thrown Molly out too when she tried to stand up to him, and cursed her to hell as he did it.

She had trusted her to keep her word.

"Do you . . . want the bath, do you?" she managed.

"I'm . . . You go first, Mam. Dunna worry."

"I'll just fetch your father his tea, then."

It was the first time Etty had used the word in years. Somewhere in her son's transformation into this man in scale, it had fallen away from them, like Santa Claus.

"Oh," said Oliver, and reached in his pocket. He straightened the petals of an Oxford ragwort, heaved himself back onto his feet and slipped its stalk into a buttonhole of her cardigan. "I found her by the railway. New one on me, she is. I did think you might like her."

1963

O LIVER REMAINED WITH his elbows on the bar top, spinning a shilling whose sphere resolved into the head of Elizabeth II. He followed the rays of the quarter-cut oak, golden beneath the beer mats and the smoke-streaming ashtrays, and once Lewis had emptied the half-drunk glasses into the barrel and returned to his place with a foaming jug, he accepted a refill and slid him the coin.

"Traitors!" shouted the boys in the door.

"I should never have been a farmer," said Griffin. "I hates fucking sheep, I do."

"Gran?" said Oliver. "Jimmy?"

"You're a good man, Olly," said Granville, his big rings clinking as he passed him his glass. "So. What's all this traitor business, then?"

There were only men in the Awlman's Arms. No local woman would ever have been seen here, and those women from off who came peering through the door every so often would rarely last a glance across the smoke-coloured walls, the soot-clouded oil lamps and Locke on his stool looking back at them skute. Besides the demolition gang, who had come by with Oliver to flog a few railway ties, everyone was a regular: the old men by the fire with their dominoes and leather leggings, the husbands and fathers, their caps tipped back on their neat-cropped hair, the various lads of Oliver's age with hair to the collar, snug-fitting trousers and shirts for the most part open at the neck. They were men from the hills, from Penblaenmilo and Pentremoel, three months of snow still weighing on their shoulders as they watched the Crickadarn boys enter the door, press between the clustered tables, push old Adam Prosser aside at the bar and stand in formation—three abreast and four in the rear.

"Cider!" said their leader, facing down the landlord.

"Two and four," said Lewis.

"Going to serve we, is it?"

"Going to pay me, is it?" He spread his hairy forearms.

The man took a handful of pennies from his pocket and scattered them tinkling over the flagstones. He looked back at Lewis, who did not move.

"Go on, then," he said. "Who's your best boy, then?"

Oliver took a draught of beer, wiped his mouth and lowered his eyes to meet the man's gaze, working his rings slowly from his fingers. His heart was running but his mind was transparent, perfectly still. He blinked periodically, and did not speak, and when the man grinned and looked back at his friends he knew already he would win.

"How are you, boy?" he asked, at last.

"So who the fuck are you, then?"

"I'm the no-good devil what's coming to you."

"Oh? Fancy your chances, do you?"

"I dunna fancy yours."

"What the fuck is that tie?" The man gave a laugh, and his friends laughed around him.

Oliver tightened the scarlet knot and patted down the vee of his waistcoat. "You hanna heard of fashion in Crickadarn, I suppose?"

"Wop fashion, is it?"

"Do you wanna say that again, do you?"

It was Oliver's calculation that the man would swing quickly. He saw the squat of his jaw, the strata of his forehead, his thinning brown hair. He kept his feet parted, the toes of his boots alone on the flagstones, and when the man dropped his eyes a single degree he slipped a step backwards so that the ball of his fist went sighing through the smoke before his face. A fresh jibe rose in the pool of Oliver's mind. He parted his lips, but already the man's left was leaving his side and he allowed them to turn into a smile. Griffin's bar stool was about two feet behind him. The next punch came in a blizzard of movement, skimming his chin with a bloom of colour, and he took his step to dodge another, then threw his right into the man's uncovered belly—sending him grunting to the end of his reach.

The pub by now was in uproar. Another fight was squaring up next to the quoits. There was pwning on the tables, the crash as a glass met the floor.

"Lamp him, Olly!"

"Lay to him, boy!"

It was a fact of chopping wood that if you aimed your axe not for the top of a log, nor even for the bottom, but for the foot of the block—the ground itself—then with no great effort you could split almost anything you met. The man had spirit, Oliver would give him that. He was long-armed, deep-chested, quick enough almost to be good. He even appeared to be thinking now, his fists up, checking the space, moving to trap him against the bar, so Oliver waited one more moment before he sprang himself with a right like the first, to wind, to disorientate, then, as the man's arms came down, he brought his left on the full through the levels of smoke now weaving and tangling over the ashtrays, and this time he aimed for the back of the man's head and heard the pipe-stem crack of the bones in his nose even through the voices and the stool that splintered as he fell.

"Ho! Ho-ep!"

Etty swung her plant against the nearest flank and sent the beasts panicking onto the Bryngwyn track—keeping their order as they turned back towards her, close against the oval wall of the churchyard where the snow lay hunched after thirteen weeks and yet another night of rain. They were a wretched lot, for all of the fodder that Oliver had bought them—their faces as dull as the house had become, their haunches making shadows on their red-brown coats. To the rasp of the rooks and the annual crop of ravens, which was one price of having Maureen for a pet, she worked her way along the bank of the prill, beneath the overhanging sycamores, whose pink-shelled buds were bursting on infant leaves and flowers. She came to Hendy and Little Hergest, the herd's contending queens, their fan-eared princes beside them in the mud, then she looked back at Panda, which was a step apart from the others, her calf on the outside, and although she could see no fault in her breathing, no swellings, no sign of lameness, still she felt a conviction framing in her belly and she moved herself carefully into that space, bringing pressure on the cow while the rest backed anxiously home towards the yard.

"Come in, Jess!" she called. "Come in!"

As the dog closed the movement, Panda and her calf sheered away and galloped up the track, past the end of the churchyard. Etty followed, her gumboots slapping, dragging the gate for the Funnon Field open and propping it on the hanging post to seal the way back. She looked again at the pacing animal, the hang of her horns, the black round her eyes, and this time caught a limp in her hind off leg.

If the spring was due, it was yet to arrive. The sunlight leaking from the bloated clouds still lay almost level with the fields across the valley, snow in the shadows of the contours and the hedgerows. The harrier was falling over Llanbedr Hill, vanishing behind the horizon to rise again in a tumult of silver, as if bouncing on a hidden trampoline, but despite this, despite the bright, sliding whistle of a blackbird and the efforts of the cattle and the rooks, the farm was quiet. The half of their flock that had made it through the winter were squeezed with their few dozen lambs in the Bottom Field and the Middle Ddole. Albert was plodding across the Sideland Field, trailed by crows, scattering grain with every other step: a sight so familiar after twenty-three years that Etty could hardly remember him otherwise. Idris was guiding Blaze around the Long Field, rolling the soil where he had stood in the snow to ward off the helicopter with its bales from the government.

The hills, he had said, must have their rent.

"Bring them on, Nell!" Etty whistled. "That's it, Jess! Good girl! Bring them on now!"

The cattle bunched, revolving in confusion, but Etty called

to them lightly, tapping her stick to get their attention. With the others behind them, Hendy and Little Hergest edged cautiously towards her, then suddenly poured into the Funnon Field, their weight in the wet ground, spreading among the peeping cowslips, the cinquefoil and the domed ant heaps with their red crowns of sheep's sorrel, capering absurdly, tossing their horns as it dawned on them that their six months' imprisonment was over.

IT WAS OLIVER alone who wore sunglasses cutting—seventy feet above the Wye at Boughrood, his shadow flexing on the churning water. They had goggles, of course—regulation issue from the Western Contractors—but if he was going to work all day in full view of the school, the post office and the houses among the sallies and oak trees on the river cliff, then he would do so with his hair in order, three buttons open at the neck of his shirt, his eyes more fashionably concealed. Boughrood Bridge was a cage of steel: four enormous, two-hundred-foot girders, one for each corner, and a mesh of diagonals in between. It was as big a demolition job as Oliver had known. Straddling one of the topmost girders, he opened the regulators, checked the gauges and looked across this next pair of braces at his mate, Jimmy Owen, who was perched with his bottles on the opposite side, scowling past his heavy leather boots. Beneath them, to the north, a couple of mooching local boys, Jerry Miles and Edward Hughes, were sitting on the frame where the rails had lain, swinging their legs and spitting at the flood-matted islands.

"I didna mean to say no harm, mister," one of them said.

"Mister, can we come up there, can we?"

"Let 'em be, Jimmy," called Joshua, the harried-looking

foreman, appearing next to the train on the bridge-end. "I'll keep an eye on 'em."

"They're all right, boy," said Oliver. "Just getting in on a bit of the action."

"Well . . ." Jimmy shrugged. He always preferred not to make the decisions. "It is your manor, I suppose."

"On we go, then." Oliver lit the acetylene with his cigarette, flicked away the butt and turned to the brace, waiting for the edge of the steel to melt before he hit the oxygen and started to cut.

Boys had been pothering them for six months now: birds to their plough as they worked their way south, following the last down-train from Moat Lane, through Llanidloes and Pant-y-Dwr, fitting the braking chains to hoist up the rails, tossing the ties about like matchsticks. They were a famous team, or so they had heard: Scotch and Paddies, work-bitten Midlanders and hard-raised farm boys who had never seen such money in their lives; £4–10 a day they were earning, with time and a half Saturdays, and double time Sundays, and all the cash they could count for the ties they sold to the farmers for gateposts. They had bought themselves beer and suits and jewellery. They had fitted the snowplough and worked through the winter, with a pair of ghosters every week— Monday to Tuesday, Wednesday to Thursday—and each of those was thirty-four hours, with no more rest than the odd cup of tea.

The river lay straight beyond the meander, narrowing away between flower-shaded oaks towards the dark, falling nose of the Twmpa. The clouds were divided by the new electric cables, which had appeared almost everywhere over the past year and, to judge by the angler near Boughrood Vicarage, had not as yet upset the salmon—whatever the calamitous predictions. Across the valley the blossom of the pears and cherries shone in the muted sunlight. Buds like candle flames coloured the beech trees. A swallow fled beneath the bridge with insect movements as Oliver's torch left the second brace and the steel cross fell the height of a train to chime and leap on the beams.

THERE WAS STILL a drab of snow on the lane up to Painscastle, and with Oliver, Joseph and Granville on the bench and the four Hay lassies shrieking in the back, Jimmy had to back up twice and gun the little A40 van to make the pitch by the track to Trevyrlod. With the clutch in the air and the chassis shaking like a half-drowned dog, they crept across the cattle grid—the headlamps grazing the few Clun lambs in the Ffermwen fields and the cars and tractors spread along the verges. They dawdled, looking for somewhere to park, then found a space by the telephone box, where the engine expired into the night.

"I lost my shoe!" called Angie.

"All right, lad, you can get off me now."

"I dunna think he wants to, Gran."

"Where's that bloody hipflask?"

"Olly, open the bloody door, would you? We cannot breathe in here!"

She was a tidy piece, was Angie Lloyd—not pretty, perhaps, with her keening nose and that fold of flesh beneath her chin, but high-hipped and big-breasted in a way that mattered. She was not shy either, or so went the rumours. If boys wore raddle the same as tups, she might have been bright red from her head to her feet. She clung to Oliver's arm as the eight of them paraded down the lane, pressing her rigid sweater to his side, and in the lee of the castle, in the cigarette-spotted darkness, with the deep notes thumping in the village hall and the week's pay fat in the pocket of his trousers, he laughed and locked an arm around her shoulders.

Painscastle always gave the wildest dances. Tony Brown would drag his black leather jacket, his record player and tractor batteries to every hall from Gwenddwr to Gladestry, but most of these places had some inclination to order. In Painscastle, there was barely a farmer not locked into some ancestral war. To have assembled any kind of peacekeeping force could have taken a lifetime of negotiations, and since the entire dance had been known to turn against them, even the police could be coaxed out of Hay by nothing less than a riot. Beneath the ball of mirrors whose shafts of light fanned through the smoke, boys were gathered in groups, by village, with cigarettes and pints from the pub—eyeing one another, eyeing the girls in their Saturday skirts who had come with their brothers and kept to the back in villages of their own. There was a story probably all of them knew, if they couldn't have given the names or the details. Years before, some girl from the Skreen had been taking a dip in the lake at Llanbwchllyn when the lord from Painscastle came by on his horse and decided he liked what he saw. He had locked her away up here in the castle, which must have been good stone back then, not merely a mound with a sheep-haunted ditch, and when the word got out every man with an axe or a hay knife had come charging up the valleys from Llanshiver and Court Evan Gwynne, and the castles at Clifford and Hay. For several weeks they had laid the place siege until, in the end, an army showed up and put the whole lot of them to the sword. Three thousand men were supposed to have died. The Bachawy had run crimson and the blood would not mingle, even with the Wye, so the news of the battle passed all the way to the sea.

Hell, thought Oliver, as he bent for the door, but those boys had wound things up.

ETTY REMOVED HER spectacles, rubbed her aching eyes with hard-tipped fingers and began to assemble the accounts and the tax forms, the bank statements and her own financial projections, and return them to their neatly marked files. She stacked them in turn at the end of the kitchen table, where the teapot shivered on the cloth.

"Idris," she said. "They will not have one more penny on the mortgage."

"He shall not have the Welfrey!" Idris repeated.

"Then lease it, at least! We had it for a song—"

"Now, look you here, woman—"

Etty hit the table and her fountain pen jumped.

"Idris," she said. "You can attack me all you like and it will make no blasted difference. I am telling you the numbers, do you understand? There are forty-four lambs. There is no money in the bank. We made the payment this year only because Oliver has work. If it weren't for him the two of us would be stuck in a council house, and that's if we were lucky! He shall keep on working down to Three Cocks, which will pay us to restock, but it will not scratch the mortgage and it will not buy us a tractor and that old horse will not go another year. I shall ask the vet to see Panda in the morning, but God help us if the foul has reached the other beasts . . ."

Idris stood above her, his long face sheer, his short breaths groaning deep in his chest. For once he said nothing, watching her take up the pile of files as if she might suddenly remember some forgotten balance sheet, some overlooked grant form he had only to sign and return. He looked, as she left them in the bread-and-cheese cupboard, as dry, as wizened as the mistletoe drooping from its thick black beam. The oil lamp failed to find his eyes. It traced the white-grey hairs that stretched between his ears—glimpses of scalp where they had slipped out of place.

It was so thick with shadows, the Funnon. The walls of the station, as Etty recalled them, had all been smooth: the rooms one level of orderly rectangles. Here there were corners and crevices everywhere; the walls bulged and cupped beneath the discoloured whitewash. No wonder the house was such a devil to keep clean. At the overlapping chimes of half past nine, she wound both clocks and blew out the lamp—the flame that remained on the mantelpiece casting long shapes over the flagstones. Her hand was huge on her husband's back as they climbed the stairs, as they would every night, and in the bedroom she set down the candle on the dressing table, whose mirrors threw rhomboids of light across the wallpaper, the moralizing samplers and the patch of the ceiling where the rain would drip and pop in the ewer. In six years Etty had not seen her mother. She did not see her son for weeks at a stretch. As usual, she and Idris undressed back to back, pulling on a nightdress and a nightshirt respectively: stiff, white garments that fell onto their upturned feet as they knelt together at the side of the bed. Beside them, in the floorboards, were the marks of knees where Oliver was not.

A fox barked its loneliness high on Cefn Wylfre.

ANGIE LED OLIVER to a tree by a vein of a stream where the blue lights blinked in the thin, fanning branches and willow gullies dusted his spilling hair. With the sogginess of the ground, her heels kept sinking so that her eyes came barely to the neck of his waistcoat, and as she took a step towards him she stumbled and laughed and grabbed for his hands— looking up at his broad, dark face, the swelling in his cheek that made him seem to smile, his teeth repeating the white of the moon that lay above the tump of the castle.

There were the ghosts of sheep in the fields around them. There was shouting in the village, the roar of a tractor. She allowed her breasts to compress on his belly, lifted her lips and, closing her eyes, saw distant, fluttering colours in the blackness. His smell was a musk, a rich allure. His heat was such that his clothes might have hidden a fire. She felt a pressure in the tightness of his trousers and touched its shape with her long, sharp nails.

"You're going to have to kiss me first, you are," she said.

Well, he was younger than she was, even if she had misled him on that little matter and her friends and her girdle would not tell him different. He was a boy from the hills, however exotic his appearance. At least he bent when she reached for his neck and brought his face towards her own, his hot breath coming almost every second. His tongue met hers and circled its tip. His hand left her shoulder and gathered her breast, which he almost contained in the splay of his fingers. Before he got any other ideas she worked on his belt and dug in his trousers until his penis was projecting towards her. She crouched unsteadily, holding his leg, balancing on her toes, and brought its stale-smelling head between her lips. And yet, when she looked back up at his face, it seemed to her that he had barely noticed—his eyes turned up to the net of the branches and the stars among the moon-framed clouds.

THERE WERE NO other horses in the stable at the chapel, although the place stank as ever of urine and hay—smells that Idris had always found soothing and held in his lungs before he climbed from the trap. He tethered Duke in his regular bay, unhackled the shafts and laid them on the ground. He collected his stick, then turned to the door, where Ethel was waiting among the few cars and tractors, in the dress she had worn these ten years gone—its blackness subsided like the colour of her hair, which now recalled sand more than fire. She had powdered her nose to conceal its redness. She had painted over the scoring round her eyes, but with the bones of her shoulders and the spareness of her waist he would not have taken her back to Watkins, the expensive tailor down in Builth Wells—even if he could have met the bill.

"Boss," said Albert, who was standing on the path by the war memorial.

"I likes your scarf, Mrs. Hamer," said his wife.

"Thank you, Dorothy." Ethel twisted its corner. "Purse stitch, it is."

"Purse stitch!"

Albert sighed and ran his eyes down the names.

Clouds were closing on the blueness of the dawn. Between the listing stones, the daffodils were the only note of colour: brilliant yellow or white with orange mouths. Swinging his stick with his shorter leg, Idris joined the line of worshippers who fed into the chapel, passed beneath the gallery and dispersed onto the pews and benches with long wooden gulfs and entire rows remaining empty. At the big seat he stood in his polished leather shoes and looked across the pew where he had once sat with his brothers to Ethel, to Ruth and the girls who were his great-nieces, and Philip's son, Griffin—his shoulders bowed and his face worn thin by five months of humping hay to their top fields. Despite urgent meetings of the chapel committee, everybody else in the place had hair that was grey at the least.

> There is a fountain filled with blood
> Drawn from Emmanuel's veins;
> And sinners plunged beneath that flood
> Lose all their guilty stains.

Incrementally, over the past few years, Ethel had begun to depart from her organ scores. Idris had spoken to her about it, even made threats, but still, when the first verse of the first hymn was over, she allowed her right hand to trace out alternatives, her feet to draw phrases of such sudden complexity that he faltered, glancing at her upright back. Beside her, Nancy kept pumping the bellows. The congregation sang doggedly as ever. His wife seemed to think she could play what she liked. She seemed to think they were accompanying her. On his raised step beneath the tall windows, Idris stood as erect as he could manage, his hands at his sides since it helped with projection and he knew the whole hymn-book by heart. The trouble was, there was an invention to her deviations; they were by no means as arbitrary as he sometimes chose to think. Despite himself, he could not help listening, nor stifle his occasional replies. He hung onto notes until his breath almost failed him. He met her harmonies with harmonies of his own. For a full two lines in the final verse he was barely a precentor at all, but once again a soloist, facing his audience—performing a hymn composed as it left his lips.

*　*　*

"You boys, I'm telling you!" laughed Jimmy, who was sat across the bridge in his parka and his woollen hat. "You don't just go to a dance, do you?"

"Well," said Oliver. "There's dancing and dancing."

"Ever try the Twist, lad?"

It was a dull, cold Sunday. They had been working at Boughrood a full week now and most of the top run of braces was gone. The bridge lay open: a roofless skeleton with the wire rope spooling back towards the crane, hauling yet another cross-piece. Besides themselves, Granville and Joseph were cutting at the north end, weary, hunched above their work. The foreman was abusing the same pair of teenaged boys who had claimed their place midway across the span, pitching stones into the deep, fleet water, the brown foam tangling with the currents.

"Fucking kids!"

"They're all right, gaffer."

"Enough is enough! I told their bloody mothers . . ."

Oliver shivered. Even with his gloves and his thick tweed coat, the breeze kept finding its way to his skin and he was glad for once for the acetylene torch, which bloomed white behind his sunglasses. On the entire length of the railway line, in the snow and the darkness, this was the only part of the job that he had resented. It was a beautiful construction, Boughrood Bridge: all Herculean spars, diamonds of air and rivets as big as his fist. It was a hundred years old to the month, or so Joshua had told him; three hundred and twenty tons of steel. It could surely have been saved for some other purpose—if nothing else, to cut a mile out of the journey to the tack.

The crack was so loud and the fall so sudden that Oliver did not so much as cry out. He was propelled from his seat by a terrible force, the blaze of the torch passing over his legs as his back and his head collided with a girder that seemed to have appeared out of nowhere. He spun, and his belly met some other shelf, which drove the air clean out of his chest. For a second he fell, and then another, and then the river exploded around him and he was freezing, blinded, wildly alert. He threw out his hands and found some sort of beam, but his fingers were rigid from the previous night and his gloves began to slide across the rust. There was the height of the hills in the force of the water. He flailed his arms, attempting to swim. He felt himself turning and remembered his mother, then his back hit a rock and, swallowing, choking, he crawled across stones onto an island of stick-woven sallies.

Perhaps not even a minute had passed. On the bank, beyond an eddy running gently westwards, the angler from the vicarage had dropped his rod. Oliver managed to roll in the saplings. The bridge, he realized, had folded in half, buckled like a thing made out of wire, so that the sides splayed sideways and most of the bed had collapsed into the river. Jimmy was somehow clinging to his girder, his swinging torch still spouting fire. The foreman was gaping, frozen, by the crane. Among the blacks and silvers of the water, Oliver caught sight of a clump of hair and he blundered towards it, splashing and shouting, and grabbed Jerry Miles by another clutch of islands. He fought his way back into the shallows, where the angler took the boy from his arms.

Half of the village was already on the bridge-end. People were scrambling down the twisted beams, calling out to Jimmy and Granville and calling for Edward Hughes. Oliver waded through the starving eddy and climbed through the flotsam onto the path, but at the gieland the ground seemed to slide from his boots and he lay without struggling beneath a fern-sprouting willow, with the pink-white faces of lady's smock bobbing and settling around him. When he wiped his face his glove streamed blood. Above him, in the tree, he could see what must have been small birds: one with a caterpillar, another warbling flurries of notes among the buds and the yellow-furred flowers.

FOR ALL THE times he had seen him in the fields, it must have been eleven years since Idris had last been face to face with his nephew. Albert had called him the spit of his mother— a heavy-timbered Cregrina girl Idris had eyed in passing when he was a lumper—but as he stood with his father in the door of the stable, the geese by the pond still acclaiming the gander and the sheepdogs joined in fury in the kennel, he looked to Idris like nothing so much as Ivor plucked and inflated to hideous dimensions. He had the same louring eyebrows, the quick-shifting eyes. He had a chest so broad that his arms were at angles and a neck like the neck of a beast.

He murmured to calm the cob and himself, running the curry-comb from his shoulder to his belly, working in circles to rise the dirt.

"How do, Idris?" said Ivor.

"Ivor."

"You was singing very sweetly this morning, I do hear."

"Oh?" Idris came to the hind leg, went easy on a scratch and stood back, checking for flaws in the gloss.

"So I do hear." His brother cleared his throat and waited. "Well, boy, I know you shanna part with the Welfrey, and that's fair enough, like. She is your place. I shanna say no more about it, but . . . Fact is, boy, the two of us, we is neither of us getting no younger, and I did come to thinking we should talk about the future."

"Oh?" Idris repeated. He picked the hairs from the comb and turned to Blaze. "Well. It is dinner time for me, it is. I'll have my food on the table, I expect."

"Fact is, boy," Ivor persisted, "the old world is changing. Them old places like the Welfrey—you canna live on them no more. In't no farmer as can live on thirty acre, not on this ground, and Cwmpiban, well, she is seventy-six and that's no size of farm neither, let's be honest. Now, I dunna mean to call young Oliver. He is a regular lushington from what I hears, but fair's fair, my own boys has done their bit of boying, and we done our bit and all—"

"Drinking," said Idris, "is no joking matter."

"Nor it is, nor it is. Don't get me wrong. What you done, taking in the boy, it was an act of charity, I sees that now. Michael Evans's father was a cousin for Mam, and if your own family goes throwing its girls on the blasted state, well, it is a sorry business, it is indeed. Young Oliver, he is a fair larper—you done the boy proud, like—but let's face it now, he binna no Hamer. And the Funnon, she is a Hamer farm. She's been a Hamer farm these seven generations, and more besides I shouldna wonder. You and I, well . . . I dunna like to get the law involved, no more than you do. You'll say you're the oldest—you've told me that plenty—and I'll say by rights as a half of her is mine—"

"So you do think."

"I hanna come to go back there, Idris." Ivor lifted his hands. "It do hardly matter now, in any case. Fact is, one of these days, you and I, we shall be slipping along and the Funnon, she'll be coming to one of my lads—that's just the way of things, in't it? And the way it seems to me, it would be a sight easier on all of us if we was rubbing along. Mervyn here, like, he is a good strong boy. With Oliver off on the railway and so forth, it would be no trouble on him to lend the odd hand, do a bit of work with the tractor perhaps, get to know the old place. Old Albert, he'll be tight on seventy I doubt, and it has been an unkind winter. He'd be thankful for the help, I should imagine. And Mervyn, well, he is just next-door with Ruth and their two little girls . . ."

Beyond the watching dogs and the quarrelling rooks, the valley was quiet, as it had been for weeks. A ewe in the Bottom Field called to her lamb and at once fell silent, as if daunted by the noise. A dog at Cwmpiban was barking at its echo. Idris went easy on Blaze's hock, inspected his work, then hung up the comb. He slung the harness over his shoulder and turned towards the door and the house, trying to ward off another bout of coughing, dragging the thick stable air between his lips. In the yard a drizzle was beginning to fall, shimmering in the miniature puddles of the hoof marks. As he passed the two men, one of the hens gave a sudden squawk, her chicks running to hide in her feathers, and Mervyn lifted his great, bald head, screwing up his eyes to scan the sky for the sparrowhawk.

IF THE RAILS had gone and no more than the impressions of the ties still jarred beneath the wheels of Oliver's bicycle, then Erwood Station did not appear to have noticed. It sat as ever between the gaping river and the nose of the hill where the electric poles stood in silhouette. The flowerbeds were bright with geraniums and wallflowers. The pond in the down-platform sparkled with the drizzle, distorting the circling goldfish. Dismounting by the white gate for the car park, he dragged himself limping past the ticket office, with its rain-streaked advertisements for Van Houten's Cocoa and seaside resorts where the sun seemed always to shine. He moved from the gas lamp to the station sign to the fence around the grand new plot of dahlias his grandmother had planted to supplement her pension, and knobbled at the door of the small, square house whose gutter ran level with his eyes.

"Olly . . ." Molly appeared on the doormat.

"It's not what it looks, Nana."

"Michael! Michael, get you here!"

His grandfather propped himself beneath his arm, wheezing as they stumbled down the hall to the sitting room, where the fire was glowing in its arch of tiles, between the scuttle and the stand of tools, and the wireless was chattering on the windowsill.

"Get the kettle on, Michael, don't just stand there!"

"Edward Hughes," said Oliver. He fell into an armchair.

"What's that?"

"Edward Hughes. He's dead, he is."

His grandmother knew the boy, of course. She knew everybody, as she must have in the past: Edward's parents and grandparents, their friends and neighbours. She even knew the demolition gang, who had come through here a fortnight earlier, Oliver among them, hoisting the rails aboard the train with displays of efficiency normally reserved for the management. She had had them sat in a line along the platform, drinking her tea and eating her cake.

Oliver saw the blood on his swaddled hands, then the patchwork upholstery, and attempted to rise.

"Covers'll wash, boy . . ."

"We been up and down the bank the entire morning." His voice sounded thin, almost child-like. "Right down to Glanwye. He never come up!"

"Whatever's happened, love." Molly sat down beside him with white, gathered eyebrows and started to unwrap the bandage round his head. "Whatever's happened I'm sure it's not your fault. I'm sure you were just doing what you were told."

It all seemed so simple, life at the station. There were no fields, no animals, no hostile neighbours. There were net curtains patterning the view of the river. There were daffodils in a vase on the piano. There was a photograph on the mantelpiece of Oliver's mother—a girl in a swimsuit on a sunbleached beach—and another of himself on yellowing paper with his fists held tight to his chest.

Molly inhaled sharply, peering at his temple. "That is some kind of gash, boy," she said. "Do you want for me to call an ambulance, do you?"

"There was one at the bridge, Nana. It was them patched me up."

"I'll say it wants stitches."

"And they did . . . Can you do it, can you?"

"Olly, it in't exactly embroidery."

"I shall find you some clothes, lad," said his grandfather, returning from the kitchen with a cup on the ledge of his belly.

Oliver waited for the iodine whose metal stink was filling the room. He clamped his teeth and closed his eyes until his grandmother tied a fresh dressing round his forehead, and he did not resist as, with thin, bent fingers, she worked on the buttons of his sodden shirt.

She glanced from his face to the chaos of his chest: the overlaid bruises in the shadowing hair, violet fading to yellowish green.

"Jesus, boy . . ." she said. "What the hell have you been doing to yourself?"

"I'm all bruises today, I am, Nana," he said, and felt himself starting to cry.

As Etty left the landing the door's wedge of shadow gave way in front of her, sending the candle flame ducking and spitting. The door frame spread until the bedroom was lit— the shape of the four-poster shivering on the walls where the damp paper rippled and, in one place, looped back to the floor. She set the tray on the bedside chair, although she could see that Oliver was asleep, and she stood looking down at the extent of his body, his ankles protruding from the railway overalls beyond the end of the mattress. As the candle settled, the lip of the pillowcase made a shadow across the bruises in his cheek and the crown of a bandage round his pollard-like hair. He was at once a man who smelt of antiseptic and cigarettes, and her baby, afflicted by his size, by forces she had tried to control and could not. Had she the strength, she would have gathered him up and held him all night in her arms.

Keeping to the rug, where her footsteps were softer, Etty untied the knots on his steel-toed boots and set them together on the floorboards. She opened the chest in the cupboard above the stairs and, peeling off the newspaper, shook out a couple of mothball-stinking blankets, which she wrapped round his feet and lay over his shoulders. She hesitated in the moving light, the shadows alive again on the wallpaper. She watched him breathe, his one hand clenching inside its dressings, then she kissed him lightly on his un-bruised cheek, picked up the cup and went to close the curtains.

There was condensation on the window: a dingle of drops at the foot of each pane. Etty pushed back the skin of the cocoa, which itself made a few pale streaks on the glass, and drank and looked past the white-peeling bars at the black-roofed barn, the hills and the retreating valley. The drizzle had passed. The clouds had parted and dwindled into scraps. A narrow moon stood almost overhead. The stars decked the sky with their ploughs, bulls and gods—shapes, as a girl, she had defined herself as a friend doing a cartwheel, a kite with a tail of glittering bows—then, all of a sudden, there were stars on the ground. There it was at last, the electric. With envy, with wonder, she watched the bare white lights, which multiplied as the minutes progressed and the car horns called like dogs between the farms, until every contour the length of the valley had a constellation of its own.

1970

MARTIN UNPICKED THE knots in the tobacco and pressed it into the bowl of his pipe, holding the stem with his teeth as he searched for matches among the nails, the bits of string and straw in the pockets of his old wax jacket. In the sun against the wall a lean young collie named Turk uncurled, got to its feet and looked down the deep, even furrows in the common, past the gulls and peewits hopping and squalling, to the place where the hill dropped out of sight. At a far-off roar, its ears became pyramids. It turned in a circle and lay back down, while the other dog, Nell, raised a half-interested eyelid to the sunlight splaying from the variegated clouds, to the luminous pools that slipped down the valley, across the green shoots of oats on the opposite hillside and the hedgerows white with hawthorn blossom.

There was smoke beyond his own, then a chimney and a pair of close-set headlamps. As the wheels appeared in the bracken, Martin saw for a moment clean beneath the tractor.

"How do, Prof?" called the farmer, turning on the un-ploughed stretch at his feet. "I didna know you was back."

Oliver Hamer was something to see. Five years earlier, when Martin first wound up the A470, following the advert, up the River Edw to this corner in the hills where the road ran out, he had wondered how such a man could possibly have sprouted from so unforgiving a place. He was tall like himself, but where Martin was wide-hipped, his pale hair fine and thinning at the crown, Oliver was grand and swarthy—and swarthier still as the spring progressed. He liked to think that he was some ancestral throwback, some peat-soaked relic of the settlers of this forgotten valley.

"We came down last night, Oliver," he said.

"Friend's with you, is he?"

"Jonathan? Yes."

Oliver dropped from his seat to the ground, frowning at some flaw in his work that Martin was unable to perceive. He came across the bank with the dogs at his feet and his raven on his shoulder—his big chest trying the buttons of his shirt, long veins scrolling from his rolled-up sleeves. His smells were earth and oil and animals.

"Well," he said, considering the sky. "You picked a fair old week for it."

"Such was my thinking."

"Holidays already, is it?"

"I did a bit of juggling, that's all." Martin wiped his glasses, positioning them again on his nose. "I have to say, Oliver, it never ceases to amaze me how the Welfrey catches the sun. And the wind goes right over. The bees can't get enough of it. I was thinking I might put up a small greenhouse, with your permission—see if I can't grow some grapes."

"Them old boys knew where to put a house."

"Indeed they did."

"What am I moithering about?" Oliver laughed. "If they'd known a damn thing they'd have stuck him down the bottom!"

"So, you're ploughing the bank, then?"

"I'm spoiling the scenery, I'm sorry to say, but it spares us the forestry. I cannot abide them bloody plantations. Full up of foxes besides anything else."

"This would all have been forested, of course, once upon a time."

"Not with bloody larches, it wouldn't."

"True."

"Elms, I do believe."

"Elms," Martin agreed. "And oaks and birches. They were cut down, for the most part, in the late Neolithic and the Early Bronze Age. Many of the other species were planted. That's why you tend to see certain trees near old houses. Beeches were supposed to protect against lightning. Elders were supposed to ward off witches."

"You wanna have a word with Albert, you do." The farmer cupped a few oats in his hand, a dome of muscle in the crook of his arm. "Right one for that old squit, he is. And he seen the roots of the old trees. They'd rise them up the mawn pools when he was a boy."

"Is that a fact?"

The birds were clearing from the last of the furrows, returning to the ground they had already perused. Through the mumbling of the tractor, the breeze brought the momentary tacking of a whinchat, the calls of the lambs in the fields above them and the fields three hundred feet below. At a noise that Martin had not noticed, Oliver dipped his eyes to Turley Wood—its oaks tinged golden, as if foreshadowing autumn—and a small blue van, climbing the track to the Funnon. Only once or twice had Martin seen the change that could come over his landlord's son. For a year at least he had been convinced that the stories he heard in the post office and the Awlman's Arms were nothing more than malicious gossip—despite the deep crescent scar in his temple, his two absent teeth and the kink in the bridge of his nose. But now again he saw the man's face close, his eyebrows fall, his jaw come forwards like the chinpiece of a suit of armour.

THE SUNLIGHT CUT Builth High Street on the diagonal, casting the shapes of chimney pots and television aerials across the Fountain Inn, where Griffin the Pant was installed on the pavement with Tom Llanowen and George Gilfach. He lifted his cap in a jovial greeting. Beyond the cars and the Land Rovers stood along the north side, a man was harrying his cattle away from the Smithfield—trailed by flies and a couple of tractors, whose drivers paused by the clecking men between the Lamb and the barbers. Weaving among them, Etty and Nancy Llanedw held their willow baskets to their chests, heavy with sugar, currants and raisins, Typhoo tea and yeast for the baking. They passed beneath the awnings of the shops and the tea rooms, and the May Fair bunting—their long skirts jangling with the coins they had earned from the sale of their eggs and bright yellow butter at the table they shared in the market hall.

"Spain!" said Nancy.

"Never!"

"Alice, she is all about in her head. You never seen a girl so excited! Well, I did say, and John said too, we said they should spend their money on getting themselves started, but everyone else gets a honeymoon, they say, and, well, it is Spain, in't it?"

"Spain . . ." Etty echoed.

"I'm only sorry as they canna get married in the chapel. It were always so handy for Llanedw, like. When Bridget married Harry, oh, that were lovely, but Trevaughan are church in any case, and Llanbadarn Church is a fine little place."

"Give us the lend of a grandchild, will you?"

"We shall have them to spare, I cannot deny it . . ." Nancy hesitated. "That Annette Mills in't a keeper, then?"

They followed a gang of Cregrina women through the kissing-gate into a field of a graveyard where the great, squat tower of St. Mary's Church stood red-hued over the circling yew trees. The grass had not been cut since the fair, and the ground between the headstones was white with daisies.

Etty stopped in the path.

"Oh!" said Nancy. "There's lovely!"

The organ reached them across an angle of paving stones: a music so rich that, for all her Sundays in the corner of the chapel, Etty could not remember the like. It seemed as grand as the church itself, whose walls here seemed suddenly, giddyingly tall, with their windows alight in the warm, full sunshine and a cross on every gable.

"Come on!" Nancy grinned and turned from the path.

"Oh . . . No."

"Well, you can stop here if you likes."

"There is the bus, Nance."

"She'll wait a while yet, girl! Get along with me now. What's gonna happen, eh? It's not like Idris is even in town."

Etty followed her uncertainly through the tall, pointed door at the foot of the tower into the cool church air, where

Nancy set down her basket and walked boldly across the long red carpet that led around the back of the pews. Except for the organist, who must have been concealed somewhere beyond the pulpit, the wrought-iron screen and the plumes of peonies and sunflowers, the building was empty. The music here surrounded her, so that it might not have come from an instrument at all but have emanated somehow from the sheer white walls and the dark beams arching at the height of the barn and perhaps that height again. It spilled and unfurled, with moments when the right hand alone darted forwards, moments when the left jumped out and went playing around it until the tune was remade and the two hands spun over the deep notes of the pedalboard, as if dancing together across the flagstones. Etty waited for the verse to repeat, but instead the music found fresh ways to build, to ascend, to renew itself. Slowly, her basket clutched against her shawl, she joined her friend in the aisle and peered around the column at the mouth of the chancel at a skein of pipes reaching almost to the roof and an ancient, lop-eared man, who sat hunched above three banks of keys, between stops more numerous than she could count.

IDRIS WAS IN the pond when the van arrived, straddling Hanoch, dragging a post through the brown, milling water and the shadows of the overhanging elms. He knew the note of the engine, and the date, and he gave no heed to the geese on the banks nor old Jess yawping from the shade of the whilcar, which had lost its snout and gained a coupling and was now no better than a trailer. He rode a steady circle, keeping the reins short, and as the water purled down the troughing towards the chain-harrowed, manure-skithed slope of the

Banky Piece he spoke soothingly to the tare young cob and barked instructions to Albert, who was hobbling between the sluices at the top of the field.

"I didna see you in court," Ivor began.

Idris ignored him.

"Do you wanna know what come of it?"

With the turning horse, his brother appeared among the ruts by the gate—Mervyn behind him like a grotesque shadow.

"Well," said Ivor, "I shall tell you what come of it, and I has no obligation in law so I shall deem it a favour. This farm is ours, mine and yours. Half the ground is mine and half of the house and all. So, I shall be taking a half of the mortgage, and I could be quibbling about that, so says the solicitor. We has drawn up an agreement as you will be signing. Since I have no plans to be sharing your roof, and I dunna suppose as you'll be wanting to move, I shall be taking on the greater portion of the fields. If you wanna sell the house we shall make the arrangements, but as things stand we shall be cutting gates to the Long Field and the Crooked Slang and boodging yours in the Tumpy Field, the Bog Field and the Sideland. Them in between, them is ours."

"Far sluice, Albert!" Idris called.

"You has the right to appeal, you do, but I'll tell you now, them fees is no bargain and it shanna make no difference in any case. All I can say is you wanna be thankful I in't putting you over the door and the whole place up for auction, which would, I imagine, put a fair penny back in the pocket of the bank and not very much in yours."

Finally, Idris drew on the reins. He rounded the cob and glowered across the settling water, the beast-trodden mud and the marsh marigolds tucked among the roots of the trees. The sun was glancing from the surface of the pond; its rippling light ascended the trunks. His brother, he saw, had cropped his hair. Keen-eyed, he was smewling back at him—his thin lips arching over spare brown teeth.

"Now, look you here," he said.

"You canna say as I give you no chances!"

"If one of your creatures sets foot on my farm—"

"You can think what you likes, boy."

"I shall shoot the dankering thing where it stands!"

"I has the law, I do! The boss died intestate, so—"

"You parasite bugger! You shame on the name!" Fighting his breath, Idris kicked on the stirrups and tushed the post up onto the bank. "I is counting to ten, you stop-at-home sod, and if you hanna—"

"Oh! Rowsel all that up, would you?" Ivor seized the bridle to hold the cob, which was snorting, pawing, trying to turn. "I wasna old enough to serve, as you very well know—"

"And that's too good for you! Stop at home and make your prayers as neither of us comes back! I knows you!"

"By God, I's a good mind—"

"I's counting to ten, and if you dunna leave go of my horse and get from my yard, I swears to God—"

"Leave go the horse, boss!" said Mervyn.

Idris felt the blood in his face, the air once more draining out of his chest.

"I shall buy the bloody place outright!" Ivor shouted.

"Boss!"

There might have been a tourniquet round Idris's body, crushing him until the pain itself was driven out of his chest, into an arm, his neck, his rising jaw. As Hanoch reared and he lost the saddle, he saw the hayfield beneath him, fertilizing nicely, the leaves of the elm trees—pointed, serrated, perfectly scored among the clusters of their disc-like fruits.

"Boss?" said Oliver.

"Dunna move him," said Albert.

"Boss? You all right, boss?"

He had a fine voice, Oliver: low, almost bass, with none of the tendency to shrill of Idris's own. It had long been his sorrow that the boy was unable to master a tune. Idris could not number the Sunday evenings when they had sat in the parlour with Ethel, her voice as pure, as lovely as she had seemed to him those first few times he had seen her at her market stall in Erwood, and the longing had come to him for one further harmony. He had always loved trios, their heady complexity, their intimation of infinity. It had been his ambition, he seemed to remember: a group to perform in the larger halls, perhaps with Oliver, his older brother, whose voice had been as deep as his namesake's, perhaps with Phyllis Jones, who would have been his brother's wife, had the world been just. His own Oliver had simply listened, turning the page at a nod from his mother. It was not his passion, but he had not complained. He was glad at least that he had been there. He would not have had it elsewise.

Etty left the bus at Rhosei Cottage, where the driver turned west towards Aberedw, and Mrs. Price's gander was hissing from the phone box—his tongue spearing orange from his beak. She lifted a hand to the vanishing women, took her basket in her arms and started up the pitch towards the Pant, between pink-speckled walls of hawthorn blossom and leaves almost emerald, promising summer. The sunlight parted over Aberedw Hill like the sun was hanging, kite-like, just above the clouds. The puffing, cycling call of a pigeon followed the plod of her old studded boots among the Cluncross lambs as big as their mothers, the cowslips, buttercups and red bird's eye that flooded the ditches with colour.

She was one bend short of the Cwmpiban turn when she heard the sound of an engine and moved to stand on the sloping verge—looking up to see a big yellow car only when she knew that it was not Mervyn's van.

"Can I offer you a lift, Mrs. Hamer?" asked Dr. Tyler.

"What's happened?" asked Etty, sharply.

"Your husband's had a fall. I had a call from your son . . . He's with us, don't worry." He leant to open the passenger door.

"Yes, Doctor. Thank you, Doctor."

Etty had ridden in a car or two, thirty years earlier, but never in one with such commodious seats, an orchestra playing softly on the wireless and a bank of dials with little red needles to indicate who knew what. She sat very upright with her basket on her lap, rolling her aching shoulders discreetly while the doctor blew cigarette smoke from his beard and guided the long bonnet around the potholes, through Cwmberllan Ford, where the floor of the wood was radiant with bluebells.

"And have you noticed anything particular lately?" he asked.

"Not that I can think of, Doctor." Etty tried to mimic his bettermost accent. "But, well, he is over seventy now, and he will work himself . . ."

There were house martins in the yard, darting and flickering among the insects in the rising air, diving on the puddles and creeping in the mud. They had a nest above her bedroom window, which some held to be good luck and others bad. The post and rope were abandoned by the pond. Hanoch was tethered loosely by the Plock, where the Fordson stood among the castrated lambs, its plough pointing back towards the orchard. After a moment of trying the handle, Etty allowed the doctor to open the passenger door and she led the way across the narrow bridge, waiting for him to rub his shoes on the doormat and then advance into the hall.

"Good afternoon, Mr. Hamer," he said, brightly. "Albert. Oliver."

"Good evening, Doctor," Idris muttered.

"What can I do for you, then?"

"Well. I'm not the one to say."

"Lungs been troubling you again, have they?"

"I expect."

Idris, of course, was sitting in his chair, his hands on the arms, his eyes some degrees to their left. His breath was a croak in the stony darkness. When, at a glance and a nod from the doctor, Etty pressed the little plastic switch by the door and the bare, clean glare of the bulb filled the kitchen, she saw his face, which was pale as the hawthorns—sparks of sweat sliding down his forehead to gather in his white horn eyebrows. His trembling lips were pink with Gaviscon. Opening his case, Dr. Tyler pushed the cuff up his arm, worked the bulb and considered the reading on the sphygmometer. He uncoiled the stethoscope and knelt for some moments, but Etty had had her year of training; she knew the symptoms well enough.

"Well, Mr. Hamer." Dr. Tyler returned to his feet. He spoke gently, precisely. "I'll say you've had a heart attack. I'd like to get you to Hereford, soon as we can, just to keep an eye on things. I'll take you there myself, if you like."

There were cobwebs in the corners, marks and stains on the bald white walls that the oil lamp would never have revealed. There were the rings of cups on the tablecloth and pockets of dust between the flagstones and in the crevices of the pot dogs on the mantelpiece.

"Well," said Idris. He blinked as the sweat ran into his eyes. "Thank you for coming, Doctor. Ethel, would you make the man a cup of tea, please?"

THERE WAS A laciness to that final furrow, an imprecision to its line that made Oliver grimace and blow the smoke from the side of his mouth into the reddening light of the Monday evening. He might, in fairness, have been ploughing a cliff, and in full view of the entire valley. Even riding up empty, climbing the bank back towards the Welfrey with the diff lock down and the plough held high, the big back wheels would spin the sun-dried ground. He could not stop himself leaning forwards, as he had in the trap—as if his weight might keep the Fordson from flipping onto its back.

The addlands at least were reasonably level. Lurching past the top of the reen, Oliver turned the tractor side-on to the slope, waiting for Maureen to hop from the mudguard to his shoulder before he collected the jug and the butter in its dock leaves from the cardboard box behind the handbrake. He waded to the gate through the crisp brown fern and the bowing heads of the new year's crop. It had been his mother's idea to put an advertisement in *The Times*. How she had known that there would be some quist who was willing to pay fifteen pound a month for this old place with its dubious spring, he struggled to imagine. It did not so much as have the electric, which Idris had finally allowed at the Funnon a couple of years before. Professor Chance was a comical sort, but his notes arrived with his every appearance and the Welfrey cottage had never looked so tidy—even in the days before Sarah died. Its face was painted a fresh, rich cream and its green-framed windows looked down upon rows of cabbages, carrots and potatoes as orderly as their own. Oliver passed the red MGB GT the professor somehow always wrestled up the track and, climbing the steps, looked back past the barn and his tractor at the long shadow leaning from Llanfraith Hill, the mountains tending faintly to the south and the clouds erupting pink at their edges. Whether it was the peace of the evening, or the whole bloody business with Ivor and the doctor, it took a word from behind him before he noticed that the door had already come open.

"Oh," he said. "How do?"

"Hello, Oliver," said Jonathan: a gangling youth whose relationship with the professor he thought it better not to explore. "I didn't hear you knock."

"I . . . dunno as I did, to be honest with you. I brung you your milk."

"That's very kind. Come in. Please."

The changes wrought on the outside of the cottage were nothing to the changes in the kitchen. That chill March morning when Oliver and his mother had come up the hill to see if John wanted his horses back, there would have been more cause to wear boots inside than in the yard—what with the mud and the rat shit and the shotgun lying among the maggoty shreds of John's brain on the flagstones. On the ceiling the stamps remained in their rows—the heads of Edward VII and the Georges, facing to the west: one for every letter

John and Sarah had ever received. But now there were book-shelves to the height of the beams, and gold-framed paint-ings of forests and waterfalls in all of the intervening spaces. There were large, sagging armchairs arranged around the fire and a low table piled with newspapers and magazines. There was a typewriter on a desk at the window—a plump cat dozing among the geraniums and the binoculars on the sill.

"How are you, Sophocles?" said Oliver.

"Martin!" called Jonathan, turning for the stairs. "Do sit down, Oliver, won't you?"

Oliver inspected the photographs hung around the man-telshelf, some of them in colour—the two men together in shorts in a city, a big-eyed, foal-legged girl on an overweight pony—then he selected an armchair and picked up that week's paper while his raven made her way down his chest, stood on his knee and yawned.

"**YOU TOO CAN RENT TV.**"

"**HOSPITAL CARNIVAL QUEEN.**"

He admired the beaming girl, her neat white teeth and curtains of long, dark hair.

"Miss Annette Mills of Llanelwedd was chosen at a dance held at the Builth Wells Hospital—"

"Oliver! I do apologize . . ."

Oliver got quickly to his feet. Even dressed in a coat made out of a towel, his bare feet leaving prints on the floor, the professor reminded him of his old headmaster at the gram-mar school. In repose his face was a studious frown and, ani-mated as he would often become, he always made Oliver feel that he should stand up straight.

"I didna mean to rise you from your bath, Prof."

"No trouble. No trouble. Will you have a drink?"

"Well . . ."

"Everything's all right at the Funnon, I hope? You set off rather briskly this afternoon." He took two glasses and a bottle of his homemade cider from the corner cupboard.

"Well. I might take a drop."

The professor waited for him to expand, but then retrieved his spectacles and turned to the window, gazing down towards Llanbadarn-y-Garreg, his pale hair wet and haloed by the sunset.

"I cannot tell you, Oliver," he said, "what a relief it is to be back here. I tell my students about it, you know? That silence!"

IT WAS THE edge of night. The darkening light of the flaming clouds fell over the floorboards of the bedroom and the ridge of Idris's legs beneath the counterpane, his head and shoulders hoisted up against the pillows, with his hands and Bible on his slowly lifting chest. Perhaps it was just some quality of the sunset, but as Etty sat the soup, the matches and the unlit candle on the bedside chair, it seemed to her that the furrows of her husband's face had dwindled almost into invisibility— as if they had not, after all, been cut by time but had been the symptoms of a tension now suddenly released. Despite the band of hair he would insist on training over his scalp, he looked young, younger than she had ever known him. The light entered the caves of his eyes, revealing them to be not so much black as brown, with rays like a cross-cut oak.

"May," he murmured.

"She's the only month," said Etty. "How . . . how are you feeling?"

"Pretty ordinary, girl, to be honest with you."

"I brung you some dinner."

"So I do smell."

"Do you want me to help you?"

"Might be for the best."

Etty perched on the side of the bed. She filled the spoon, the pork fat glistening on the meniscus, and emptied it carefully into his mouth. He swallowed with an effort and his breath became hesitant—the lines returning briefly to his cheeks.

"I dunno . . ." he said.

"It will keep. I can bring it up again later." She replaced the spoon on the tray, but felt for once that it would be wrong to leave and followed his eyes to the bedroom window: the shadow-flooded valley, a martin still busying over the yard. "It must have been terrible," she ventured, eventually. "To be gassed."

He nodded slowly. She did not move.

"The gas was the least of it, girl, to be honest. I dunno. You thinks on times as you's made it all up. The bombs and the aeroplanes and the shells and the bullets. You canna think as there could have been so many. Why would they trouble, like?" He paused to breathe, a tremor in his jaw. "Me and Oliver, we was there. And Albert. We was with our own, like. Better for morale, I suppose it were, that manner of thing, though Oliver, he'd volunteered a year before me. Two year perhaps it were? Two year older than me, my brother . . ." He paused again. "The rain, mind. I tell you. Never stopped, it did. Just raining pouring, all day, all night. With the mud and all, it was all you could do to blasted walk, and there we was, trying to get back to the line. Then there were this pillbox, see? He opens up with his blasted machine gun. Like hail it were, all spitting from the puddles. Well, two of the lads, they was goners for starters. Me, I made the trench just, but this one bullet comes and clips my helmet and round I goes and another, she comes clean through my shoulder. Clean through him! You never felt the like, girl, I'm telling you now. Fire in't a half of it. So, there was this barbed wire had my gas mask. Barbed wire everywhere, there was. I's always hated the damned stuff since. There was gas in the trench and I had me a lungful . . . Lucky I was, to be honest with you. Most of the lads as was gassed, they gone blind and burns all over them— once the stuff took effect, like. Took a day or so, it did. That bit wasna so concentrate, perhaps. I dunno. Any road, Albert, he had me back on my feet, after a fashion. Oliver, he sticks his gas mask on me. I dunno if it got to him or not. We hanna gone no distance when a shell come down and a nub of shrapnel goes in his eye."

He coughed for a moment, almost retched.

"I canna remember so much after that. Albert, he dragged me up the first-aid station. The both of us stopped there a day or two. Mostly you only gone home if you had yourself a head wound, but what with the gas and all—the shell shock, like— I were sent up to hospital in Epsom a few month. Terrible place. In't nothing much to be said about that. By then, any-way, it were the Armistice, so I come back here and mooched about a year or two till the boss had me doing him pictures of trees. Water colours. Mam used to do them, see? That's where he had the idea, I expect. We still had the kit. Done them by the hundred, I did. There weren't no scrap of paper as didna have an oak on him, or an elm, or a hawthorn. Not so bad, some of them, though I do say so myself. That sorted me out some in the end."

The room had grown dark. The martin was gone. The clouds above the black line of the barn were swollen, bloody, ripe with night-time. Idris took another slow breath, feeling the levelling weight of his chest. On the edge of the bed Etty waited; then, not knowing what else to do, she turned and bent and kissed him on the forehead. She hesitated, then brushed out her skirts and returned her eyes to the window.

THE THING ABOUT collies was that they were clever. The old dogs, you couldn't fault them for heading and driving, but they didn't have the same eye. Cousing the ewes and their big-boned lambs up the bank beneath the beeches that Thursday morning, Turk and Nell never lost concentration for an instant. Turk, in truth, was given to set; he would lie down sometimes if a sheep merely turned. But the flock knew well enough where it was going and the dogs kept back, their tails at their feet, their ears alert, watching them trot through the pishing rain without a face to be seen among the well-dagged rumps. Since there was nobody to offend besides Hanoch beneath him and a whinchat giving its name from a gorse bush, Oliver sang the chorus of a pop song repeatedly. His mail-order jeans were clinging to his thighs, water was running and sloshing in his gumboots, but his new wax coat had a tall wax collar, which folded tight against the back of his cap. His chest and shoulders would not have been drier in the kitchen. Across the valley, Cefn Wylfre was a murky impression, with the Funnon and the Welfrey scars on its side. At Cwmpiban, Mervyn was topping thistles near the boundary hedge, which neither he nor his father had yet attempted to breach. The rain was sniping through the unfurling fern, shuddering the red globe flowers of the wimberries. As they came to the common and the sheep dispersed among the quarries, the wary yearlings and the bare hawthorns ring-barked by the wintering sheep, Oliver crossed the rutted lane and turned his back to the wind to scrutinize the hilltop: the lambs dog-shaking, their mothers weighted by their wool.

Under the green crowd of larches at the Island, Dick was leading his cow on a bridle—his sister straddling her bony back—so Oliver kicked up the cob and rode to meet them.

"How do, Miss Davies?" He raised his cap to Dilys, who scowled at him from beneath her umbrella, her lank hair blowing across her face. "Where you off to, then? Picnic, is it?"

"Market," said Dick, with his usual grin.

"Oh?"

"I have had it with beasts, I have, boy. It is the scything, see? Plays merry havoc with my back, it does. I canna cut the bloody hay no more, so, there we are. Maggie has got to go. We shall miss the milk, like, but she's feeding well enough just now."

"Well, if you needs a bit of fodder?" Oliver offered.

"You's a good lad, Olly. We shall just have boughten milk, and shanna be the worse for it, I expect."

"How's the old Island?"

"Middling, boy, to be honest with you." Dick pinched his eyes beneath his dripping hat. "Maesllwch, they dunna want a gamekeeper no more, see? They is none of them shooting, not this new lot, though I says to them, where the grouse goes, there goes the songbirds. The foxes, they'll be full of it, for sure." He shook his head. "We do get our pensions, like, but it is only a few bob and the bedrooms do get terrible nesh. I put a bit of zinc on the roof, but the wind come under him, and the windows, they'll be a hundred year old if they're a day. Plastic bags, they dunna do for glass, I'll tell you that for nothing!"

"Maintenance grant," said Oliver. He kept the reins tight.

"I never could do them blimmin' forms."

"I shall have a word with Mam. Very greet with the Ministry, she is."

"So," said Dick. He gave a slight nod. "Idris scratting on, is he?"

The umbrella rose an inch or two.

"Not so good, to be honest with you, Dick. It is his lungs, see? Tremendous strain they do put on his heart. That's what the doctor says . . . Hanna stopped him bossing me about, mind."

"Aye." Dick laughed. "Hard as a toad, that boy!"

The umbrella fell until his sister's face and her wind-scoured hair were concealed altogether.

Oliver remained with the dogs in the lane and the rush of the rain on his back. He watched the procession continue across Llanbedr Hill: the thin cow lumbering through puddles and over tractor ruts, the umbrella low above the cowering rider, as slowly the three of them became a single space in the rich green heather, black against the shadow of the mountains—hardly to be told from the gaunt little trees.

THE GEESE AND the dogs suggested a stranger. Etty moved her bare arm slowly round the bread oven, feeling the heat of the bright yellow bricks, the fine hairs rising from her skin. She set the tins on the long wooden spade and slid them into line on the floor of the oven, brushing a last few embers against the door to keep the heat in the mouth before she fastened the latch, glanced at her clock, hung up the kettle and untied her apron.

"Who's that, then?" asked Nancy Llanedw.

"Well, if the dogs don't know . . ."

"There'll be visitors, I doubt. Once the word gets about."

"I suppose there shall."

At a knock on the door Etty rinsed her hands, rolled down her sleeve, checked her eyes in the mirror in the larder and started for the hall across the flagstones Nancy had scrubbed and finished with milk. The bedroom above her was perfectly still. The chairs in the parlour remained in their arches for the Methodist faithful who observed their Sundays in one another's houses now that the chapel was closed.

Idris's best hat was sitting on his chair—as if he had suddenly vanished from beneath it.

"Hello, Mrs. Hamer," said the woman on the step.

"Mrs. Hamer," Etty repeated.

Always a big girl, Ruth had grown still more with her children. Her coat was tight across her breasts. Her skirts spread over broad, round hips to tumble finally to the ground. She looked at Etty hesitantly through the sheet of water that fell from her umbrella, a cloth-covered basket on the other arm.

"I wanted to see if I could help, I did," she said. "I fetched you some food, look."

"Oh," said Etty. She glanced beyond her. "Ivor send you, did he?"

"No no. He is up the Vron, he is. I come on my own."

The rain was drumming on the umbrella's tight black fabric; it roared in the flem and sighed in the yard, where a bantam and her half-grown chicks were pecking in the grass beneath the eaves of the barn.

"Idris is gone," she managed. "Not two hours ago."

"Oh," said Ruth. "I'm very sorry to hear it."

"Thank you for the thought, but we are only the two mouths to feed now."

"If you's sure . . ."

"There is one thing, if I may?"

"Anything, Mrs. Hamer."

Etty took a long breath. Although the doctor had left, she had not quite shed his accent. "When you do see Ivor, I would be grateful if you could remind him of his recent visit. I was at the market at the time myself, but Oliver was present, as was Albert. I would like him please to reflect on his actions, given his interest in the law."

"I SHALL FUCKING kill him!" said Oliver.

"You'll do nothing of the kind."

"I shall go by there—"

"You will start, Oliver, by not using that language in front of me."

"By Christ, I shall throw him bare-arsed—"

"Oliver!" His mother whipped the grass with her plant. "You will control yourself, that's what you'll do. You will control yourself and think. What do you suppose'll happen if you go down there waving your fists? They'll have an assault charge on you before you've made it home."

Oliver snapped at Turk, which was crowding the cattle, setting just feet from the nearest calf.

"Think!" said Etty. "Monday, Ivor had every card going. He could have sold this farm from under our feet and bought it back at a blasted song. No one in this valley is going to bid against him—no one save us—and he's got the Vron and Cwmpiban for surety. We've only got the Welfrey, and not a lot of that neither. Now we have got ourselves one single card. This whole business, it looks like trouble—that's the thing, that's why Mervyn's done nothing with his blasted gates. You put one more card in his hand and he's got us, do you understand me? You do your farming and leave the business to me."

The rain at last had broached Oliver's collar; it was leaking down his neck and spreading on his shoulders.

"Yes," he muttered.

His mother held the gate to seal the Bryngwyn track while he drove the beasts up the Funnon Field, through the poochy rushes beneath the spring. He sent Nell back for Doris—an ill-omened animal that would stray from the herd at any opportunity and had once got stuck to her chest in the bog— then stumped up the slope among the trampled ant heaps and the remnants of the trefoil. By the church, the rain beat the five-pointed leaves of the sycamores. It set the bluebells trembling and him along with them, as if they were hairs on his body. The boss was dead. God knew that they had had their differences, but this was no less than an attack on their farm. It contravened the world's proper order, its justice, its right and wrong.

The cattle massed at the top end of the yard, chavelling the cud, staring dull-eyed into the rain. Oliver held the gate for his mother to pass, then watched her stalk down the bank of the flem, skirting the herd, her long plant swinging, her headscarf wet around her downturned face. When they had the two flanks covered he whistled to the dogs and closed on the animals, slapping the shoulder of the first that turned, following them slowly as they fed into the beast-house to spare the grass for a day or two.

"Ho-ep!" called Etty. "Ho-ep!"

At the tail of the herd, Doris pitched and wheeled. When Turk darted forwards with a warning bark, she came at him with swinging horns and udder slopping and, breaking past him, cantered to the pond. Running himself, Oliver went to head the animal off. He shouted threats and scattered the geese, and while Doris retreated back into the yard she paced and snorted and tossed her head and, as he approached with arms apart, she tried again to escape down the slope. Diving sideways, Oliver grabbed her horn. She thrashed his arm but he brought her round and, seizing the other, stood before her with his feet spread wide—feeling her heat in his straining hands, staring back into her white-lashed eyes. The muscles showed in her fern-brown neck. With gumboots dragging and quick breaths wheezing in the bridge of his nose, he threw his weight backwards and twisted her big head slowly to the left. He fought for his balance and then, with a lunge, he heaved her sideways, flat on her near side, and before she could make it back onto her feet he knelt on her shoulder and, with both hands joined on her long off horn, forced her head into the streaming ground. The near horn cracked and broke in two. Her wild white face turned dark with mud. As she bellocked and twisted he thrust her head into the underlying stone—three times, four times—until the hulk of her body lay twitching and shuddering.

Oliver rose and, looking around him, jumped knee-deep into the flem. With a grunt he locked his arms beneath the bridge and pitched it out into the yard. It must have been a sod to dig out of the hill. The bloody thing had the heft of two men. It was near enough as tall as himself, deep and straight and distantly red, with scratches running down one of the corners he had once thought the scrabblings of a troll. He had to hoist one side onto his toecaps to get a grip with his fingers, but he managed to lift it as high as his shoulders, and then above his head, and brought the narrow end down on the skull of the beast, which erupted blood from its eyes and its earholes, imploded like a bad egg on a wall.

MORE TIMES THAN she could number, Etty had seen her son come home with an eye bruised closed or a finger broken and twisted out of line, but whatever he did she had never had to see it. It had never happened here. Oliver stood above the shattered carcass, his big chest heaving, his stubble-shadowed jaw pushing into the rain. At his feet the dogs lapped at the prill of blood, which was winding its way towards the pond. She stared at the scene with the cattle behind her, hiling their cratches, then she crossed the yard quickly and jumped the flem at the narrow place beneath the parlour window—her breath spasmodic, spots of light confusing her vision.

"I'd best rise the tractor then, boss, had I?" asked Albert from the barn.

In the kitchen Etty seized the newspaper and, by instinct, the wood basket. Turning, she saw a redstart on the sill outside the window, framed in a pane, dipping his head and tabbering his tail as if he wanted to get in. She shouted at him, but he continued to dance, fixing her with his bright black eyes, and she almost ran as she headed for the larder, out of the back door and into the orchard, where the apple trees had been through their pink and the rain-fallen blossom lay white and sunken in the grass. The wood basket. She only carried the damned thing in case Idris saw her and she could pretend to be rising bruns from the woodpile, and she hurled it away into the potato patch before she ducked into the privy and locked the door.

TO KEEP THIS PLACE BOTH CLEAN AND SWEET, said the notice, OPEN THE DOOR AND CLOSE THE SEAT.

Etty was forty-seven years old. Two laps of skin hung loose

from her neck; she could flick them with a finger. Her red hair had become dull and pale. As she weed and shivered in the rising stink, the thin, chapped hands either side of the newspaper looked less freckled than mottled.

"**Parents. Is your daughter interested in nursing?**"

"**61 Mediterranean holidays to be won!**"

She tore at the string of newsprint squares, wiped herself and looked back at the paper, which showed, drop-spotted, a girl reclining in a two-piece bathing suit—a pair of sunglasses dangling from her hand.

"**While your new fridge freezes you can lie out in the sun.**"

Above her, the rain was pummelling the thin zinc roof.

1976

THE OAK IN the Oak Piece bore leaves in such numbers
that it was only when Oliver climbed the gate into the
Funnon Field and passed into its shadow that he could see
against the high, hot sun some memory of its whorling skeleton. Thirty-five times now he must have witnessed this phe-
nomenon, this rebirth of the year, and still it seemed to him
as unlikely as the dead returning from their graves. A warm
breeze fled up the tightening valley, ruffling the tall grass and
moon daisies in the Banky Piece, running among the pale-
bellied leaves of the great tree, which shimmered, seeming to
shiver with pleasure. A lark was trilling somewhere in its
depths. A vapour trail passed straight through its crown, like
an arrow through a cowboy's hat.

"Boy, Turk," he murmured.

He swiped at a horsefly and continued up the slope, following a rack between the ant heaps bleached on the south
side, mossy on the north—the thyme on their heads just
thinking of flowers. The rain was tough a-coming, as Idris

would have had it—the Far Top Field was pale as hay—but the ground beneath his gold-framed sunglasses was pink with loosestrife, purple with self-heal, and he whistled lightly to the raven on his shoulder, which whistled lightly in response.

He was almost at the gate when he stopped and turned, frowning back down the slope towards the funnon, which had grown a few brambles these past few years. A damp, dark hole in the sunlit field, he had thought more than once about fencing it in, since at least one creature had drowned in there. He glanced at the dog, whose ears had risen. He took a few steps in its direction and saw a hat evolving from the shadows—climbing haltingly into the sunshine.

"Oh, hello!" said the girl. "You must be Oliver, right?"

"Might be," Oliver admitted.

She smiled uncertainly, set down her plastic barrel and wiped her hands on her denim dungarees, which were cut at the thigh so that her legs led bare to her sandals. Since it would have been awkward to have done otherwise, he shook the hand she offered in his big, grubby fist.

"I'm Naomi."

"Are you, then?"

"I hope you don't mind my taking some water. I spoke to your mother. She suggested I come here . . . So. This is Maureen, is it?"

Oliver felt a frown trace across his forehead. He glanced at the raven. "I expect."

"I know all about you, you see?" The girl tipped back her broad straw hat, looking up at him with blue and dark-lashed eyes. "Dad's been on about you for years—ever since he first came down here. To be honest, I did wonder if he was making you up . . ."

"Your father . . . ?" said Oliver.

"Martin. Martin Chance."

"The prof? Isn't he—"

"Well. He was married once, to my mother. Obviously."

"Well!" He looked at her again: her face still flushed from the steep stone steps, the rounds of breasts in her glimpse of a T-shirt. "I cannot say as I see the resemblance."

"He hasn't mentioned me, then, I take it."

"To be honest with you, Naomi," said Oliver. He gave a low laugh—his geography corrected, extended, back in his control. "To be honest with you, the prof doesn't really hold towards people in his conversation. Not with me, in any case. Things, that is more his line. Bees. Vegetables. Churches. Tree roots. Funny-shaped stones he's dug up. Barrows it were, last time I seen him. He reckoned he'd found one up Penblaenmilo, though I'll say it's just where they used to keep the rabbits. Between ourselves, like."

"He tells me about you," the girl observed.

Oliver inclined his head. "Among the other things?"

"Oh, I didn't mean . . ."

"I'm pulling your leg, girl." He smiled and pushed the sunglasses back up his nose. "Got a car here, have you?"

"Yes. In the yard."

"I'll lend you a hand with that then, shall I?"

"Well . . ." She lifted the barrel two-handed, then put it back down. "OK. That would be kind. Thank you."

"We do have a spare tank down in the barn. I'll fetch him you up when I gets a minute."

Taking the handle, Oliver noted the pleasing swell of the muscles in his chest, the breeze in the mouths between the buttons of his shirt. He held the barrel six inches clear of his legs without a tremor or trace of its weight and, flicking the rope from the falling post, followed Turk onto the Bryngwyn track.

Naomi watched Oliver in the ring of the binoculars standing on a ladder in the sheer green bracken—his scale unarguable even at this distance. He peered down the hill in his garish shades until, at a signal she could not see, he reached again for the top of the pole and turned the aerial another degree. Beneath him, his raven was fidgeting on the tractor: an ancient machine of once-blue bodywork, which, to all appearances, might itself have been unearthed. His dogs were spread in the evening sunlight, one of them wagging each time he shouted.

"Mam?"

It was a good ten miles to the nearest town. It was half an hour's walk to the nearest phone box, which was as close to a centre as Rhyscog possessed, and, in any case, had a resident goose and was all but impossible to use. The village, it seemed, was rather a space. The nearest pub was five miles distant, and the nearest shop. It had a primary school, but its only church was the ruin at the Funnon, which was a place on the edges by any definition.

Along the hillside, the farmer climbed back into his seat and turned the tractor in a long, slow arc, revealing a tank roped onto the back. Naomi looked past him, at the valley that billowed from this crevice in the hills. On the hilltop opposite there was a yellow digger on the bank of a scar of a track. Despite the sunlight glancing from the end panes of the conservatory, she felt the chill of the rock in the flagstones—the stubble was trying to rise on her shins—and, returning the binoculars to their marks on the windowsill, she pulled on a shirt she had found in the wardrobe and settled in an armchair next to the fireplace. In this air tainted faintly by pipe smoke, this silence so total that she could hear a man's voice quite clearly some quarter of a mile away, without a phone, without electricity, without so much as a serviceable spring, she seemed to begin to understand her father. This house was a den, she could see that much. Little wonder it had taken her a year of wheedling and him every excuse from loneliness to the condition of the track before he had allowed her the key. There were varnished stamps in rows on the ceiling. There were landscapes in between the bookshelves. There was a single photograph of herself: ten years old on a plump bay pony, on a birthday he had remembered.

She tucked her legs beneath her, opened her notebook and waited for the tractor to arrive.

THERE WAS A vertical line to the left of the screen, which bulged, like a spoon, so that Oliver's nose pushed out of the reflection and his forehead resembled an egg. The speaker fizzed through the rasp of Etty's brush on the plates, their clinking on the rough stone sink. As he twisted the dial, there came a sudden hush, then the voice of a man who might have been talking in a blizzard. She glanced again at the television. Perhaps that was a head she saw, or a gesturing hand, but then all trace of the picture dissolved and the man became a half-heard murmur.

"Bloody thing!" said Oliver.

Etty said nothing. She would have liked, of course, to know what the man was saying, but she had spent an hour now traipsing between the set and the yard to wave at her son up his pole on the common. There were better things to do with her Sunday evening. She scrubbed the cutlery in the bare inch of water she had already used twice that day, wiped it dry and returned it to the drawer in the bread-and-cheese cupboard. She chased a fly from the left-over mutton to the open window, where it prospected the pane between freedom and the flypaper. She carried the bowl into the larder and set it on a shelf in the grumbling refrigerator.

"I shall take the bugger back!"

He prodded the button so that the blizzard retracted to a point of light, and disappeared into his bellying image. Collecting his cider, he went to lean on the bar of the Rayburn, which she had not lit since the previous afternoon—his hair black and tumbling among the hooks in the beams, the gnarled white berries and droplet leaves of the mistletoe.

"Fetch a bit of water up the Welfrey, did you?" Etty asked.

"Well, we canna leave her up there without."

"No no."

The mood seemed to lift a little from his shoulders. "A daughter for the prof, mind!"

"I know."

"I didna think I'd heard her right."

"You'd have thought he'd have mentioned her."

"You would!"

Removing her apron, Etty opened the long drawer, took out a jigsaw and emptied the box on the table. She propped up the picture of the carthorse on the lid and sat in her chair to turn the pieces face upwards. Whatever Oliver said, she had never believed that the professor was a queer—he was a professor, after all. Surprised as she was to find he had a daughter, she was hardly less surprised to find her stopping alone up the Welfrey: a girl no more than twenty, with her legs bare for everyone to see. Of course, she saw half-clothed girls every time she went to town—there had been more than one in the church that morning—but Builth was one thing and Rhyscog another.

A curlew passed over on its way to the Rhos, crooning more sun for the following day.

"Up there for a spell then, is she?"

"All summer, she reckons."

"All summer!"

Oliver pulled up his chair, which was a little too small for him. He lit a cigarette with the scratch of a match and assembled the pieces for the horse's jaw. "I did say Nana might find her a job," he said. "Down the café, like. Student she is, see? Nothing better to do, in't it?"

In the fiery dawn that following Saturday, the burning heather on the distant mountains appeared to be a fissure: an eye in the horizon revealing the approaching sun. Llanbedr Hill itself was dark. The valley they had left showed a couple of night-time lights. Beyond the sharp-tipped, red-trimmed ears of Naomi's cob, the three other riders stirred and turned against the sky: Harry Llanedw, hunched in the lee of his cap; Griffin the Pant, alert and looking around; Oliver, erect on his tall black hunter, surveying the silhouettes of the firs or larches, the extent of the open hilltop.

"Well," he said, "it shanna rain."

"As is best, boy."

"Nettle to it, then, shall we, Funnon?" Harry spat in his hand and doused his cigarette.

"All right, girl?"

"Not so bad, Oliver."

"Not so bad! That's the way!" Oliver barked at the quarrelling dogs. "You mind them lambs in the quarries now, Panty. We had a couple of legs broke last year, and it was my fault. They'll be uncommon vigorous, I expect."

"I expect," Griffin agreed.

"You come along with me now, Naomi."

The trench of the lane where the digger had been working stretched the whole way over the common, framed by piles of dried hard earth. Their horseshoes sparked as they stepped through its shadow. To the right, a tree marked the corner of the farm's furthest field—the fence dissolving into its bark. At Oliver's lead, Naomi gave a flick to the reins, her arms absorbing the nod of the cob, the jeans she had taken to wearing round the valley beginning to slip on the saddle. She watched his gaze shift quickly between sheep she saw and sheep she supposed. She watched the dawn on a pond and the other men fanning away into the bracken, stark on the contours, vanishing again and then altogether.

"Well," he said. "At least we know why they dug them quarries."

"Why's that, then?"

"Some old stone road in the lane there, in't there? Best tell your dad, now I do come to think of it. They'll be laying the tarmac in the week, I doubt."

The hill here was narrow, no wider than a mile, squashed between Penbedw ground and the standing walls of Pant-y-Ffynnon, which, like most of the old, remote houses, had gone down between the wars. The Island alone remained of those places, and that had housed no more than the beasts since they had bought it off Dick and Dilys. Oliver took stock without particular distinction—noting the families of ewes and lambs as he noted the creatures for Cwmpiban bolting back to their territory, the ponies in a hollow, a barn owl floating pink across the heather, the piercing notes of a pipit in a hawthorn. The low light picked out the old copps and reens, which Idris had told him were cut by the Denes, or the Danes, as the professor would have it. As they came to the ridge where the ground bowled west towards Garreg Lwyd and Craig-y-Fuddal, the dew-settled track opened in front of them and the breeze cleaned the last sleep from Oliver's mind like some benign cousin for the lazy winter winds. Almost without realizing, he rose on his stirrups, brought his hands and his balance forwards and released Devil with a kick of his heels. He gave a yawp, which was taken by the air. To the drumming of hooves beneath him and behind him, he felt the flying mane of the horse on his neck and fled for the cliffs as if running from the sun.

"You done your bit of riding, then!" he said, grinning, turning on the summit to watch the girl guide the cob towards him up the scree—the grey stone crumbling and rolling from his feet.

"It's been a while," she said, breathlessly. "Comes back, it seems!"

They sat together on Garreg Lwyd: the highest point on the whole, long hill, where the sidelands and the hiding places were best exposed by the coming light. Naomi had lost the band in her hair, which now fell sun-streaked over her shoulders. She was quite a girl, it had to be said. Her eyes were large. Her lips were full. There was a childishness to the freckles on her nose, but she carried herself so effortlessly, so confidently, that he was reminded less of other girls he had known than of the first proper thoroughbreds to arrive on the farms down in the Wye Valley, five or six years before.

He kept that to himself.

"Not such a bad spot, is it, really?"

Naomi smiled and nodded in agreement.

"Right, then." He took a breath to steady his thoughts. "There'll be one or two past the edge there, down towards Cwmoel, but the dogs'll find them, I expect. The finding's not the problem so much as the keeping." He levelled a crooked finger at the yearlings tight round a mawn pool to their left—aware of their presence, calling in concern. "That hog there, off to the side, look—she'll be a dodger. Her mother was a dodger and she'll have picked it up, sure to. You cannot be expected to know that manner of thing, of course, but I tell you now, she'll be running off ahead of the others and the first hole she spies—whoosh—she'll be squirrelled away in him, waiting for us to go on home. Cunning buggers, sheep. Some of them, in any case. A sight more cunning than folks gives them credit. Keep your eyes about you, basically. Keep to the high ground, keep checking behind you and Nell'll do the rest. She'll gather in her sleep, that dog. Turk, she is a bit more tare."

"Tare?"

"Tare . . . Excitable, like. Sorry, I was forgetting."

"No, I like it."

The farmer hesitated, briefly uncertain, his dark eyes moving in his high, carved face. Suddenly Naomi could imagine him as a boy: his will not yet in tune with his body, his size an encumbrance rather than a strength.

"Do you know all of them, do you?" she asked.

"The creatures? Yes, I expect."

"How the hell do you tell them apart?"

"How do you tell people apart?" He shrugged, looking back along the common to the far-away conifers and the sun, which was rising from a seeming plain: liquid, trembling, throwing its light across the jumbling hills. "That ewe there, she loves her swedes. It's an obsession, almost. She'll hop a fence for them, if you give her the chance. That one, she's got black on her nose and eyes: touch of Beulah in the bloodline some-where. That one, she is touchy as hell. Burnskin, you call it. Let a dog close and you cannot handle her at all. Some I know well, some more, like, in passing. Same thing, in't it?"

EVEN WITH THE windows and the back door open, the an-cient cold in the walls and the flagstones, the kitchen was as stifling as the oven in the Rayburn. The hands of the grand-father clocks were hidden by mist. Droplets fell from the boards of the ceiling to make little circles on the floor. The faces of the women were bright with sweat: Etty, Nancy Llanedw and her daughter Bridget, and Ada, who was the wife for Griffin and a daughter for Lewis, the landlord at the Awlman's Arms, which told you a thing or two about her. The professor's daughter was washing up steadily, and if she was wearing bell-bottomed trousers then she was at least not exhibiting herself and was enough of a novelty to distract the children and keep them out from under their feet.

"Well," Naomi was saying, "I'm a girl and I wear jeans."

"I wear a skirt!"

"Do I look like a boy to you?"

"No . . . How come you went gathering, then?"

"Because Oliver asked me."

"Why?"

"Because I said I wanted to."

"Mam?" Faith turned to Ada. "Mam, can I go gathering, can I?"

"Ask your father."

"That means no," she told Naomi, sourly.

"How come she can go gathering and we can't?" Lucy demanded.

"It's different, that's why." Bridget set down the rolling pin and began to chop the pastry. "Anyway, she's a grown-up. Now why don't you stop pothering the poor girl and rise me the spuds?"

Whatever the costs of this long, hot spell, it did look for once as if they might shear on time. It was six years now since they had last been able to stick to the calendar: two days for the Pant, two for the Funnon and two for Llanedw—one for the hill sheep and one for the valley. Normally the rain would not be so kind. Since there was no shearing a sodden ewe, they would either waste hours with the creatures pressed into every available bit of shelter or abandon the work for days on end and cut into weather they needed for the hay. The trouble this year was that everyone had lambed well. With the pasture parched and the hayfields wilting, the prices at market had gone through the floor. With luck the wool clip would pay for itself—if the Wool Board's assessment was halfway reasonable—but once again they would be struggling for the mortgage, and the big new shed with its fine zinc roof would remain in the realm of Etty's dreams.

"You know what I reckon, Naomi?"

"What do you reckon, Lucy?"

"I reckon Oliver's soft on you. I reckon that's why he wanted you to come gathering!"

"Lucy!"

"You think so, do you?"

"Is that true, Naomi? Does Oliver fancy you?"

"Oliver's old!"

"Do you fancy Oliver?"

"No, I do not."

"She does! Look, she does!"

"Faith!" Bridget snapped. "Lucy! You are overstepping the traces, you are! You say sorry to Naomi right now or you are going home, the both of you, do you understand?"

"Cider time, Ets," said Nancy, wiping the condensation from the window of the clock. "Ten it is."

Etty slid the gravy to the warming hob and headed for the larder, almost waddling in the tight brown stockings she wore for her varicose veins. She collected the tumblers from the shelf above the salting stone and set them together on the tray. She stirred the cider jugs, whose rotten-apple smell rose into the steamy air. Naomi, she saw when she turned, was standing in the door—her face a little pink, her hair tied back in a baler-twine bow. Etty dropped her eyes; she hardly knew why. It was not as if gathering was much of a romantic gesture, and besides, how many names had she had to digest over the years? Amy and Megan, Annette and Angharad. To be fair to the girl, she was trying to help. She was wearing a shirt as long as a smock, which all but disguised her young woman's body. There was nothing she could do about the smoothness of her hands or the poise of her shoulders: her education, her life she could choose.

The racket redoubled as Etty opened the front door and arrived in the stench of the crowded sheep. Half or more of the flock remained shut up in the Bryngwyn track, but still she and Naomi had to wind across the yard. Inside the tall, open doors of the barn, Albert was folded round his tally stick. Most of the men were hard at the shearing—the good, sprally animals kicking between their legs. In the catching pen, Oliver took a ewe by the wool to replace a yearling that sprang away naked—his muscles oaken in his filthy vest.

"Now then, Ethel," said Griffin, "that in't Llanedw cider now, is it?"

"And what the hell's wrong with it?" asked John Llanedw.

"You got to be held down to drink the bloody stuff, that's what!"

"It'll make a man of you, Panty." Oliver rolled the fleece, tucking the neck wool back into the rope.

"If I got any more manly, boy—"

"Cut!" called Harry.

Griffin's boy, Philip, shot forwards with the tar.

John looked sideways at his son-in-law, his pinioned sheep nicked just by the shoulder. "Someone bring the poor thing some grass," he said.

"And you're the one to call me slow!"

"Well, then, Panty," said Oliver, "I shall have yours gladly."

"I didna say I didna want it," said Griffin. "I'd drink my own piss, I'm that thirsty!"

As the women reached the hurdle with the fly-plagued jugs, the apparent chaos began to resolve itself. Harry daubed the cut on the ewe, which leapt, with Turk a pace behind, to join the others in the pitching pen. Albert added her notch to the stick. Philip rose the broom to start sweeping up the pell wool while, one by one, the machines fell silent until the soundbox walls of the yard had only the sheep to repeat.

OLIVER DUCKED FOR the branches of the sycamores, riding home between Pentre Wood and the shaley wall around the hump of the churchyard, which they rarely grazed at this time of year to spare the twayblades and spotted orchids. The evening air smelt strongly of garlic. He kept his eyes on the track before them. He did not like to look at the bank. Of all the flowers that grew in their valley—and in these days of herbicides and reversible ploughs there were many he rarely saw anywhere else—it was the bluebells that seemed to him most like hope. To see them fading, shading to brown, served somehow to remind him of his broken bones, his broken nose, the scars and sprains that littered his body. Swinging from the saddle, he opened the gate and led Devil into the long, dusty yard.

"Quoits!" he declared.

The mood of the farm had become comfortable, familial. The last of the ticks had been removed, the last hooves pared and the last ewes maggoted and marked with his initials to run again on Llanbedr Hill. They had finished two hours short of sunset. The prospect of sleep before the next dawn assignation had eased the lines around Nancy's eyes, brought a wagging carelessness to the dogs at his heels and a swagger to both Harry and Griffin as they led the three horses to the puddle of the pond. Oliver rose the twenty-pound sledge-hammer and drove a steel bar into the stony ground beside the mixen. He strode down the yard to the door of the barn, where his mother was cooing to Ada's latest baby and Lucy and Faith were treading down the fleeces. Naomi was with them in one of the sacks, jumping with her shirt in a knot at her waist, which revealed her midriff, a hint of her hips.

"Girls!" he called. He took down the horseshoes from their peg among the tarnished scythes.

A wash of anger came over Naomi that must have shown in her cheeks. She tied back her hair and climbed from the bag, lifting the girls to the cobbled floor, barely remembering to return their smiles. As she entered the yard she did not look at Oliver, who was scraping out a line with his boot, who perhaps really did think of her as a girl, who, for all of her father's effusions, really stood apart from the few people around him only by virtue of a few extra inches.

"Whenever you're ready, Panty," said John.

"You look and learn, Llanedw." Griffin rubbed his hands in the dust, spread his legs and scowled towards the church. "Bloody master at work, I am!"

He hurled his horseshoe, which drifted left and landed in the pile of manure.

"You must be sure and give us a lesson sometime."

Griffin grimaced. "Kink in him, look . . ."

"Come on then, John!" called Nancy. "Let's be seeing you!"

Again, it seemed, this was a pleasure for the men, who were cheerfully passing around cigarettes, bold with cider, which Naomi, of course, had not been offered. The women were sitting by the wall of the barn, on a long, flat stone half-buried in the grass, which seemed to be cut faintly with letters: an *S* perhaps, perhaps an *A*. The girls were crowding close to her feet, calling and gesturing to a place beside them. They cheered then sighed as John flung his horseshoe, but none showed any sign of playing herself. It was Etty, of all of them, who really surprised her: a woman of rather beautiful, cattish eyes, of red hair coiled among the grey in her bun, who was reticent, even awkward, but instructed the men in the handling and the prices of the wool as if it were she, not her son, who was really in charge. After three days working in the Station Café, Naomi had a far better sense of her mother, Molly, who might not have joined in the game, with the state of her hands, but would certainly have been smoking and most likely drinking as well.

"Can I have a go, please?" she asked, calmly.

Oliver was weighing a horseshoe in his hand, the low sun on his wool-greased skin, the golden rings he wore on his hands and the golden chain around his neck. He paused and turned with a grunt of amusement and gestured at the pile on the ground.

"Come a bit closer if you like."

Naomi said nothing. She stood at the line, rotating her shoulder to loosen the muscles, then pitched the quoit overarm. It did not spin neatly like the others, turning side over side, but it bounced as it landed and continued to roll, bounding across the slope beyond the barn, keeping its course over the dusty ruts to stop within inches of the post.

Despite herself, she stuck out her tongue.

"Dad!" said Lucy. "I wanna go!"

"And me!" said Faith.

"Christ, boys," said Griffin. "It is a bloody revolt."

PALE AS THE grass in the Banky Piece had become, the moon daisies, the scabious, the cranesbill and birdsfoot trefoil made the hillside into a splendour of colour: whites and pinks, blues and yellows. Oliver led Naomi down the path by the Middle Ddole hedge, which, despite some trimming earlier that month, was itself festooned with flowers, bright with the songbirds hidden in its leaves. The curlew came over, singing no rain for the rest of the weekend. Towards Cwmpiban a snipe was winnowing—its strange vibration filling the warm evening air.

"Oliver?"

"Olly," he corrected her. He drove a way round his old Escort van, flattening nettles with his boots. "Oliver is more for my mother in a mood."

"Olly?"

"Yes, Naomi."

"Where did your father come from? If you don't mind me asking?"

"Idris? Funnon boy."

"No, I mean . . ."

"Oh, you knows about that, do you?"

"Dad did mention it."

"Oh. Well." He checked over his shoulder. "To be honest with you, girl, I don't rightly know where my father came from. I can't say I know who he was."

"Aren't you curious?"

"Well. Mother doesn't much care for the subject, and I don't much care to upset her. Some bugger who ought to have known better, I imagine."

"Dad never knew his father either," said Naomi, after a moment. "Or his mother. Did you know that? He was found, as a baby. That's where the surname comes from."

The air was cooler among the trees around the stream, which continued to leach, stone-paved, out of the bracken-rich hills and filled a pool where the banks came apart that seemed to have been dammed at some point long in the past. Oliver stopped on a thin pebble beach pitted with his own footprints. He pulled off his boots and his sweat-stinking socks and pushed his big, wrinkled feet into the water.

"This here's the wash-pool," he said, with a sigh. "We'd use him for the sheep years ago. When Idris was about, like. We'd wash them for the shearing back then, see, and we'd dip them here and all—chuck in some horrible brown stuff as did for half the fish from here to the Wye, I doubt, though I cannot say as the crap we use now is much better. Any road, he's clean enough. I'll just have a splash then I'll let you get on. No one wants their waitresses reeking of sheep."

Naomi sat against a nearby tree, unbuttoning her shirt

from her tight white T-shirt, catching his glance as she dug out the pouch and the Rizlas from her pocket. "I've been after one of these all day," she said.

"Make us one, would you?"

She hesitated.

"Oh!" Oliver chuckled. "Joint, is it? Well, I'll have a go on yours, then."

"You don't mind, do you?"

"Now, look here," he said, "I am going in this pool, though I am not a sheep, and being as how I shall not be perving on you I would be grateful if you would look elsewhere."

He fought with his vest and exposed his chest, which was dark and defined between still-darker arms. His waist was taut and tapering, shaded with hair. A moment passed in which Naomi tried again to place him—to find his kind among the oceans of people back in the city, around the tall, terraced house on Neville Street where she had grown up. Then she smiled and shuffled round the tree, tearing a roach from the Rizla packet, watching the swallows, which could still see the sun—the bare sky sparkling where their wings caught the light.

With a splash and a gasp, Oliver fell into the water.

SUCH WAS THE depth of the unearthed road that the sheep now climbing onto Llanbedr Hill appeared to Naomi to be no more than heads, like the ghosts of Roman soldiers in the stories. She stood on the bank in the rich green heather, and when the first of the animals arrived at the corner— bony-looking without their wool, the letters *MH* blue on their sides—she tried to count them as Albert had shown her: pairs on her left hand, tens on her right. A collie came coursing over the hilltop, veered between the digger and a mound of earth and sent the flock scrambling onto the track she had taken with Oliver the previous morning. Behind them a Land Rover slowed and stopped. A bald, hulking man jumped down to the stones, looked her over, nodded a greeting and then, with a boy of similar dimensions, followed them onto the common.

Naomi regretted not changing her waitress skirt.

"So," said a second man, who remained in the passenger seat, his eyes on a level with her knees. "How many we got, then?"

"Oh," she said. "I don't know. I can't really work out how you do it."

The man was small and gaunt with age. Cropped white hair and a band of speckled skin surrounded his flat tweed cap. His face, whose lines the evening light could barely penetrate, appeared to move on the right side alone, giving him the impression of a grimace.

"Me," he said. "I counts their legs and divides by four."

He gave a gulp of a laugh so Naomi smiled in reply.

"Actually," she said, "I was really just looking at the old road . . . Did you know it was under there, did you?"

"Well." The man mopped some drool from the side of his mouth. "I'll have said there was something. He would dry uncommon easy in the sun."

"Do you know anything about it?"

"Well. He were a drovers' road, like, back in the day, but there's no news in that. He were a drover's road even in my father's time. Stop by the Rhosei, they would, for cueing the cattle."

"Cueing?"

"Wore shoes, they did. Plates, like. Not so much like horse-shoes. Cues they called them. You an . . . archaeologist, is it?"

"No, no. It's my father's thing, really. He'd never forgive me if I didn't come and look. Perhaps you know him? Martin Chance? He rents the Welfrey from the Hamers, at the Fun-non." She waited. "You know them, I suppose?"

The old man blinked, his left lid drooping, then turned to the windscreen, the scooped-out banks with their lines of strata and the stone-paved road, which showed a little convex on the horizon, against the mountains in their habitual haze.

"I knows who you mean," he said.

THE SUNLIGHT FILLED the valley precisely. The greener north, the pallid south, the encircling bracken, all shone equally, all leant their shadows towards the pass between the hills. There were church bells ringing somewhere to the west. There were new-shorn sheep in the Funnon fields and, in the yard, the murmur of engines as a van and a tractor turned onto the track with a trail of glimmering dust. As Naomi continued back down the lane, heading for the car she had left by the phone box, she saw Etty fill a watering can in the pond, among the already-yellowing elm trees. She saw Oliver on his path to the brook—his bag and his raven on opposite shoulders—and, on a moment's decision, she pushed through the bracken of the verge beside her, hopped a sag-ging fence and crossed the corner of a steep, bare field. Again she would have fared better in her jeans. The crop in the next field hid nettles and thistles—and brambles too, spilling out of the hedgerow, no less painful and surprisingly itchy for their cascades of pink-white flowers. Birds surrounded her here, more heard than seen: one so expressive that it might have been talking, another, a wren she spotted in the leaves, repeating streams of quick-fire notes. The ground was dry and run with cracks—it fell into powder beneath her sandals—but the sun had lost its daytime ferocity, become an easy pleasure on her back and her shoulders. Even with the stings and scratches on her legs she would, if she could, have kept the valley just like this.

Oliver was lying on his back in the wash-pool, so that his ears were submerged and his golden head with its black, spilling hair appeared to be floating on the water. He was humming to himself, and although the song was far from tuneful, still Naomi found herself thinking of Orpheus, drifting downriver to the Aegean Sea. She sat by a tree that might have been an alder, her legs hanging bare among its exposed roots, and began to assemble the pieces of a joint while Maureen watched her from a nearby rock, clicking her fierce, curved beak.

"Tea and cake, please," Oliver said. He lowered his eyes along his nose.

"And for you, madam?" asked Naomi.

"The lady will have a dead mouse."

"How was it today, then?"

"Hot." He splashed his face and pushed back his hair, ripples spreading outwards to the banks, distorting his long and opaque body. "How this bit of water's got the strength to run away I do not know. I tell you, girl, if it don't rain soon . . . I'm finding crayfish dead already and we in't even onto the dipping. Them organophosphates. You can spread them on the fields, do what you like, and they will get in the streams. What'll come to the salmon I don't care to think. October time, not ten years back, they'd run up the Edw like a bloody bore. Turn the whole river white, they would!"

Naomi jotted a few lines in her notebook. She went to mention the old man on the hill, then decided against it.

"Olly?" she said.

"The pool's all yours in a minute, if you want him. I do not mean to put you off."

"Your cob. Hanoch."

"Hanoch," he agreed.

"Would you mind if I rode him again sometime?"

"Aiming to do some exploring, are you?"

"Well, yeah. I thought I might . . . I can pay you, if you like?"

The water again had become almost still, and since Oliver was looking into the near-circular leaves of the trees above them she glanced from his face to the dense, dark hair of his crotch.

"When was you thinking?"

"Well, I'm working for your grandmother again tomorrow." She spun the lighter, held in the smoke and exhaled into the unmoving air. "Tuesday, perhaps? Or Wednesday?"

"Hang on till Wednesday and I'll come with you. We'll be two days at Llanedw if the weather doesn't break. I could do with a day off, in any case. If you ride up north, on from the Welfrey, like, well, there's Glascwm and the road at Llanfihangel-nant-Melan, but elsewise you can go, what, fifteen, twenty miles? Open ground the entire way. Radnor Forest. There's barely a farm once you get out there. The odd ruin, that's it. Proper wilds, it is."

The smoke was working on Naomi's mind, bringing her a slight, calm sense of elevation. She didn't care if she had somehow offended the man on the hill. Oliver could say what he liked about the brook, but this was still no lifeless, concrete channel, no river of pilings and stinking mud. His voice was sonorous among the cloaking trees, whose leaves she saw on the surface of the water, cut from the piercing blue of the sky, containing his head still tilted backwards with his body hardly hidden beneath. Her eyes moved between these different fields and, in moments, slipped out of focus so that they became indivisible.

"WHAT'S THAT ONE, then?" Naomi asked.

"That was a bullock, from what I recall."

"And that?"

"Sod with a bottle."

"And . . . that?"

"I couldn't say, to be honest with you, girl." Oliver shrugged. "I woke one morning and there it was."

She moved to his face, her nipples hardening as they brushed through the hair on his chest. There was a mark in his lip, near the incisor with the broken point. There was a brief, pale line in the day or two's growth on his chin, like a comet, and a longer arch beneath the black hair tumbling on his forehead.

"What happened there?" She touched it with a nail.

"Fell off a bridge."

"Is it true you once threw a policeman off a bridge, in a sack?"

Oliver gave his grunt of a laugh and put a hand on her hip, looking from the pink curve of her mouth to the white vest lines running over her collarbones and the cleft of her breasts just touching his chest. He inhaled deeply to see them swell, inspected her thin arms parted round the pillows. "What's that?" he asked, with a nod.

"Inoculation," said Naomi. "I screamed, apparently."

She dropped to her elbows, her fine hair falling like curtains around them, and brought their lips together—her tongue sliding down between his teeth. His taste was rich, a distillation of leaves and earth, the hot summer air and the last cigarette he had smoked. She put her fingers in his armpit and pressed them to her nostrils. She had thought at first, when they shook hands, that his heat was an aberration, some factor of the sunlight, but here as well he might almost have been feverish. She found his hand and guided it past her navel and his slack, moist penis, between her legs, and as he moved his hard-tipped finger as she had shown him she shut her eyes then held it fiercely—closing around him with a groan.

The stars were hidden by a sea of cloud. Beyond the candle flame on the warping glass, the only lights were deep in the valley: one at Cwmpiban, another at Gilfach. All day Oliver and Naomi had been here, in the bedroom at the Welfrey, venturing downstairs only to water the horses they had still yet to mount, to find another bottle of cider or whatever sustenance was provided by a tin of baked beans. The only sounds were the yelp of a fox, far away on Glascwm Hill, and a badger down in Turley Wood—its cry like a distressed child.

Naomi slid over him, to the foot of the bed. She stood a little weakly, then tipped back her shoulders so that the shadows vanished beneath her breasts, which rose and shone as the ribs showed over her belly.

"By Christ . . ." Oliver murmured.

"Nice?"

"Well." He collected himself, dragging the pillow under

his head. "Naked women are two a penny in these parts, of course. Panty saw eleven of them up the Bailey the other week—hippies, like. All of them starkers aside from their gumboots."

"Griffin," she said, "is full of shit." She pinched a pair of knickers between her thighs and took two cups from the bedside table, which was scattered with Rizlas, an ashtray, a notebook, a candlestick and a plastic ring of pills. "I'm going to make us some tea."

Oliver swung his legs onto the floorboards. He got to his feet, his head an inch or two shy of the beams, bunched his chest and turned to the candlelight, which picked out the muscles of his stomach.

"Well?" he said.

"You," said Naomi, "have quite a high enough opinion of yourself as it is."

THERE WERE FIRES on the hills: sparks at an untellable distance. That one perhaps was on Radnor Forest, somewhere out for Kinnerton or up on the Creigiau. That one must have been on the Epynt, where nobody knew the names anymore. The only one Oliver could place for sure was the peat fire on Gwaunceste Hill, which had been burning for days: a necklace for the hilltop with sudden adornments of gorse or scrub and even an oak, whose low-hanging branches wore flames like candles.

"The oak tree blossoms on Midsummer's Eve," Oliver remarked. "Albert did tell me that one time. Ups and blossoms and wilts and falls, and all of it over by sunrise."

"Is that an oak, then?" asked Naomi.

"I expect."

"Olly, it's about five miles away."

"Well, I know him, don't I?"

His arms were like an armoured corset: a thing of warmth and leather and metal. His hands were large enough to cover her breasts. He stood with his chin just touching her hair, his half-rigid penis a stripe of heat against her back and her buttocks. They were breathing together—a tint of smoke in the night-time air, the fern moving softly on their legs.

"I cannot believe," he said, "you have got me up here unhackled."

"I let you wear your boots, didn't I?"

"If Llanowen was to see me . . ."

"Right, you can warm my front now." Naomi revolved, put an arm round his waist and arranged his penis between her legs. "OK. That's nice."

"So," Oliver asked. "What you going to do then, girl?"

"I shall stop right here until my back gets cold."

"I mean, in life, like?"

"In life?" She could see the firelight faintly on his face, a shade apart from the surrounding clouds. "You won't laugh?"

"I won't laugh."

"I'm going to be a poet."

"Why would I laugh at that?"

"I don't know. It just seems—"

"Good place to write poems here, I imagine."

"Well, that's one reason I came."

"Going to write one about me, are you?"

Naomi smiled invisibly, returning her head to his neck. "I might have written one or two already."

"Only one or two?"

"You really are the vainest man I ever met."

"Things to be vain about, see? Do you know they write poems about me?"

"Limericks, I heard."

"Bloody epics, look. Heroic exploits, that manner of thing."

It was the first time Oliver had ever been on Cefn Wylfre at night. The shapes and smells of the sheep on its slopes, these all belonged to Llanowen and Llwyntudor, and even on those moonlit evenings when some activity or punishment had kept him back at primary school he would never have dreamt of coming up-over. The fairies and the corpse candles, well, Albert had always told his tales a little slantwise, but the tales of the chapel—their undying worms and unquenchable fire—still they remained, after all this time. He put a hand gently through Naomi's hair, felt her belly, her thighs, their indivisible warmth. He could have expressed no more plainly his thoughts in the bedroom—that he found something abiding in her beauty, unlike the likes of Angie or Annette, whose appeal had been vernal, precisely in the fact that it would fade. There had really only ever been Amy to compare, and she had belonged to a separate lifetime.

"I never did think I would become a farmer," he said, finally.

"How could you not have done?"

"I was aiming to be a vet. Or a doctor. I did get the grades at O-level, like. No thanks to old Idris. It might have happened. Or a boxer. I could have been a boxer. Good, I was. Three Counties Champion."

"I saw the picture in your grandmother's house."

"There you are, see?"

"Do you still do that stuff, Olly, do you?"

"What stuff's that, then?"

"Fighting."

Away to the north, the fire had found a few higher branches of the drought-seared oak at Cwmtwrch. It was threatening to turn into a candle of its own.

"I never did think I would become a farmer," he repeated.

"I'm warm now," said Naomi. "Let's keep going!"

The fires extinguished as she led him down the slope, her wellies flapping against her calves. In a bowl of grass, a moth was floating: a glitch in the darkness. Sheep hurried away from them, hollow on the dry ground. Naomi picked her way among the ragged trees—sudden shapes against the reddish clouds—following her spare hand, testing the space. The first few nights she had spent at the Welfrey she had listened to the void of this hill. In the moments when she was falling asleep she had seemed to be floating with nothing more than the creaks of the house to remind her where she was—and these might equally have been the sounds of some intruder who knew she was alone with no way to raise the alarm and with nothing to defend herself besides the wine bottles her father used for his cider. She would never have come up here without Oliver. She would not so much as walked about the house in her underwear had it not been for him, so pleasingly scandalized by their nakedness—his hand like an anchor in the night.

"Mawn pools, girl," he said, in a murmur.

They were working their way across a level in the hilltop where the grass had risen into tussocks or reeds and, as she peered ahead of them, Naomi seemed to see a glaze to the ground and a flickering movement—perhaps a sheep, perhaps the invention of a joint.

"What have they got to mourn about?" she asked.

"Mawn, not mourn. It's an old word for peat, it is."

"Oh, *mawn*."

"Best not to go too close. Deep they are."

"No swimming, then?"

"No swimming." As she took another step, Oliver caught the faintest light, a blueness in the path beneath her boots, and he touched his chest although she was holding his hand.

"Can we go between them?" she asked.

"I'll show you in the day, how about that?"

"I don't know what it is about you, Olly. You tell me to do one thing and I feel a powerful urge to do the opposite."

"You're trouble, that's why."

"It's only with you. I'm quite good normally."

Oliver smelt the damp in the soil here, a wealth of age and decomposition he had almost forgotten these past few weeks. He felt the thirst in the hills and the fields. He drew the girl towards him, the sensation almost painful as her breasts pressed cool against his ribs. For a moment again there was light where she had been standing. There was a paleness too, close to the water, which must have been sheep, although it was no more than an hour till dawn—the hour that Albert gave to the fairies. Then, out of the blackness, a line unfurled between the half-seen pools, growing rapidly as the sheep fled away from them, brightening into a soft, pure blue.

"What . . ." Naomi breathed. "Is that luminescence?"

"That's your path, girl," said Oliver.

1977

THE CRY WAS a fracture in the midsummer night: a new note in the music of the party, which sounded to Oliver less like songs than some machine wanting oil. He glanced across the cramped little sitting room, past the young men sprawling in the armchairs with leather sandals and skeiny beards, the women in T-shirts, draped on the men's laps or cross-legged on the blim-pocked carpet. Had he known that Naomi's friends would look like this, he would have thought twice before polishing his shoes, combing in his Brylcreem and choosing his waistcoat with the prancing deer on the left-hand panel. He would have thought twice about coming at all. The gabbling woman, or rather the girl, who had him pinned against a sheet-covered wall was wearing a deep-cut, velvet dress, but to her it seemed to be some kind of joke. Leather boots showed under its hem. Her face was made up almost like a clown.

"You . . . got to excuse me," said Oliver, trying not to spit, since the ceiling forced him to lean above her. "I have a baby, see? Upstairs he is."

"That waistcoat!" she exclaimed again.

Oliver was always able to hear Cefin. He could wake him with the slightest noise. Once, when Naomi had gone to see about her next year's studies, taking the boy with her, Oliver had still woken regularly throughout the night and would have bet money that his son had woken too, in his basket, wherever he was.

He grappled his way towards the door, stepping over people and ashtrays, avoiding the light in its spherical shade, but he could not remember, he realized, how to get to the hall and arrived instead in the thin, dirty kitchen, where bodies were crowded on the lino and the sideboards and Naomi was leaning on the fridge, talking to a man in yellow-lensed glasses who might have been an old boyfriend for all that Oliver knew. She smiled when she saw him—her eyes black-rimmed, her jacket tight to contain her belly and make the most of her milk-heavy breasts—but he turned and then caught his head on the lintel, so that the people around him looked and winced.

The hall seemed narrower than he had remembered, although perhaps it was just these numberless people. It was a wonder that there was air enough to breathe. They sat in lines against either wall, their legs interlocked, their knees in ridges—some of them surely not half of his age. At least here he was able to stand upright, and with the staircase slanting high to his left he held onto the banisters as he stretched for each space, muttering apologies, awkward, conspicuous. One man looked up and caught his eye: a lecturer possibly, his hair run with grey. By the front door stood two men in leather, one with a ring in his nose like a bull, and a black man with long hair fashioned into snakes, who grunted a greeting as he passed.

There was a couple having sex in the bedroom, moulded half-dressed over the bed so that at first Oliver mistook them for the bedclothes. Their noises joined the lamb-like wail of his son. He tried not to look as he took the basket and hurried back onto the miniature landing, into the women who were waiting for the toilet.

"Oh! What's her name?" They gaggled round him, putting out their fingers.

"Cefin." He wrapped him in his arms, held him to his chest like some part of himself restored. "He's called Cefin. Like . . . Well, like Kevin."

"Hello, little Cefin!"

"I like your accent. Where are you from?"

The front door now stood open to the street, giving a glimpse of space beyond. Lying the baby on his forearm, his small legs working, his dark, angry face enclosed by his fingers, Oliver picked up the basket, the nappy bag and the bottle of milk that Naomi had pumped before they left her mother's house that evening. He hardly noticed if he trod on anyone as he clambered back down the stairs. The air outside did seem to bring Cefin some measure of calm, although the street was no better than a strip of tarmac between terraced houses like great, dead hedgerows. There was a weed or two curling out of the pavement, but there was not one tree, not one patch of grass. The houses were distinguished only by pebble-dash, the colours of the doors and the way that the light fell from the craning streetlamps. At either end were yet more houses. As Oliver stood, rocking backwards and forwards, he looked up, through radiating telegraph wires and the television aerials on the chimneys, into the slice of tainted sky, down at his Land Rover in the line of cars.

"Olly!" Naomi appeared in the door behind him, fighting her way through the crush on the step. "Olly, where are you going?"

"Home," said Oliver.

"No," she said. "No, no, you're not."

"Naomi, he was screaming, he was. There was two people fucking half on top of him! You think that's all right, do you? I don't think that's fucking all right!"

"Olly, I didn't know. I didn't hear him. I only checked on him ten minutes ago! We'll . . . What are you even thinking, anyway? You can't leave me here. Can I have him? Please?"

"I do not want him going back in there. I shall fetch him home and you when you're done."

"Olly, I'm . . . He's two months old! I'm breast feeding, for God's sake!"

"It will be dawn in half an hour or so. I have got the bottle. I shall pick him up some of that powder."

Cefin was starting to cry again, his voice dividing the lifeless street.

"Olly . . ." Naomi stood before him, her lips almost quivering, a line slicing into her forehead. "Love, come on. Please. It's all right. We're both of us exhausted. He's hungry, that's all. Please. I need to feed him. We'll . . . We'll go to my mum's house—"

"And what? September, he comes back to this, does he?"

"It's a party, Oliver! For Christ's sake, I've not been to a party in a year! You don't live in the bloody pub, do you? I'm sorry this is hard for you—really I am—but you do have to make a bit of an effort, you know? This is where I come from!

It's not like I've ever had you come here before, and I've bent over backwards to fit into your place, haven't I?"

"Well," said Oliver. "I'm here, in't I?"

Naomi took the baby with a noise like a whimper and at once the pain subsided in her face. She tugged at her jacket, pulled the scarf from her hips to hang over her shoulder and put him to her breast, his cry a mewl as he smelt her milk. The two of them became a single entity: a thing self-sufficient in the unnatural light, in the music still spewing from the too-small house, by the mud-striped Land Rover where Maureen was watching them, hunched and black on the steering wheel.

BY THE TIME that the sun scored the clouds to the east, Oliver had already crossed the Beacons. The mountains were black and crested to the south—where they should have been—above knitted hedgerows, stirring creatures and the sky-framed trees on the ridges of the hills. He must, he thought, have made choices in his life, but for the life of him he could not remember any. He had asked Naomi to marry him but she did not, she said, agree with marriage. She had suggested that he sell the Funnon, or suggested it was something they had to consider, since no place was more important than a child having parents and she was damned if she was going to abandon her degree. But even if he could have consigned his mother to some bungalow in Aberedw or Builth Wells he did not have the deeds, whatever his name. With half of the farm gone to Ivor or Mervyn, and with the mortgage paid, he would have been left with barely a pocket full of change. Perhaps, in the end, that was his choice: nothing the one way and nothing the other.

"What do you think, girl?" he asked Maureen, quietly.

The raven clicked her sharp black beak.

"It's not so bad, is it, eh? They're only stopping at her mother's for a spell. And we always knew she'd go back to university. It's not like that's any news . . . We done all right. We've had her to ourselves all year."

Blank as he was, with the passing of the city and those long valleys choking with houses, Oliver felt the strength returning to his body—to his hand as he flipped down the visor on the windscreen and pushed his sunglasses onto his nose, to his arms and his legs as he dropped through the gears and turned by the Griffin, into Llyswen. There were no other cars on the Wye Valley road. The sunlight surrounded the Radnorshire hilltops, picking out the ditches of Twyn y Garth, striping the high Ty Isaf fields with the shadows of oaks and hawthorns. Coming out of Erwood the ground rose slightly and the light poured into the window beside him, turning Maureen from black to a welter of colours, like oil on water, while beyond the bridge, the shelving rocks of the urgent river and the picnic tables of his grandmother's café, the fern was green around the long, dark head of Llanbedr Hill.

1983

THE 4600 HAD no shadow at all on the level ground at the foot of the Bottom Field, or none at least that Oliver could see. It grew again only as he climbed and crossed the slope—the front-end loader, the bonnet and the chimney flowing across the tedded grass, the buttercups, yellow rattle, self-heal and globe flower, their colours as muted as the pressings in his mother's books. He stopped periodically when the baler turned shrill and a bale arrived like a monstrous egg. Through the oil and smoke he smelt the churning hay and, with nothing to do but to follow its spiral like water vanishing down a plughole, he thought about Amy perched on a hayrick, about Albert with his scythe—his Isaac—keening the blade on the long leather rhip with a pinch of sand from a pocket of his old sleeved waistcoat. In the days of the boss, haymaking had seemed to go on forever—mowing and raking, rowing and cocking. Once or twice they had not finished until October. Hard it had been, and hot as hell, with the sun on your neck and the hayseeds itching, clinging to your skin, but if nothing else it had never been lonely. Even with the baler they had bought that summer after Idris's death, which had had no sledge and left square bales at random on the lattermath, they had still been working with the Pant or Llanedw. Now it was not so much the sweat he remembered as eating his bait in the whilcar's shadow, a gang of them descending on the wash-pool by the yellow light of a low, round moon.

He was cutting the lines at the heart of the spiral when Etty appeared on the Fordson in the Banky Piece. She drove inchingly as usual, her narrowed eyes spreading shadows to her temples, steering two-handed as she brought the trailer side-on to the hill and killed the engine—not, as Oliver knew, to save diesel but because the brake had given once in the Top Field and she always felt more confident in gear. Oliver paused for a bale, then finished the field with the baler still short of capacity. He knew she was watching as he pwned the valve to lower the drawbar and climbed stiffly to the ground to uncouple the PTO, unscrew the hydraulics and roll the concrete weight into place. They did not speak. There was nothing to say. They moved around each other here like they always moved, like those spangled dancers he would see sometimes on the telly in the Awlman's Arms—certain of their purpose, their place in the space, following the music of the year.

Once the trailer was loaded, Etty lugged the bales back through the Banky Piece, which Oliver had mown in part in the week, since neither of them would have started the baling on a Saturday. She pulled into the yard between nettles and foxgloves, moving so slowly that it seemed the weight might defeat the old tractor, but at last she passed the barn and the sapling sallies and stopped again by the fence for the Plock, where Devil and Hanoch came over to greet her—twitching their ears and puckering their skin against the horseflies.

"You're really aiming to use them bloody things, are you?" asked Oliver, arriving on foot, pushing his damp cap back from his forehead.

Etty ignored him. She returned from the barn with the black plastic roll and dropped it in the yard with a smack.

"Good hay this lot'll be!" he insisted. "Give him a few days."

"Olly, it has to go in wet, I've told you already. Wet and seal it up to keep."

"Mam—"

"It makes no odds. We are doing it anyway." She pulled out the first of the enormous bags.

"If it is such a good idea, then how come nobody else is onto it?"

"Olly." She looked up, squinting again. "These things weigh a ton. Are you going to get over here and lend me a hand or not?"

It was only the changes that required discussion, or at least gave the two of them something to talk about. There had been her decision that he should drive all the way to Kelso to buy a Border Leicester ram, when there were tups in their multitudes in Builth every Monday. There had been her decision to buy the New Holland baler, when the money might have finished off the lambing shed. Remove her subscription to *Farmers Weekly*, it seemed at times, and they might not have spoken in months.

ETTY DRAGGED THE toy box the length of the landing, wincing as it squealed on the floorboards, leaving little scratches in the polish. Reversing through the door, she shoved it against the old, striped wallpaper she had glued back in place with some success. She stood to breathe—upright again since the operation, which had, after all these years of discomfort in her legs, been over in barely an instant. Besides the dressing table, which she could not move, she had effaced almost every trace of herself from the bedroom: the washstand, her chamber pot, the breach of magazines, even the embroidered Bible verses she had brought with her out of some sense of duty when she swapped rooms with her son on Idris's death. There were picture books on the bedside chair. There were clothes for a boy in the chest-of-drawers. The impression of her body remained in the bed, however hard she had tried to plump it flat, but it was concealed effectively by the counterpane she had been stitching all winter, with snow-white sheep, a lattice of hedgerows and herself in the yard holding hands with her grandson, while Oliver beamed from his big blue tractor.

Beyond the chamomile in the vase on the sill, and the window cleaned both inside and out, the hills were as green as the tight little fields.

THE SILAGE MADE a mountain at the end wall of the barn—regular as honeycomb, the sun in the west on the lip of each bale and the folds converging on the ties. A hen could have hopped from the slit above the hayloft and stepped out onto its summit. Working his way across the final level, Oliver sealed the bags as he had sealed them all—wrenching on the twister to spare the gripe in his back and the finger he had broken on some man's head the previous weekend, which was going badways and would have to be seen to. From here he could see across the ring of young willows pawing at the pond, sprouting among the stumps of the diseased elms, down the open valley to the white speck of the church in Llanbadarn-y-Garreg. Cwmpiban, he noted with some satisfaction, had burst a tyre on their long-bed trailer and were wearily unloading while one of the girls rolled a fresh wheel down the bank from the yard. The long-horn cattle in the next-door field were watching sleepily. For years now this had been the way between the two farms: a series of battles contended at a distance. Once or twice Oliver had found his hill sheep driven far off their territory, wandering helplessly on the grass for Llewetrog. Once he had found a hole in the wall for the Panneys that neither the weather nor the creatures could have forced. He had himself shot Mervyn's dog, which had sclemmed into the Long Field and taken four lambs, but even on those occasions when they had met in the lane, each of them daring the other to reverse, they had neither of them uttered so much as a word. Instead they had vied with the lambing and the shearing, the hay and the harvest, rising at three to be the first to finish, and both of them waited and waited for Ivor to die.

"Olly!" called Etty.

Oliver grimaced and looked at his hand. "All right, all right!"

This was the thing about a job like the hay—the silage, as he now had to call it. Tedious as it was, it did at least serve to justify the moment. As he slipped from the bales and tramped up the yard, the chill of tomorrow was back in his belly. With his eyes on the ground he crossed the concrete bridge, kicked his boots against the step, passed the telephone on its table in the hall and climbed the stairs to the transformed bedroom, where his mother was standing at the carcass of her dressing table—its drawers and its mirrors removed. She had done what she could, he noticed that much. The window, free of its moss and its cobwebs, threw perfect diamonds across the patched-up wallpaper. There were toys arranged on the big rag rug he had not seen in thirty years: cars and trains, jigsaws and Noah's Ark animals.

The back bedroom, by contrast, was a gloomy little place. The view itself was pleasant enough—the sunlit orchard and the weeded rows of the vegetable garden—but its ceiling was black from a leak in the roof and its air was heavy with the rot in its floorboards. It was all they could do to squeeze the dressing table between the sagging cot, the stacks of magazines and the boxes of worn-out, old-fashioned shoes.

"Not much fun in here," said Oliver.

"It is only for a week."

He gave a nod, turned back towards the door.

"Olly," said Etty, quickly. She pulled her lips into a kind of smile, arches in her cheeks where there had once been dimples. "I know all this is awkward on you, I know it is . . ."

"You're not wrong there."

"You'll be about tomorrow now, won't you?"

"I dunno." He glanced at his finger. "I'd best get to the doctor, by the looks of things. And there's the TB testing in the afternoon. I've the vet to meet up the Island."

"Olly, you told me you'd change it!"

"Must have slipped my mind."

"For God's sake, I . . ." She looked away from him, scraping the loose hairs back into her bun. "What am I supposed to say to that, eh? He's your responsibility, isn't he?"

"So I do hear." Oliver shrugged.

"And what does that mean?"

"Means as it sounds."

"He's your responsibility, Oliver! End of blasted story."

"Oh," said Oliver. He produced his cigarettes and tapped one on the packet. "Paternal responsibility. Right one to go lecturing me about that now, aren't you?"

ABOVE THE SINK and its long-necked tap, a three-day moon showed pale between the bars of the clouds. Etty stood on the kitchen flagstones, their cold air on her naked legs as she could hardly have felt it in a decade. Through the open door she heard the clatter as Oliver lifted the seat in the Land Rover, unbolted the plate and poured red diesel into the dummy tank that Harry had installed in his garage at Llanedw. She listened to his weight in the springs, the thud of the door, the bark of the ignition, and it was only then that she let herself cry—the tears escaping her shut-tight eyes to pool in the lenses of her spectacles.

There were times, in spite of everything, when she wondered whether Oliver could have been Idris's son, after all. He had all of his meanness—took a penny prisoner, as her mother would have said—and he was mean enough to her as well. She wiped her eyes and blew her nose, and looked again at the moon in the window. It was not as if she had not been changed by her husband herself. She had not always inhabited this labyrinth of signs, which brought some meaning to every nest of the swallows or the bees, to the oak leaves coming before the ash, to the phase of the moon when she trimmed the dead ends of her hair and to any of the trimmings she had missed to consign to the fire. In truth, she did not know if a moon concealed by cloud for its first two days still qualified as new, but she had, as ever, quite enough to worry about as it was, so she rose a coin from the biscuit tin on the mantelpiece and went outside to stand on the doorstep, where Maureen descended with a puffing of wings and landed gently on her shoulder.

A raven on the roof; there was another one.

"Well, old girl," said Etty. She ruffled her feathers. "Just the two of us again tonight."

The dogs were calling for their supper in the kennel. The chickens were poothering along the wall of the barn, on the grassless ground where the old bridge had lain, among the red steel uprights of the skeletal shed at the top of the yard. She waited some minutes for the high clouds to move, but then the moon appeared again—a toenail clipping in the distant blue—and she made her offer of the ten-pence piece, gave her bow and continued down the yard, round the silage stack to the gate for the Banky Piece.

"Dill! Dill! Dill!" she called.

It was an evening to the height of music—the furrowing clouds converging on the west, fiery with the falling sun. The valley for once seemed open to its light: a bowl of birdsong, murmurous streams and ripening oats. If only she could have felt it, risen for a moment against the gravity of time, like a buzzard on an updraught, and been a part of it fully. As a girl, she remembered, she had sat by the river on the stretch of grass where her mother now had her picnic tables and watched the teeming rings of the rain with such wonder, such transportation, that the water could be running down her chest before she even noticed she was wet. So what if there were more cuts in the limits and quotas. The Funnon perhaps had never looked more plenteous. Her grandson was coming. The air was sweet with the scent of hay. The farm went on and they had kept their promises. They had not pulled up the hedges. They had not drained the bog with its watercress and ragged robins, its nests for the peewit and the curlew.

"Dill! Dill! Dill!" she repeated.

This time the drake gave his quack of acknowledgement and led the ducks out of the trees around the brook—the nine of them waddling in single file, back up the field towards the pond.

IT WAS NOT that Oliver was fat, of course—not like he had been as a boy. Erect he was every bit as imposing as ever; but that bulge in his shirt in the cramped Land Rover, it showed beneath the frame of his sunglasses and intruded on the evening like his thoughts of his mother and his son. It jarred with the man he saw in his mind, who was lean and indomitable, and black-haired still, if only with the help of a dye bottle. He crawled between hedgerows of pink and white dog roses, driving the daggy Nelsons for the Pant, which Griffin would insist on grazing on the verges as if he had no grass of his own. His mother was right, that was the size of it. She was right about Cefin, as she had been right about the tup, which was, after all, one half of the flock, whose big, white-faced crossbreds had no rival on any farm he knew. No doubt she was right about the silage too—even if, this year, their neighbours would be making hay successfully enough. Oliver might not see his son from one year to the next, but even to think of him made his heart seem loose in his chest.

In the yard of the old forge in Llanbadarn-y-Garreg, a shaggy-headed man was working on a motorbike. His T-shirt read GET IT TOGETHER, JUNKIE. In the uncut hayfields for Pentwyn, where at least half of the hedgerows had been bulldozed, the only flowers were the red and white clover. Branches were trailing over the Gleision, where once he had come on these summer nights to flick brown trout from their refuges under the bank.

He never saw the trout anymore.

"Line 'em up!" Oliver called, striding through the door of the Awlman's Arms, the buttons restored on his waistcoat.

"I shall have you tonight, Funnon!" Lewis chuckled and found a glass.

"Oh, you think so, do you?"

"Weights, look." He curled his arm to show off the muscle.

The locals' bar reeked of smoke and sheep-dip, with a faint undercurrent of perfume. It was noisy with the wireless, which stood on the shelf beneath the bottles of spirits, its back in the mirror that covered the wall with the black and gold letters of Guinness. Oliver received his beer. He opened his packet of Porky Scratchings and leant against the bar to consider the room: the few lads bunched at the peeling tables, with cigarettes and dolled-up girls—one of whom, he noted, looked quickly away. A lass for Pentremoel, if he was not mistaken, although he had thought her to be about twelve.

"I seen you made silage," Griffin remarked.

"I seen you made nothing."

"Dipping we was. Tight as you like they are this year."

"Don't I fucking know it."

"Forecast's fair, in any case. You's wasting your money, if you asks me."

"Time will tell, Panty. Time will tell."

"So," said Griffin, after a moment. "Your boy's tipping up tomorrow then, is he?"

Oliver grunted and reached for his cigarettes.

"By Christ!" Griffin whistled. "I still canna believe as you tupped that girl!"

"Right then, Funnon!" Lewis poured a couple of pints and headed for the corner and the Pac-Man table they used for their arm wrestling. "Beat me this time and it's drinks for a week."

The ache was gone from Oliver's back. His finger continued to burn like hell—it looked like a sausage in a golden girdle—but a single beer had given him distance and he was almost able to ignore it. He kept it straight as the two of them sat and he levelled his eyes with his customary purpose. Lewis was old, as old as his mother, but there was a blacksmith under his landlord's bulk, and the wiles of a charmer, and few men could hold him for long. As the two of them locked hands he threw his weight behind his arm before Oliver had even parted his boots, and it took all of the strength of his left abdominals to restore him slowly to the vertical.

There were, there had always been, rules to the war with Cwmpiban: boundaries, if only for self-preservation. The farms might compete to finish the hay, but if the weather was kind then they shared the same pressures and kept out of one another's way. Oliver came to the Awlman's Arms; everyone knew that. If Mervyn went anywhere, it was the Black Ox in Painscastle, where Oliver had not been since the place burnt down some twenty-five years or so before. When the door swung open, creaking softly, Lewis seized his opportunity. A growl arose in the depths of his chest and, with a sudden roll of the ball of his body, he drove him almost to forty-five degrees. Oliver found himself frozen briefly. His eyes had not left the face of the landlord, but he could see the door beyond his shoulder and it was a moment before he controlled his muscles and drove their hands so hard into the Pac-Man screen that he must almost have shattered the glass.

"Fuck!" he exclaimed. He closed his eyes and held his breath.

"How are you, Lewis?" said Mervyn.

"Cwmpiban."

If Oliver's finger had been healing at all, it was broken again for sure. It was throbbing madly inside its ring—its pain in his head like somebody was pwning on an anvil.

"How's your old man?" Lewis asked, wincing, shaking out his arm.

"Pretty ordinary, to be honest with you."

"Oh?"

"Had another stroke, look. This morning, it was. They's took him to Hereford . . ."

Mervyn had followed him, Oliver realized. He had been waiting and seen him leave. He watched from his corner, cradling his hand, the Pac-Man blinking blue and white beneath his chin. His neighbour must have been all of forty-six years old, but with no hair to lose, no part of his body that could possibly have expanded, he seemed as he had on the first day he ever saw him, in the mist, with Idris and Ivor. Even his trousers with their baler-twine belt, his tartan shirt and dingy brown jacket appeared exactly the same.

"Right then, boy," said Mervyn, as he approached. He settled himself in the empty chair. "Let's see what you got then, shall we?"

It surprised Etty now that Idris had brought the stone to the farm at all—given his superstitions, given his aversion to the little ring of stones on Cefn Wylfre, which was hidden by the fern but still, she suspected, had kept him away from the hill at night as effectively as the mawn pools. It was Oliver who had turned it into a gatepost when the man on the digger broke one of the old ones, clawing back the banks to make space for the shed. He seemed happy to use it however he liked. Herself, she would have been more cautious. For her the stone belonged to the hills. Like them, it was something separate, unknowable—however many times she might have crossed it, back in its days as a bridge. As she flipped the rope from its head and opened the gate by the wall round the abandoned church, she was careful not so much as to touch it, and barely glanced at its lichen-clad sides—its mysterious scratches faint in the marginal moonlight.

She had wished so many times that, on Idris's death, they had simply sold their half of the farm, divided the change and gone in search of their separate lives while Oliver at least might have found himself some other line of work. She had been angry, she remembered that. They had sold the pig and the Hereford cows, bought machinery and dragged the Funnon into some distant quarter of the twentieth century, because there had seemed to be no other course, because without children there was no purpose but progress. But always, always by the grace of Ivor, who could on any day, at any hour, have put the two of them over their door.

Bats were flitting between Etty and the stars. Her slight shadow moved across the colourless flowers: helleborine and green-veined orchids. On Llanbedr Hill, a tractor was returning from the Ox. Its headlamps turned between the yews in the churchyard; its driver's song was thin beneath the half-asleep rooks. Once she might have heard the rerp of a corn-crake in the Rhos, or the churring passage of a nightjar, but those night-time birds were all gone. She entered the church and, feeling her way along the pews, sat down in the same place favoured by her mother, before the pulpit, in the moonlight piercing the shattered roof—falling through the bat-smelling air to the grass and the holly tree sprouting from the flagstones. A regular little dressed-stone building it may have been, some Victorian replacement for whatever must have stood here before, but she had always loved this church. From its porch the valley appeared to be landscaped; the hillsides harmonized in such a way that the first ancient person to worship here, descending perhaps from the forest to the spring, might have chosen the place because it was here that he saw God. Even in St. Mary's, on her bench at the organ, Etty felt the need to express her prayers—if only in her head. Here alone that need was gone. She could sit and know her thoughts understood as she did not understand them herself.

TWENTY MINUTES THE two of them had been here, now the night had come and the battle could wait no longer. The cheers of the crowd had died into murmurs: remarks on the relative lengths of their arms, Mervyn's advantage in terms of leverage and the dreadful condition of Oliver's finger, which rose black and askew from their dribbling fists. If anyone was giving odds in Oliver's favour it was only because they knew his history: the five men he had beaten at a disco in Gladestry, the anvil he had hurled more than sixteen feet one year at the Erwood Show. Mervyn simply would not move. His scalp was red and welling with sweat, his bicep strained at the rolls of his shirt, but he neither met Oliver's gaze nor tried to ignore it—seeming, if anything, to be gazing beyond him, as if admiring a far-away hill.

"All right, lads." Lewis leant on the table. "Let's break it up now."

"Break it up," Oliver muttered, "and I shall break you up."

"Mervyn?" Lewis hesitated. "Funnon, you needs an hospital, you do . . ."

For the first time in his life, Oliver looked away. It was one of his rules to lock eyes with his opponent until the other gave—fight or arm wrestle, it had never once failed him—but then he had never faced anyone so inscrutable. He lowered his head until his hair touched his forearm. In his mind he built an arch between his left boot and his right hand, whose jutting finger seemed the pivot of the world. Images came with his tabbering eyelids. His mother again had hair like fire. His son was five, was two, was three—his life thrown into wild disorder. Mervyn's breath arrived in quick, stale gasps; he had no choice but to breathe it himself. Without stubble, without brows or even lashes, his face appeared to be melting, resolving itself into the long, trench-cut face for Idris— and when he closed his eyes against this terrible vision the images redoubled: Naomi in tears, Cefin as he had first seen him as a baby, dark and screaming and unmistakably his. They were fighting for their children, he saw that now. That was why the old ways no longer worked. The real protagonists were not even here. Cefin was in his distant city. Mervyn's one boy was working with his uncle Vivien, who would visit Rhyscog barely once a year. That was why Oliver could never capitulate, would die before he allowed his hand to move a single millimetre.

1989

A HUNDREDWEIGHT MEANT NOTHING to Cefin—not in terms of stones, of which he weighed six, nor in terms of the kilograms they used at school. In terms of the sacks they had brought back at lunchtime, he could move these only by wrapping his arms round their rope-tied necks, jamming his trainers in the barn's cobbled floor and reversing in a series of jerks. Cefin was not a physical boy—if he had his father's hue, he had none of his bulk—but still he doubted any boy in his year could have dragged eight of these bloody things all the way up the stairs into the granary. He stood in the hot light falling from the door, while a dog named Blackie pushed her wet-tipped nose beneath the hem of his shorts. What he needed was a machine, or failing that some kind of mechanism to help him. The barn, like the farm, was all but empty. For years he had thought that, with all of this space, his father must have been a millionaire. There was the elevator leading to the white-iced hayloft, but he could never have moved the thing and, besides, he did not know how it worked. There was a long canvas belt in a heap near the swede chopper. There were scythes in a line on the deep stone walls and a set of scales hanging almost above him—their blocks and loops reaching high up to a beam.

The solution, when it came, was so obvious that Cefin felt foolish not to have thought of it before. Unwinding the rope from its cleat on the door jamb, he lowered the pulley, removed the heavy scales from the hook and speared instead the nearest sack, which, with the hiss of shifting grain, he found he could now lift quite easily. The welder fizzed in the workshop round the corner. He took the canvas belt and speared that too—hoisting the sack some feet into the air before he swung it over the topmost step, tied it to the handrail and let it down.

The granary was dark and sweltering: a windowless room above the stable—or what his father called the stable, since it housed only the Ford 4000, whose cab was pocked by collisions with the arch. Perhaps it was these that had damaged the wall. As Cefin backed across the oil-slick floorboards, gripping with the cracks, passing through the light streaming thinly from the roof tiles, he cleared a path in scattered bits of mortar and stone. He steered round a pot of grain dyed blue and the stiff, long-tailed body of a rat, and almost trod on a little roll of paper, which, once he had recovered his breath, he opened and angled to inspect.

```
A B R A C A D A B R A
A B R A C A D A B R
A B R A C A D A B
A B R A C A D A
A B R A C A D
A B R A C A
A B R A C
A B R A
A B R
A B
A
```

The words were written in faded pencil and around them was a series of signs, which reminded him of horoscopes in the newspaper. One was the sun. Another was the moon. Others were less certain—the paper was almost brown with age—but, wiping the sweat from his glasses with his T-shirt, he made out a couple of three-line stars and the circle and cross he knew from his mother meant a woman.

SIX YEARS HAD passed since Cefin had last stayed at the Funnon. They had stayed at the Welfrey, of course, he and his mother—once with his grandfather, once with Adrian. But to be with his father alone; Cefin was reminded of a story his mother had written about a boy with a dragon: a vast, winged creature of knotted eyes and knife-sharp teeth. It was not that Oliver had not tried to be nice; he had given him a fishing rod, he had taken him for a ride on his tractor and sat with him and a jigsaw after supper. He was just so big, so alien, with his foreign words and his scar-mapped face—his hair, black as rubber, sweeping onto his shoulders like a film star.

"We never had no combine when I was a lad," Oliver told him, leading the way between the silage bales and the drooping trees around the pond. "A binder we used in them days, pulled by a horse, like. I cannot say as I miss the bloody thing. Them days we'd cut before the grain was ripe, not like now. That way it wouldn't fall, see? We'd leave him plem to ripen in stooks—like sheaves, you know? Like . . . like bundles." He opened the gate into the Banky Piece and slung the cutting bar over his shoulder. "Turn them to dry, we would, and a right bloody business it was and all."

The sunlight was fanning from the black-bottomed clouds, across the daunting hills and the deep green valley, which seemed to Cefin to belong so completely to his father that he could hardly tell the two of them apart. The shorn sheep grazing the short, mown grass were all emblazoned with his initials. Beyond the brook, on the opposite hillside, the girl continued to drive his father's tractor—the baler chattering behind her.

"All right, then." Oliver turned and looked at him sideways, his dark eyes buried in gathering cracks. "Who helped you? I was joking, I was. You know that, don't you? I never did mean you to move the damn things. Them sacks weigh a hundredweight apiece!"

Cefin glanced at his face.

"The scales!" Oliver said, suddenly. "The blasted pulley!"

"I thought . . . that was what you wanted."

His father gave a gulp of a laugh, hesitated, then rubbed his head with his claw of a hand. "You canny little bugger! I shouldn't have thought of that in a million years!"

It had been his grandmother's idea to invite Ada, who was the youngest of Griffin's five children: a surprise for the Pant, whatever that meant. So far that day Ada had granted Cefin three words exactly, talking only to her father and Oliver, and she had passed the entire afternoon on the Fordson—following the straw left by the combine harvester, hopping from the seat to the pedals whenever she needed to stop. She must have seen the two of them climb out of the trees round the stream, but she did not once look away from her work: a sturdy girl with corn-coloured hair, her chin set, jutting in front of her.

"How do, Panty?"

"Not so bad, boy." Griffin humped another bale onto the trailer.

"I ment this thing, or near enough. We should be done afore it comes to rain."

"Two hours, I gives it."

"Aye, and I'll say as Cwmpiban wants four."

Cefin stood awkwardly next to his father, who lay in the stubble beneath the cylinder of spikes, grunting and wheezing through the bolts he held in his teeth. Compared to the machines he had seen elsewhere, the combine was not much of a size. It was red, or had been, with a steering wheel upright on the roof and a spout on the side where Griffin would fill up the sacks. As Ada baled the final row, tugging the string to empty the sledge, a dark shape swept between themselves and the clouds—the scream of its jets came an instant afterwards; it must have been travelling faster than sound—and she ducked and puckered her face.

"Thousand foot, my arse!" she exclaimed.

"Now then, now then," said her father.

"I tell you," said Oliver, "I shall give one of them bloody planes a barrel one day, you see if I don't!"

He dragged himself back out of the combine, dropped his spanners in the box and brushed the dust from his denim shirt, which he always wore buttoned up to the neck. He took one of the shotguns from the Ford 4000 and rummaged in his jeans for a couple of cartridges.

"You ever fired one of these things, boy, have you?" he asked.

Cefin shook his head.

"Nothing to it, look. Well, she'll give you a bit of a kick, I expect, but so long as you're not leaning on a tree nor nothing she shall not do you no harm. Twenty bore this is, your nana's gun. Nice little piece." He crouched down behind him, and Cefin smelt his ripe sweat stink and the chemical reek he'd been told was sheep-dip and better than the carnage you'd get from the blowflies. "You hold her like that, that's it, lean into her a little, and squeeze the old triggers there when I gives the word—one then the other. Keep her on the corn now. That's it."

The last square of corn stood alone in the golden expanse—its bowed heads rippling although the day was almost still. The others had fetched guns of their own from the tractor: Griffin purple-faced, still in a sweater, Ada's T-shirt tight enough to show she wore a bra. Had Cefin moved a muscle he might have forgotten where to put his hands, but the barrel was shivering in spite of his efforts; the sweat was collecting between his eyebrows and the frame of his glasses. He felt as he did on sports day at school, poised on the line among the boys who would win, his stomach contorting, his mother at the rope in her tracksuit and Aertex shirt. When a rabbit erupted from the back of the square and set a wild, zigzagging course for a hedgerow, he grabbed at the triggers out of surprise, but the clap of a shot came only from his father as the animal threw its tail over its head and landed twitching on its back.

"And there's one for starters," said Oliver, with satisfaction. He caught the cartridge and dug out another. "Safety catch," he added, flicking a switch on Cefin's gun. "Ready now?"

There was smoke all round them, sweet and blossoming. Cefin staggered with the recoil as if he had been punched. Struggling to right himself, trying to keep the barrel on the wall of the corn, he heard through the ringing silence a voice calling to him by name. Another rabbit had burst into the open—his father was hurriedly trying to reload—and as he turned his gun across the naked slope for a moment, his eye, the safety catch, the little black sight and its weaving course made a single line, the stock jumped again and the white, dancing tail came suddenly apart.

ETTY ALWAYS DID the clothes on a Monday. Any later in the week and her hands would not recover for the service on Sunday, and even then, especially in the winter, she could bite her lip until she tasted blood before she came to the end of a hymn. She dunked Oliver's jeans in the scum-covered bath, rinsed them thoroughly and began to feed the colours through the mangle—turning the handle with slow, stiff movements, collecting the water to use on the floor. In the window over the salting stone the clouds were congealing; the creatures were pressing round the fences on the hill. But still, when she heard the noise of the geese, she removed her apron, mopped her face and went to stand on the front door-step to watch Oliver on the combine, grinding round the corner of the barn. Behind him Griffin drove the Ford 4000 with the children on the trailer among the bales, the sacks and the rabbits swinging from the lade. They reminded her of the floats at Builth Carnival—the four of them parading through the yard, acclaimed by the chickens and the burn-skin dogs—and she smiled at the thought and waved to her grandson, who slipped to the ground and trotted towards her: too old for hugs or kisses these days, although really he was no more than a boy, a tadpole where Ada had her first hind legs.

"I shot a rabbit!" he told her, standing straight in his shorts and T-shirt.

"You never!"

"This boy . . ." Oliver stopped the combine in the lambing shed. He returned to the yard with his belly before him, a swing to his stride whose recent absence Etty noticed only now. "I tell you, Mother, he is a crack shot!"

"Course he is." She let her hand touch his shoulder. "You'll be hungry, I doubt. Do you want a bit of tea, do you? Ada?"

"Yes, please, Mrs. Hamer."

"Yes, please, Nana."

Etty looked from the clouds to the low-glancing martins and the chawms around the tyres of the trailer, in which she almost expected to see pink flesh, as she did in the cracks in her fingers. "Best to come on in, by the looks of things," she said. "The rain shan't wait for the kettle."

The anxiety of the morning was gone—and that was nothing to the days of hay, when they had been slaves to every turn in the weather and the winter waited dark and uncertain. The silage, the combine, these things were like blessings—as the binder had seemed after the reaping that she alone re-membered: the long nights working by the waxing moon, its light just enough to see the faces of the men, the grey of the hills, the rabbits by the hedges and the farmhouse white across the valley. Change would come and sometimes for the better, but it was not this, nor the fact that they had brought in the harvest, beating both the storm and Cwmpiban, which sent her lightly back into the kitchen to recover her apron, spoon tea into the pot and take the cake from the oven to sit, still steaming, on a plate on the chipped blue tray.

IT HAD BEEN so many weeks since Cefin had last seen rain that he could hardly remember how it happened. Beyond the barn the hills seemed vague, as they would without his glasses. There were spots in places in the yellow-brown yard: sudden spiders of water and dust. A drop ran down the side of his neck. With Blackie crawling after them, he and Ada shuffled backwards from the doorstep to sit by the telephone table.

"You like Def Leppard then, do you?" Ada asked.

Cefin finished his mouthful. "Don't you?"

"Philip likes them," she admitted. "My brother. I like Madonna."

"Well, you're a girl."

"My friend says I look like her."

"She's got hair a bit like you. Sometimes." Cefin stroked the dog's neck—her muscles hard beneath the reeking fur. "Do you . . . want to see what I found?"

"What is it?"

He reached in his pocket and extracted the roll of paper.

Away from the grown-ups a certain fierceness had left the girl's face. Her lips had parted. Her eyes had ceased to be the slits of her father. She slithered towards him on the seat of her shorts.

"Where did you get that?" she asked.

"The granary . . . Do you know what it is?"

In this gathering twilight the stars, the moon and the beam-circled sun seemed more mysterious than ever.

"Magic," said Ada.

"Magic?" He smiled.

"Yeah, and what would you know about it?"

"How old are you?"

"When's your birthday?"

"April . . ."

"Mine's January, so there you are."

The hall felt something like the entrance to a cave. The rain was growing, blackening the yard, scratching an angle from the wall of the barn where the bale elevator was spluttering steadily. The hills seemed to crane in successive waves of shadow, and at the first hint of lightning the wretched dog tried to climb into Cefin's lap.

"Oh, come on," he said. "You're not serious, are you?"

"Of course I'm bloody serious." She was scowling again. "Move!"

"What?"

"You heard me. Budge out the way."

Cefin shrugged and slid onto the doormat as she took his place, crossed her legs and leant over Blackie, murmuring in her ear. She ran her hands round her neck and along her back, tickled her chin and caressed her nose, and slowly, weirdly, the animal subsided. She lay on her lap like something deflated and appeared to have fallen asleep.

"Well?" she said, and lifted her eyes.

"How . . . did you do that?" he asked.

"So you believe me now, do you?"

"I didn't say that."

"Well." Ada checked behind them, her fingers working on

the dog's neck. "Magic's what it is, if you like it or not. That's a horse charm, I expect, since you found him over the stable. What you do is you hide him above a door—stick him in the wall is best—then you say a prayer on whatever's coming through, and there you go, your prayer comes true."

"Do you think he still works?" asked Cefin, finally.

"I don't know. Might do. You're not supposed to look at him first, that's the only thing. My grandad, he is a charmer, see? And my great-grandmother was. He's got her book. That tells you everything. He's going to give it me when I grow up."

Out across the hills there was another glimpse of lightning, and the rain turned white momentarily. It was some miles closer to judge by the thunder, which might have been a tremor in the earth and brought to Cefin a feeling of giddiness that made him want to run outside and stand with the rain falling full on his face. He could feel somehow the relief of the ground, which seemed to be breathing this fresh, new air—opening itself, even to him.

Blackie still did not so much as twitch.

"When I was a kid," Ada remarked. She wrapped her arms around a sun-brown knee and watched the water spilling past the doorstep, creeping along a crack between the flagstones. "When I was a kid my mam used to tell me as thunder was just Olly Funnon making a racket. I believed her too. I always thought your dad was a giant."

OLIVER MIGHT GRUMBLE that if she wouldn't take her test then she ought at least to take the 4000, but Etty knew where she was with the Fordson, which she always kept in the exact same gear and controlled with the lever by the steering wheel, and even that she preferred not to touch. She liked the feel of the air on her face. She liked her red, white-spotted umbrella, which Cefin was holding, squeezed against the toolbox on the mudguard, like the bearer for some visiting queen. To the throb of the engine, they followed the course of the long-gone railway between the sodden fern on the spur of the hill and the fat lambs grazing the lattermath in the fields. At times the Wye wove almost beside them, frothing through the ashes and hazels on the bank. With the harvest and the ploughing, the broad Wye Valley was flowering in its way. It was green, red-brown and luminous yellow—and every combination where the grass or the earth pushed through.

There was old man's beard in a Tir-celyn hedgerow.

There was light on the silage clamp at Coed-yr-Aber.

Had the road not veered to the left, they would have driven straight into the garden of the café but, as it was, Etty turned with the line of its fence and, waving past a lorry in a wash of tyres, guided the tractor round the big SOLD sign and came to a halt among the cars and puddles.

She tugged the black button, and the lid on the chimney tabbered and fell.

"Where's the river path, Nana?" asked Cefin.

"Just by there, look." She pointed. "You come and get yourself a cup of tea and I'll show you."

It was astonishing, really, the transformation her mother had wrought. The station looked much the same as ever, except that everything was new: the smart white fences that ran along the platforms, the panes of the gas lamps, which now contained bulbs, even the glass-faced posters for seaside resorts, "K" Boots and GWR Summer Extras. The beds and hanging baskets were alight with geraniums. Goldfish shimmered in the rain-pitted pond. For the restored siding she had found from somewhere a pair of green-and-gold carriages, which she had turned into a shop selling tea towels, paintings and books of local interest. Where the rails had lain there was now a lawn—its dribbling umbrellas dwarfing their own.

"So," said Molly, admiring the rod and jar across the table in the café, "you're a fisherman, are you?"

"Dad's been teaching me," said Cefin.

"Where'd you get all those worms, then?"

"Well, Nana Molly, what you do is you wriggle a crowbar in the ground. Then the worms all think an wnt is coming and they head for the top to escape him."

"An wnt, eh?"

"An wnt . . . A mole."

"I know what an wnt is, bless you." She stroked his cheek with her bird-like hand, which made him shrink minutely backwards. "Your mam OK, is she?"

"Yeah. Well. She was OK last week."

Molly lowered her voice. "Best waitress I ever had, your mother."

"Mum was?"

"Talk about an advert! You never seen so many boys wanting tea in your life!"

Cefin smiled, a little politely. He drained his Coke.

"It is no wonder you're so blasted handsome." She beckoned to Lucy, who was collecting plates from a table near the counter. "Now then, what else will you have? The millionaire's cake's very good, I'm told, though my old teeth won't take it, I'm sorry to say."

For the time being, it seemed, Molly remained in charge at the station. Twenty-five years or more had passed since she had bought the bungalow near Erwood Bridge—Etty's father had given up waiting to retire and died—and even now, with

223

the tenants gone, she had not left the station cottage. Still, three times a day, she would hump her frame the length of the platform to preside at the till, to scrutinize the takings and keep an eye on the customers inside and the customers out in the garden. She sat across the table, old and alert, watching her great-grandson through her owlish spectacles and the close white bars of the ticket-office window as he vanished down the steps among the long, serrated leaves of a sweet chestnut.

"An wnt?" Molly repeated. "How long's he been here? Six days?"

"The professor dropped him . . . Saturday."

She sipped her tea and dabbed her lips, considering the timetable beside them on the wall, which offered services to Moat Lane and Three Cocks Junction. "I did speak to Miles the Solicitor, Etty," she said. "He told me he'd help, though he is retired or near enough."

"I . . . don't know as Olly'll go for it, Mam."

"Then you tell him to come and talk to me."

Etty turned her headscarf in her hands, flattened it again on the vinyl tablecloth. Although the two of them were speaking again, their words still came out forced and hesitant.

"I don't know," she said. "It is your money, it is. You ought to . . . You ought to enjoy it."

"I'm eighty-eight years old, girl. What am I going to do? Go on a cruise?"

"It is my problem."

"It's our problem, Etty." She met her look with the sparks of her eyes. "You're my daughter, aren't you? It was me as made you go up there in the first place—"

"Mam, you know that's not true."

"You were just a girl, Ets. You were no kind of age. I . . . I

224

know I came back here, and I did say I wouldn't, and there's nothing more I can say about that. But it doesn't mean I've forgotten what happened. I knew you was seeing someone, or I guessed in any case, like in how you was dressing and how you was acting, and I could have told you about the dangers, and I didn't—I was too bound up in the work and your father—"

"It was my decision," said Etty.

"But I pushed him, see? I did. When I told him about you, well, of course he was always going to go crazy, but I rose to it too. I was so bloody sick of him. I all but told him it was his own fault. I called him a drunkard, and a lazy bugger, and no kind of man when there was soldiers dying, and no kind of father when it came to that. So, is it any wonder he come on so hard? I never gave you a chance, Etty. That's the truth of it. By the time I was done we was both of us leaving and you'd not even got to say your piece . . ."

"Dad was never going to let me stop here," Etty said, in the silence. "I knew that. I told Idris even before I told you . . . That same Wednesday, there he was, hanging round the market like normal, using up coupons to buy our eggs like he hadn't got none of his own. I knew he liked me. I could hardly have missed it. I knew he was a good man, in his own way. So I told him everything. I told him I would be having a baby. I said I would marry him if he would have me."

"It's . . ." Molly swallowed, dropping her eyes. "It's just money, love. Money for Olly. Money for Cefin. That's all I ever wanted for it. Give Miles a call. Please. He'll speak to Ivor, if Ivor can be spoken to. He'll speak to Mervyn. There's got to be a price as'll buy them out the Funnon, get everything square. He'll sort something out for you, you'll see."

Beyond the lip of the bank, Cefin was standing on the exposed rock: a crink of a boy in an old green anorak and plastic trousers, his gumboots together, his black hair erupting from his baseball cap. With a flick of the rod, he sent a worm through the rain into the teeming current, watching it sink with a fierce concentration.

"He looks like him," Molly added, more softly.

"He looks like them both," said Etty.

"Yes." She nodded. "Yes, I suppose he must."

THERE WAS A third pool at the Gleision, on the Edw, between Martha's Pool and the old wash-pool for the neighbouring farms. The Middle Pool it was called. It was an eddy on the north side, almost still, with a little spring trickling down the bank into an arch of ripples. On Friday evening with the rain long past and the sunlight falling skute from the trees, it sparkled clean—so perfectly transparent that it might hardly have been there at all. Oliver sat with his son on the still-damp grass, watching the pair of coachman flies they had tied out of newspaper that afternoon. They had yet to catch anything but it didn't seem to matter. There were, surprisingly, a few trout about, mooching in the shadows. One of them would come to the lure in the end.

"What's that tree, Dad?" asked Cefin, after a time.

"That one? That's a hazel, that is. See the nuts?" He pointed to their heads, peeping out of the dense veined leaves.

"Can you eat them, can you?"

"Eat them?" He laid down his rod and got to his feet, picking a bunch that he peeled with the nails of the three fingers on his right hand.

Cefin flicked his fly upstream to save the lines from getting tangled. He chewed on the nuts, which were soft, almost creamy, and watched a trout flexing slowly under the opposite bank—the water so clear that he could see its open mouth, its eyes like the spots that patterned its sides, its fins like vertical wings. He was not so bothered about catching the fish. He was happy to watch it. He was happy just to be sitting here with his father while the water turned and wandered past them. From the tousled grass that hung around the spring, a spider appeared on the surface of the pool: a minute creature, which scampered at speed across the drowsy eddy, pursuing some invisible insect. It seemed for a moment to consider their flies, then darted back to the dark, muddy shelter of the bank.

WITH THE RED light extinguished on the corner of the Walkman, the dark grey window stood apart from the wall: a frame for the chamomile flowers on the sill. In his dressing-gown and Batman pyjamas, Cefin sat on the counterpane his grandmother had embroidered, on the bed he realized now was hers. At home he might have switched on the television and given a few minutes to Super Mario Bros., but here he just sat with his fishing rod, scraping a nail between his teeth and watching the hill above the ridge of the barn, which seemed in the night-time to look back at him.

His father crossed the yard with a creaking bucket: a man a little stooped, but powerful and purposeful as he always appeared in the day. The dogs in the kennel greeted him rapturously. They burst upon him in a formless mass.

Cefin sipped his cup of hot chocolate, which normally he was not allowed, but then normally he was not allowed meat—Adrian wouldn't have it in the house—and he had eaten little else all week. He fiddled with the handle of the reel. It was bad enough, he thought, to have left their flat, where he could creep from his bed in the never-dark nights and curl up in his mother's warmth. It was bad enough that she was now his teacher, in the high school where he would once more have to go on Monday—and a teacher too who got whistled by the older boys and used in taunts that followed him in the corridors. There were bats in the yard: scraps of the blackness come suddenly to life. There were stars among the ruptured clouds. As his father retraced his path to the house, he imagined the three of them together, here—as they would have been when he was a baby.

Once the radio was talking in the kitchen, Cefin set down the rod, turned on the light and retrieved the penknife from his fishing bag. He had already examined the cupboard in the corner: a narrow space above the hall, crammed with magazines and linen that smelt of his grandmother. It was only by squeezing round the sheet-laden shelves then stretching over an old leather trunk that he was able to reach the stones at the top of the front door. Leaning on his side to allow in the light, he scooped away the bodies of cobwebs and used the knife to bore a hole in the mortar. He pushed the roll of paper deep into the wall, then knelt on the rug on the floor of the bedroom with his hands joined flat in prayer.

THE PARLOUR AT the Funnon was like a hole in time. Its piano might have been exchanged for an organ, bought perhaps from some defunct chapel, but its walls were whitewashed, as Naomi remembered them, heavy with samplers, a photograph of the coronation and even a dusty portrait of John Wesley—a Bible in one hand and the other held open to a sepia sky. There still was the stiff black dresser, unsanded, unpolished, with empty spaces for the floral plates that lay across the white lace tablecloth. As she worked her way back around the wall to the window, Oliver loomed in his chair at the head and Cefin looked pale as she had ever known him, for all of his week in the air. The formality she found almost unbearable. She was afraid she might start laughing or crying, just to crack it all open and breathe.

"I . . . like your loo," she said.

"It is an improvement," Etty agreed.

"It's a mercy in the winter," said Oliver.

"Are you . . . all right, Mam?" asked Cefin, his accent torn between his father's drawling vowels and his vagabond version of hers.

Naomi did not feel all right. She did not like driving at the best of times, and as if the vomiting that morning had not been enough she had been forced to stop three times on the way. These smells of her past, this stone and damp; they worked on her darkly. Perhaps they were working on her son as well. Although she was sure that she must look ill she could not understand the alarm she saw, half-hidden by the frames of his glasses.

"I'm fine, love." She touched his arm.

"Are you sure?"

"Course I am . . ." She pulled on a smile.

"And the teaching was a success, I hope?" Etty asked.

"It was fine, thanks, yes."

"That's good."

"These residential courses, they can be very intense."

"I can imagine." Etty set down the book of poems Naomi had given them and reached for the teapot: a horrible thing in the shape of an acorn. "Will you . . . Will anyone have another cup? Cefin?"

The boy at least was picking at his cake.

"Well," said Oliver. He set a hand on the table, its second finger gone beneath the knuckle. He appeared to be trying to hold in his belly. "I shall have to go round the sheep before the show. I am sorry we cannot tempt you along for an hour, Naomi. We could find you some manner of fancy dress, I expect?"

"Thank you, Oliver, but it is quite a long way . . ."

He nodded slowly, his eyes on the door. "Last go round the fields, boy?" he asked.

The shapes of the sash window fell across the table. Its light revealed cracks in the handles of the polished silver cutlery, a trace of copper in the bowls of the spoons, distortions in the tines of the forks. In the yard there was the slap of wellies, the murmur of voices and the cackle of chickens retreating from the tailing dogs.

"Well," said Etty, when the two of them were alone. "You have my congratulations."

Naomi flinched. "Is it that obvious?"

"I know it's none of my business, girl, but if . . . if you did feel you could talk to him about it?"

"Etty . . . I really don't feel I owe him anything."

"No no . . ."

"It's only his business if he makes it his business, and he doesn't, does he? When has he ever been to visit his son? Never. Not once. It is the sheep this, the cattle that, it is best to come here—like none of the rest of us has anything better to do."

"I . . . I don't think that's what it's about." Etty's voice had died almost to a whisper.

"Then he needs to grow the . . . hell up. It was years ago, for God's sake! Years! There's only so much I can do, Etty, you must see that? God knows I've tried to make things work, but, what can I say?" She put a hand through her hair and looked at her cake, which she had still not brought herself to touch. "I'm sorry," she said. "I'm sorry. It's been such a hard week and I'm . . . I'm missing my cigarettes like you wouldn't believe. It's not fair to take it out on you. I only found out on Sunday myself. Nobody is supposed to know. I've told Adrian and that's it. I haven't even told Cefin."

"He looked . . . He did look worried."

"I'll tell him in the car."

"Well," said Etty, quietly. "I do mean it very sincerely. It has not been easy on you, I am sure."

"Nothing you don't know about, I imagine."

"Well . . ."

"Did . . . Oliver ever see his father, if you don't mind me asking?"

The effort in Naomi's eyes had collapsed, become a weariness, an emptiness that Etty had not suspected. A cloud moved over the valley around them. The shadow leaning from the barn grew faint, the swallows bright only in their bellies. The window's pattern dwindled, vanished, and with the shadow gone from the face of the girl the table seemed less like a barrier, more like the connection perhaps once intended.

"No. No, he never did." Etty looked at the spots on her hands where there had once been freckles. "It was all so different in them days, girl. Back then there was the shame of it, see? It was a mortal sin, everybody thought so. There was only the one other woman I knew who had got herself in the family way, outside of wedlock, like. Glenda her name was. I stopped with her for a while, I did. I mean, there was nobody else. She, well . . . When she told her parents, they packed up her things in a brown paper parcel, gave her a ten-shilling note and said they never wished to see her again. Well, there was no maternity money in them days, see? Nothing of the kind. So off she went to the Mission of Hope, as they did call it, to repent of her ways and get marched off to church with all the other naughty girls through some town where she did not know a soul. I forget its name now. Somewhere away. She came back, of course, a year or so on, but her baby was adopted. She never did find out where she went." She looked up at Naomi, who was watching her in silence, sucking her lips so the pinkness disappeared. She was so young, she thought, not thirty-four. Perhaps, for her, all this would still be an episode. "Me," she said, "I was not going to lose my baby. Not for anything. But I had this other option, see? I was fortunate, really—that's how I look at it. You might not believe me, but I do."

THE BLOW TO his head did not hurt Oliver so much as confuse him, since his long blond wig fell over his eyes and he stumbled on a plant pot, into the trellis round the door of the hall. He righted himself with the prefab wall, which was flexing faintly with the fight inside, and growled, and looked into the white-striped road. His face, which he always kept clean shaven, was pallid with powder, picked out with his mother's lipstick, mascara and blue eye-shadow. Beneath the waning moon and the streetlamp on the opposite pavement stood four big lads in jeans and boots—one still holding the neck of the bottle.

With a sigh, he slipped off the sovereign rings he used strictly for display.

"Well?" he said.

"That's Olly Funnon," hissed the boy at the back.

"And?" The one with the bottle was a Painscastle boy—perhaps a son for Archie Powell.

"You never said it was Olly Funnon!"

"It's a fat old farmer in a fucking dress!"

"A gown," Oliver corrected him.

"You fucking what?"

"It's a gown." He ran a hand down the silver polyester, the panels he had stitched himself.

"You, mate, put me in hospital for two fucking weeks! Do you remember that, do you?"

"I cannot say as I do."

The road was broad and empty for the moment, although there were headlamps in the trees towards the bridge—the noise of the engine drowned by the pounding of the disco. The slope was just in Oliver's favour. There was a line of cars beneath the houses in front of him, a telephone box, the wide plate window of Williams' Store.

"Are you sure it was him, are you?"

"Are you going to shut the fuck up, Dicey?" The Powell boy dropped the remains of the bottle and locked his fists at either hip. He was short-armed, full-chested, his close eyes fierce in the light of the hall. "Well, mate," he said, "you are going to learn it now. We're going to teach you a lesson, we are. We're going to grind your nose in the fucking road!"

"You screwed up with the bottle, boy," said Oliver, evenly.

"How's that, then?"

As the headlamps appeared on the brow by the Wheelwrights, he came forwards suddenly, judging the space to the length of their arms. He feinted once to make the boy waste his right, then sent all of the anger and frustration of the day into a cut to his jaw, which pitched him clean into the lorry's path. There were almost no rules in a four on one—fewer still when it was started with a bottle. Oliver was religious about these things. It was always the opponent who set the terms. Whatever goading he might have faced, he had never, or not since he was eleven years old, hit anyone who had not hit him first—although as the lorry swerved and sounded and a narrower, crop-headed lad arrived on his pavement, he allowed him merely to graze his arm before he drove his elbow into his ribs and left him retching by the crowd now massing on the step.

There were men dressed as women, women dressed as men: the order of the world upturned. Erwood Show—it was ever the same. Faces peered greedily from waking bedrooms and the windscreen of a car, which slowed and stopped and closed the road. Oliver's sequins shone in its headlamps. His shoulders thrust from the straps of his gown. Dicey, he had turned up only for the sake of appearance. Plump, mild-eyed, he stood sideways ridiculously, like he had once seen a picture of a sideshow boxer, and Oliver had only to show his broken teeth to send him scurrying behind a Daihatsu. The one lad left was exposed, uncertain. He shielded his eyes against the gathering cars. He was a log of a boy and hit him with strength, but no one with a brain above his neck would have aimed for Oliver's hay-stuffed bra, and he left his face so easy a target that on another day Oliver might not even have bothered. As he crumpled backwards into the window of the store, the glass bowed momentarily around him—its image contracting almost to a halo.

Blue lights were turning on the walls of the village. A siren rose above the thunder of the pop music. With the fighting that evening, it was hardly to be wondered at. By the door of the hall the Powell boy was upright, the neck of the bottle once more in his hand, although his jaw was hanging askew from his head and blood was dribbling from his mouth.

Years had passed in which Oliver might have gone to Naomi. Her new baby might have been his. He might have lived with her, with Cefin, who could watch a six-inch trout with such eagerness that he felt eager, alive himself—and instead he was left only with this child who staggered towards him with his bottle and dreams of revenge.

Oliver let him have a single cut, to feel its punishment, to see his own blood flooding from the tear in his gown. He did not look at the blinking police car. With the crowds and the shouting, he did not even notice the officer who seized his arms and clamped them at his back while a skinny little policewoman tried to move into the Powell boy's way. If others had a mind to get involved he was long past caring who they were. Freeing his one hand, he revolved on the spot and, grasping the policeman by his belt and tie, threw him helmet-first through the windscreen of a Datsun Sunny. The policewoman backed away with her truncheon, shrieking into her spluttering radio as he stepped another attack from the Powell boy, seized his ragged hair and tripped him flat into the road. He told him his plans in a series of grunts, forcing his face into the jagged tarmac and working his nose across the stones. The boy was shouting, writhing and kicking. The cartilage folded beneath his weight. The thin bones splintered and gave. There were the hands of men round Oliver's shoulders as the blood wove away down the shallow hill—purple when the blue light passed.

1990

IN THE NINE dead months that her son was away, Etty had fallen out of step with the electric, had come to find its light too hard, too unforgiving. That Friday night, in his chair in the kitchen, Oliver looked no more than the frame of himself—she could hardly believe he had become so thin— but still, in the tremulous glow of the oil lamp, he looked as much refined as reduced. She had never much liked the way he dyed his hair. The grizzled fuzz that covered his skull was sparse towards the temples but sat more naturally with the lines beginning to divide his cheeks, to swallow at least one of his scars. It was his eyes that alarmed her, fixed on the Rayburn like the flames were still visible—not so much weary or evasive as bereft.

In the fields the ewes were calling continuously, their breaths concealed by the cries of the others.

"Market today then, was it?" he asked.

"Market," said Etty.

"How was that, then?"

"Not so good, Olly, to be honest with you."

"Thirty-eight?"

"Thirty-five."

"Thirty-five . . ." He squeezed his cigarette against the lip of the coal scuttle and pulled the packet from the pocket of his jeans.

"The two-year-olds did come a little better."

"And three fields gone to blasted Cwmpiban."

"At least we don't have to worry about all that now. At least it's legal, us and them . . ."

The grandfather clock reached half past nine: another bar in another gate. Prising himself back onto his feet, Oliver stooped for the drooping mistletoe. His shadow shivered on the rough white wall. It had been so long since Etty had last hugged her son that at first she did not know what he was doing. She had never found her face against his chest, his grown-man smell in such proximity—strange without a whiff of animals, just cigarette smoke and some bitter soap and a trace of starch that made her think of hospitals. She winced at the pressure of his ribs on her hand. She turned her head one way and the other, as if looking for a way out, but then, haltingly, she allowed her ear to rest on his shirt, whose neck for once was open, spilling grey hairs, disentangled her arms and wrapped them round his waist. Even now she could only join the tips of her fingers. His stubble cagged in her tied-back hair, his shoulders were above her, but there was his old, familiar heat, the progress of his heart, the sigh in his nose as, at length, he inhaled and her fingers came briefly apart.

* * *

SETTING DOWN THE newspaper, removing his glasses, Oliver rolled his fists in his aching eyes and dragged his bare feet out from the covers and onto the bedside rug. The calls of the ewes had grown sporadic, hopeless. They afflicted him in a way he had not known since he was a child. The candle was playing on the flowers of the wallpaper. Perhaps, he thought, the three-day week had returned. Perhaps the farm had fallen into such straits that they could no longer afford the electric. But he had seen enough bulbs and strip lights to last him into the next millennium. He was glad for the flame as he trod across the floorboards—his disfigured hand in the tunnel of the stairwell, in the glass by the coat hooks and the windows around the front door.

At last, it seemed, Oliver understood why his grandmother and his mother had each in her turn been drawn to the abandoned church, which was, after all, not old, not beautiful, not packed with their neighbours—the only compensation for their weekly condemnation in the chapel. In his long flannel nightshirt, the candle guttering, he stepped over the hurdle tied in the lychgate and climbed the rack among the stones for ancient Hamers, the sheep with their rabbit ears and large Greek noses grown quiet at his approach, as if he might be returning their lambs. High above the sycamores and the hard, wizened yew trees, the thin moon fled through the pell-wool clouds—a chip in its arch, which Idris had told him was a man sent in punishment for gathering firewood on the Sabbath. Its pallor lay along Llanbedr Hill, on the limb reaching down almost to Cwmpiban and the three good fields they had lost. Squat on the circular summit of the tump, the church had fared no better than himself in recent times. Brambles groped against its walls. The bell still hung from its bar in the belfry, but the ridgepole had folded almost in the middle; the roof was a valley of jumbled slates and pools of blackness that turned into stars as he passed through the porch and sat on the pew at the front.

At times he had tried to explain to Naomi why he could not join her, why he could no more crawl out of this valley and live than he could have crawled out of his own skin. She had not understood and he did not blame her. Had she been here now, by some turn in events, he would doubtless have run to the usual excuses: the fern to be cut for the beasts up the Island, the ewes to be fed since the tup was journ and another year would need to begin. What he had not said; perhaps it could not have been said at all. He set down the candle on the rotten wood beside him and held his hands to his chin, watching the light on the nettles and saplings that were pushing through the broken slates. If it was the church, then the building itself was nothing more than a marker. The cross on the altar, black against its window, was as transitory a thing as the leaves. Perhaps it was the cold on the soles of his feet, bringing its memory of the ground underneath, the rocks and the dark little spring.

All life, he thought, passed through this place: these closing rings of wall and trees within this hoop in the hills.

BEYOND THE YEWS, the headstones and the strange, ornamental trees of St. Mary's Church, the morning wedding was beginning to convene: men with new haircuts and unfamiliar suits, women in dresses that bellied from their tight-calved legs. Oliver paused on his return from the police station, where he was obliged to report every day without fail, and leant his elbow on the sill of the Land Rover, waving past a couple of cars. Maureen came pattering over the seats and hopped from the gearstick onto the steering wheel. His mother was standing at the foot of the tower: a woman tight on seventy years old with grey hair parted and bound in a bun, nodding her greeting to the ushers and bridesmaids, where Nancy and the vicar shook hands. She entered the door with her fingers joined as if cradling a chick or some fragile artefact, and as Oliver checked his rear-view mirror, peered round the raven, and continued past the park, the Groe, he decided not to steer for the bridge and instead turned left into the municipal car park, where for once he put ten pence in the machine.

Strand Electrics had not changed at all during the past year. Not that the town looked particularly different, but there were boys at the bus stop with jeans that made his own look tight and caps turned backwards, as if warding off fairies, and these, like the H-reg post vans on the corner, gave him a disquieting sense that this was not quite a place he knew. The shop, in any case, retained its sign and its blue-and-white awning, its windows packed with advertisements and boxes. The man he saw reflected in the glass of the door, pushing his bootlace tie between the collars of his shirt, was again black-haired, and if he was craggy he was at least no longer fat.

"Good morning," said the girl at the counter. Her fingers stopped then resumed on her calculator.

Oliver nodded. After all this time the crack between her breasts, the shape described by her tight pink T-shirt, made him forget for a moment the purpose of his visit. He noticed the wheeze of the breath in his nose, but to breathe through his mouth might have looked like panting, so he looked away to the plugs and wires that were hanging from the pegs just behind her.

"Washing machine," he remembered as he came to the first of the large white boxes by the wall.

"Pardon?" said the girl. She looked again at Maureen.

"Washing machine," he repeated.

"Oh." To judge by her accent she was not a local. "Well, the Hoover is an excellent machine. Twelve hundred spin. Four-point-five-kilogram load."

Oliver breathed through the gaps in his teeth. "How much you want for him, then?"

"How . . . Oh." The girl smiled briefly. "You'll find the price on the top."

There was, indeed, a piece of cardboard folded on the lid of the machine. Oliver took a couple of steps backwards. He narrowed his eyes until its number became confused with his lashes, and then, since the girl had returned to her calculations, he turned to face the window and took his glasses out of his jacket. It had not occurred to him that one of these things could cost anything like five hundred pounds, which, with the dismal condition of the market, would have left him change from a dozen ewe lambs and all of their fodder for the winter. Slipping his glasses back into his pocket, he gave a thoughtful grunt and considered a cooker, a clock, a pair of headphones and something else made of plastic. He followed the wall to the last of the machines, which resembled the first but was a third of the price.

"I said," said the girl, "do you have any particular require-ments?"

"Oh?" Oliver frowned. He had been having trouble with his right ear.

"We do offer a generous payment plan, if that's of any concern to you?"

"How much for cash?" he asked.

"Cash?"

"Cash." He removed the breach of notes from his jeans, patting the lid of the cheapest machine.

The girl hesitated. As she drew back her shoulders her cleavage bulged. "Actually," she said, "that one is a dishwasher."

THERE WAS REALLY no need for Nancy to come to every service at St. Mary's. Etty herself was paid little enough to accompany the Eucharist each Sunday morning, and while the flat fees for weddings did add up over time, the cut received by the organist's assistant must barely have covered their petrol. She sat in her place at the end of the bench, drew the stops and turned the page at Etty's nod, but, with no bellows to work these days, otherwise she just followed the staves, listening to the wind of the great pipes above them—the wonder of an instrument able to possess these grand, pointed arches, this vaulted roof, this plain of an aisle, where the bride and her father were processing into the mirror.

In truth, as ever, it was largely courtesy, or the simple fact that she liked her friend to be there, that made Etty use the music at all. She could have played "The Arrival of the Queen of Sheba" blindfold. Her hands fled of themselves across the manuals, her left on the swell and her right on the great, the two of them together on the choir when she came to the fluting intervals. Her feet danced weightlessly over the pedals. The whole piece lasted only three and a half minutes—less if the bride reached her destination before her—and the

245

hymns to come were no less familiar, with a full congregation to carry her along. With the two co-codamol she had taken in the car, she could still feel the abrasion in her wrists and knuckles, the muscles beginning to quiver in her forearms, but the pain for the time being seemed unimportant beside this stately tempo, these skeins of semiquavers.

With the last, tailing note, the two women turned to face into the church: Nancy white-haired, high-shouldered, proper in pearls, Etty in her blouse and her long grey skirt, discreetly holding her hands in her lap. Unnoticed they might have been, as given as the place, but their bench was level almost with the pulpit. They looked down on the altar, on the stalls where choirs would join them on high days, on the two hundred people now watching the couple through the filigree screen, the pink hyacinths and yellow alstroemeria. The girls of Rhyscog all had jobs, of course. Bridget worked in her husband's garage, Lucy managed the Station Café, Faith was in the office at Brightwells. But for women like them, who had seen it all different, who had known the weeks as a year-round cycle of washing and cleaning, churning and baking, with a few, fevered hours of conversation at the market and chapel, perhaps the thrill of such a position would never entirely pall.

AT A GLANCE the high Edw Valley was green, almost generous. A tractor was ploughing the straw stubble at the Vron, trailing seacrows and off-true furrows. A tup was busy in his harness by the river, mounting ewes, daubing them with his stark red raddle. On the Little Hill the gorse was burning. Its smoke rose over purpling heather, paler fields and darker hedgerows, tending away into the mottled clouds. It was only when he slowed the Land Rover to inspect a glat or climb a verge to make space for a car that Oliver saw no flowers but the odd meadow saffron or the fingers of honeysuckle, the leaves of the hazels grown yellow-fringed, lank.

Here was Penarth Mount, where he would walk with Amy Whittal in the days when he was more than a middle-aged farmer on early release, when she was less than an anaesthetist in Cardiff or Birmingham or some city of that sort. Here was the barn where he had never persuaded her to remove her knickers. Here was Penarth Wood, where, it was said, the last wolf had been killed in the reign of the Tudors, its four paws nailed to the door of Cregrina Church. With the cost of white diesel, he would never normally have thought about coming this way. But he felt a need to see these hills, to recall how they billowed from this rising lane, how the trees parted on the bank for Llwyntudor to reveal his own corner of a valley: the tumbling fern of Cefn Wylfre, the near-bald head of Llanfraith Hill. There was the Old School: now a house for some retired teacher, grey above the keeling posts and browsing ewes of the football pitch, which would still get used from time to time. There was Llanedw, half-farm, half-garage, where Bridget was working in her oil-smeared overalls—a torch in her teeth beneath the hydraulic ramp, among the masses of waiting cars.

Even hung with clematis, divided by a floor, the windows of the chapel seemed tall and forbidding as ever.

At first Oliver did not recognize the boy: the gangrel with a rucksack who was picking his way over the stones in Cwmberllan Ford. He put his boot on the brake only so as not to splash him, dropping into second with a roar from the engine. His wheels were already parting the water when he noticed the black hair beneath the boy's woollen hat, the tan of his skin as he turned to look back at him across the bonnet patterned with the tunnelling trees.

He hesitated, then pulled on the handbrake and leant across the seats to the passenger door.

"Good God," he said.

"Hello, Dad," said Cefin.

"Can you . . . Can you fit them things by your feet, can you?"

"I'll hold onto them."

Oliver nodded. He put the Land Rover back into gear.

"I like your hair," said the boy. "It's better short."

"I shall tell Vidal."

"You're . . . back in one piece, then?"

"Well," said Oliver. His voice was level but his hands were trembling. "To be honest with you, boy, I've not had the time of my life just lately."

"Is it true you threw a policeman through a windscreen?"

He gave his grunt. "Who told you that?"

"I heard Mum talking to Adrian."

"It is a lot of noise over nothing, boy. Why do you think they wear them stupid helmets, anyway?"

There were Limousin cattle in the Crooked Slang: healthy, full-square, pedigree animals. Mervyn was ploughing the last of the Long Field, coming to the addlands, his furrows swaying slightly behind him—although no one seemed to bother so much about the line anymore. Quantity not quality, that's what they said. At least he had not grubbed up the hedgerows. Oliver stopped in the yard at the Funnon, unwound the twine that kept his door closed and greeted the dogs, whose noses pressed hard into his legs. He stroked their heads, buying a few moments to compose himself, then he opened the gate at the back of the Land Rover and pulled the machine through the straw and scraps of wool.

"Lend us a hand with this, would you, boy?" he asked. "She is no weight, just a bit of a lump."

With Oliver reversing and Cefin holding the pipes and cables, they shuffled over the mud-striped bridge, up the steps and into the smells of dust and stone, coal smoke and discarded gumboots. The wireless was singing to itself in the kitchen. There was a space beside the fridge in the larder, in the corner under the white-speckled mirror, so they stood the machine there on its four thin legs—twisting the nuts until its surface was level—then stepped back to consider its alien whiteness, its mysterious buttons and controls.

"So . . ." asked Oliver. "Are you stopping here, then, are you?"

"Dad?" said Cefin.

"Boy."

"What do you need a dishwasher for?"

Oliver pushed the one hose onto the tap and hung the other on the edge of the sink, as the girl had shown him in the shop. He put the plug in the socket by the door, piled the shirts and underwear in the laundry basket on the white wire shelves and then turned sideways, putting a hand on the breezeblock wall around the toilet. It was the self-same boy, stretched perhaps and gruffer in the voice—there were the bones of a man in his chin and his cheeks—but there, that inimitable tangle of Naomi and himself—all doubtful shoulders and blue, watchful eyes.

"Do us a favour, boy," he said. "Keep that under the tail of your coat."

*   *   *

In the past twelve months of his mother grown laborious, then the baby like a siren at every hour of the day and night, these falling fields and red-tinged hills had come once again to seem like things imagined. Once, as a child, Cefin had tried to dig a tunnel from their garden to the Funnon—he had been waist-deep before his spade met the rock—but even then he had never quite believed that it was possible simply to travel here, at least without his mother or his grandfather, whatever strange powers a grown-up possessed. The idea there was a bus that went all the way to Erwood, to a stop across the bridge from his great-grandmother's bungalow, still seemed improbable—although he had taken it himself. He looked on every detail of the Bog Field, on these reeds, these puddles, this pile of logs by the scruffy little wood in its camouflage of blackberries and tooth-fringed leaves, with a sort of astonishment. He remembered a teacher who had one day told his class about love, which meant, she said, wanting always to be with somebody, thinking about them all of the time.

"Philip, he has not done bad, to be fair to him," Oliver remarked.

"Ada's brother, Philip?"

"He's been minding things, he has, with thanks to your great-grandmother. It was him cut the bruns, see? I was afeared we'd be burning green all winter . . ."

Cefin's father was thinner than he had been. His jeans were hanging from his old leather belt, and his buttoned-up shirt was loose on his chest. His hair was thinner too, if black as ever. As he climbed from the cab of the Ford 4000, found them each a pair of gloves and began to wrench out the brambles from the woodpile, he moved with his usual, steady conviction, but still, Cefin had grown several inches since the previous summer. His father seemed less vast, less absolute.

"Are these . . . rowan, are they?" Cefin asked.

"You dunna cut the wittan, boy."

He picked up a log and looked at the leaflets, wizened, clinging to a twig. "What are they, then? Ash?"

The long lines deepened round Oliver's eyes. He produced a pair of glasses, which he used with the arms still folded, then shook his head and set down the log for a block.

"Rowan," he agreed. "Fair play to you . . . Bloody Griffin. What he has been teaching that lad I do not know."

Oliver swung his axe as if it were weightless, his hands together at the end of the handle as the blade met the grain and the logs came apart. Now and then one of them would refuse to split and he would spin the blade round and drop it on its head so that the log seemed to burst of its own accord. The halves went bounding away across the grass. In his best black jeans and zip-up top Cefin hurried after them, trying to keep up, stacking them in the box on the back of the tractor. He had almost finished the first of their loads when he heard somebody in the scrubby wood beside them, the Rhos as it was called: the sucking of wellies, the crack of a branch. He glanced at his father, who did not seem to have noticed. He looked through the feather-like leaves of the ash trees and the willow leaves with their tapering tips and among them saw an approaching man: a great, fleshy figure with a hairless head that at another age he might have thought an ogre.

Following the eyes of his son, Oliver straightened and pushed back his shoulders.

"Not happy with my fields then, is it?" he demanded. "You after my fucking wood and all?"

"My wood," said the man. His voice was sharp but not un-friendly.

"You think so, do you?"

"My wood. Your hedge. You have a look at the papers." He turned to the trunk of the willow beside him. "You can rise your bruns, like. I shall not bother about that."

"You hearken to me, you." Oliver's voice had sunk into a growl. "That wood is mine. Them fields is mine. You can think what you wants to think, but I never signed them bloody papers. So far as I'm concerned I shall be using them to light the bloody chats. I tell you now, if you so much as touches that wood. If you tries to fell him or you tries to drain him—"

"Flycatchers," the man interrupted.

"What?"

"Flycatchers." He opened the neck of the sack on his shoulder and nailed up a bird box with quick, chiming blows. "Three of these things you wants for them, really. The great tit will be taking one of them for sure, but he'll be out and patrolling and keeping the rest of the tits away, so the pied flycatchers shall get the other two. They needs them, God knows. It's been awkward as hell on them these past few years."

Cefin stood with a log in his arms, his muscles already beginning to ache. The man, he supposed, was the neighbour, Cwmpiban; he knew nothing else about him at all—although he could not mistake his father's look as he took a step towards the hedge, as if coming between them, the axe in his one hand, his chin held high, a certain grey beneath his skin. For a moment the two men were facing one another, then Cefin took a step forwards himself and arrived at Oliver's side.

The man looked back at them with sunken eyes.

"You has the Funnon, boy," he said, finally, "and fields enough. They drives a deal, your mother and your grandmother. It in't as I'd have chosen it, but there we are. It's over, it is."

1996

"Y ou'll mind the headstones now?"

"We'll do what we can, Mrs. Hamer." John Watson sipped his tea with a pensive nod. "We have had a few of them up, like—we couldn't get ourselves up there otherwise—but Ken here, he did mark them. We'll have them back the minute we're done."

His son stood silent by the gigantic truck, the smoke draining half-seen from his cigarette.

"It is a shame, like," John continued. "If it was up to me, like, I'd be all for fixing her up, but you know how it is. That roof. If it were to fall on some poor bugger, well . . . Something must be done, like, and she can't have seen a service in, what—"

"Not in my lifetime," said Etty.

"Not in thirty years!" His big red face recovered its grin.

The mist was thinning a little with the morning, shading to blue as Etty looked upwards. She watched the digger crawl through the cavity at the top of the yard, through the hole where there had been a lychgate, its tyres slipping then biting the slope. The bucket rose, its weight coming backwards. John was shouting through the riot of the engines. As he reached the level ground on the top of the mound, two metal legs descended from slots. He leant from his cab to beckon to the boy, who reversed the bleeping truck between the limbs of the yellowing sycamores.

The bell chimed once with the swing of the backhoe, and again, more dully, in the grass. A second swat removed the remainder of the belfry. The digger's claw reached into the roof and scooped up a skeleton of rafters and ridgepole, the last slates falling like leaves. High above the yard, the church perhaps was in the open sunlight. It appeared to grow brighter where the rest of the world was opaque. Etty had thought somehow that this would all have been more difficult, that it would, at least, require another visit. The idea that the building could fit in a lorry, whatever its size, made her brain seem to press against her skull. She watched the gables wobble and fall. She watched the porch go the way of the roof, the windows implode, the altar itself, which even Oliver had refused to touch, rise through that unreal light and tumble into the still-hollow back of the truck until, suddenly, the church was gone and the mound was crowned with rubble alone.

It was funny, almost, that it had come down to bats. Had the colony survived, so the Church Council woman had told her, they would have had no choice except to rebuild. The Greater Horseshoe was endangered, apparently. Neither of them had spoken of God, nor had Etty said that something ought to mark this place whose yews, according to the professor, were probably two thousand years old. She knew well enough how she would have sounded. There was nothing to be gained from a sympathetic nod or some observation on the sorriness of the times. As the engines continued, she made her way slowly past the pillars of the lambing shed and followed the flem up the side of the house, dipping her head for the old wireless aerial, which appeared abruptly in the pearly air. In the orchard by the nailed-shut privy, she found her market basket and dragged the wooden ladder from the garden shed—moving uncertainly from rung to rung when she propped it against the first of the apple trees.

On Garreg Lwyd, where he always stopped, Oliver killed the engine of the quad and looked back across the hollows and sidelands—the bank for Penbedw and the gieland spilling towards Cwmoel. Llanbedr Hill was an island this morning. The shallow light lay over its back, measuring each lift and fold in the heather, turning silver its dew-heavy cobwebs. The ocean around him might have been the light condensed; it boiled and broke on the distant mountains, curling away into the east, where there was, they said, no hill worth the name before Siberia. In his own valley, the churchyard provided a solitary islet: a nub of ground on the brink of the shadow, its trees like reeds, its summit marked only by John Watson's JCB.

"Get away off out!" he called to the dogs.

The Island itself sat alone above the mist: a dim little cell with tattered plastic windows and a stench of beasts that a day with the pressure washer had done almost nothing to dispel. It had silenced Oliver, to discover its value. How that rascal of a cottage could be worth fifty grand when the cattle in its fields would lose him three or more was more than he was able to fathom. With occasional whistles, he watched Dee couse beneath the far-off beech trees, the bronze of their leaves conferring to the grass. He watched Meg vanish and appear in the quarries, driving the usual couple of dodgers, then run out wide round Llyn y March until every yearling on the whole long hilltop was hurrying towards him—startling a flock of plovers, which sheered together across the rust-coloured fern, the berry-spilling wittans and the snag of a cliff where he sat.

He rejoined the track as the sheep crowded by and followed them west towards the grave for Twm Tobacco: a roadster, or so he had been told, who had been carrying tobacco in the days when smoking was bad, like drugs today, and had been killed for his wares in this desolate place. Nowhere in this archipelago of hills could he see another person, or a house, or even so much as a mountain pony. A skylark in the radiant sky poured its frantic song across the common. Coming to the crossroads, he put his hand to his chest and took a stone from his pocket for the pile in the grass. With a word he brought the dogs in yawping, dividing the two flocks so that the sheep marked *OH* scattered into the heather and the sheep marked *MH* fled away to the north—spilling into the lapping mist like the pool, the Henllyn, down to their right, which had, it was said, one noon dark as midnight, disgorged itself of its water and fishes to form Llanbwchllyn Lake.

THE SUNLIGHT LEAKING from the bare stone tiles streaked the dust disturbed by Etty's feet. It made bright little patches on the sagging tunnels of ancient cobwebs, the various pieces of the four-poster bed, a grouse in a case, the toys, the tools, and the apples she had already arranged across the sheets of last week's newspaper. A hand on a joist, she knelt down carefully on the floorboards of the attic. Two floors beneath her, the washing machine was making ineffectual noises; it astonished her the things had ever caught on. In the yard the two men were talking, dragging the gates back across the mouth of the Bryngwyn track.

They had not, of course, replaced the gateposts.

"Teachers may flush drugs."

"Gay voters could determine the next MP."

"Many believe telematics will provide the biggest opportunity for pro-active development in rural areas since the agricultural revolution four hundred years ago."

"Mrs. Hamer!" There was a pwning at the door. "Mrs. Hamer, we're heading off now."

The world, it seemed, had moved on without her—if she had ever been aboard in the first place. Etty had never even heard of telematics. She had not, to her knowledge, seen a drug in her life. She took the apples from her basket and laid them out in the remaining space, keeping them upright, neatly apart, then she sat down to wait in a prolapsed armchair, leafing through the paintings in the box beside her: the trees in which Idris had found his consolation. She had thought at times about getting some framed. He had been right; they were not bad at all. Here was a birch tree naked with winter, half-silver, half-shadow, with twigs that shrank and divided the sky. Here was a wittan on the open hill, its trunk and branches twisted left, as if reaching for something past the edge of the paper. Here was an oak in the fullness of summer: a tangle of limbs clothed in emerald leaves.

"Mrs. Hamer!"

"It's pushing two, it is, Dad . . ."

"I'll scribble a note, look. She's a good old girl."

When, at last, the truck began to move, its engine bellowed; its brakes hissed and howled. Etty felt its weight in the bones of the house. The apples were trembling. A couple of glasses were toasting one another in a cupboard. Following the wire from the satellite dish, a squirrel appeared suddenly from the eaves but stopped when it saw her—its small eyes black, its fur the same white-grey as her hair. For several moments they watched each other, neither of them so much as twitching, then the vehicles reached the smoothness of the tarmac track and the squirrel whisked its tail back outside.

"I DREAMT LAST night I went to the moon," said Oliver.

"Was there any grass?" Griffin asked.

"Aye, there was, and you'd bloody had it." He leant past the line and cast his quoit, which floated through the steep light falling from the window of the pub and the shadows of its guidebook stickers, bounced from the peg and settled at the edge of the dish.

"One." Lewis marked up the board with the chalk. "You better come some shape sharpish, boy!"

"I did lease some ground off Llanedw, as it goes," said Griffin. "Too busy with the cars they are, see?"

Oliver resumed his stool, dipping a chip in his pool of mayonnaise while Angie Lloyd flattened her cigarette—her face all paint, her hair in coils. She stood on the line in jeans so tight that her knickers showed plainly beneath the pockets, balanced, scowled and flicked her wrist.

"And two."

There was a girl in the corner where there had been a Pac-Man machine, where Lewis had once pulled Oliver and Mervyn apart. She was a walker by the looks of her boots, a tourist in any case: not thirty years old, lean and smooth-skinned with yellow-white hair, her thin lips moving as she read her book and speared another mouthful of salad.

"Come on, Panty!" Griffin gave the cockerel dip of his head.

He threw his quoit, then crowed and made a lap among the people eating dinner, in the old brown sweater he wore year-round, his grey hair flapping on his ears.

"And five!"

Oliver peered at the cover of the book, which was leaning towards him so that it was hard to read more than a letter or two of the title. He peered at the girl. The only line anywhere on her face was a crescent of concentration between her faint, pale eyebrows. He wondered what path could have brought her to this place, which was surely no more than a stop on her way, to be remembered only for the quality of its lettuce, for some chance witticism from the fat old landlord or the way that the shadow cut the tightening valley. Perhaps she would continue by Cregrina, Glascwm and Colva and slip from his map somewhere beyond Lyonshall. Perhaps she would follow the route of the old railway and from Builth travel north by Rhayader and Llanidloes and disappear only when she passed Moat Lane.

"Oy!" said Angie. She took one of his chips and put her elbows on the bar, her tan leather jacket pressing cool against his arm as her wire-bound breasts thrust into the smoky air.

THE TELEVISION WAS a wonder to Dilys. After twenty-two years of life in Aberedw, she had still not quite got used to the thing. If she was trapped here, in her bungalow, as she had once been trapped in a snowdrift at the Island, at least she had seen in this distended window the jungles and the oceans, the terror of earthquakes and buildings so tall as to shade a Scots pine. And if she tired of a programme she had merely to press another of the buttons in her lap to see a game of football or one of those nice old black-and-white films in which an hour and a half would disappear. And then there was the window itself: the sunlit lane and the squat little house for Angie Lloyd, her feeder for the tits and the pie-finches in the garden, and the two fields banking to the yellow-red wood on the ridge.

The bungalow was warm, that was the main thing. Dilys had sat here in tempests and felt no draught at all—and when, in its season, the winter came, she would just make the journey across the smooth brown carpet, between the sofa and the armchair where Dick's narrow backside could still be seen for all of the nurse's work on the cushion, to the lino squares in their chessboard pattern and the dial on the wall by the door to the kitchen.

Angie Lloyd, well, brassy hardly covered it. Five children she had, all of them flown, and still she had no ring on her finger. Flicking the lever on the arm of her chair, Dilys reversed to watch her return, piert from her Saturday dinner at the Awlman's, with that big-sorted scrat who called himself Hamer although he was black as a Jew or worse. She had seen the paper that week. She might not have been so good at her letters, but she knew her numbers well enough. Five hundred pounds he had paid for the Island, and all generosity when he'd had those men up fixing the roof. Even Dick might have had something to say about that, had he not been listening to the wnts—him and Idris and Ivor, and Albert, who had gone that year in his cottage in Llanbadarn-y-Garreg. Close on everyone she had ever known.

Dilys had seen them once in an upstairs window, grimacing equally, Angie's great dugs swinging like two bags of shopping. Dipping her spectacles, she watched the man call his dogs and tie them to the gatepost, with the woman beside him, clecking and laughing and all but unhackling her trousers. She sat in her chair with her lips wrought tight, but when the curtains closed she remembered the pain in her back and her feet, which were as bad today as they were in the nights. To the whirr of the motor she turned back to the screen to wait for the nurse, who would be coming at four to make her tea and run her bath.

A TREE HAD fallen clean across the track to the common—bowed and leafless, so strangled by ivy that Oliver could scarcely see the bark. It lay almost flush with a pair of old gateposts, one of which still bore the burn-mark of the Glanusk Estate. He might, he thought, have pulled it up by hand, but if he was taking no chances with a breathalyser on the lane he was not about to give himself a hernia. He stopped the quad and got to his feet, frowning into his well-scratched sunglasses while Meg and Dee hopped down from the back. There was pell wool in the twigs where sheep had passed, a honeybee or two on the ivy flowers that could have travelled all the way from the Welfrey, since you never saw the wild bees now. There was a slapping across the little field behind him and he turned to see a pigeon leave the green-gold hazels of the bank where some prince had hidden seven hundred years earlier, and then been betrayed by a man in Aberedw. Seven hundred years and the cries of "Traitors!" had still not left the village in peace.

"Hello, there!" said the girl from the pub. She ducked out of the trees. "I'm sorry. I hope you don't mind me crossing your field."

"Well," said Oliver, and turned his left ear. "Since it's not my field."

"I was just visiting Llywelyn's Cave."

"Oh, yes?"

"Not much of a stronghold is it, really?"

"Standards has risen, I doubt."

The girl, he saw, was surprisingly tall, and scarcely wider than a telegraph pole. Her face was a startling shade of pink. Pleasantly depleted though he was, this being a Saturday afternoon, Oliver presented the dome of his waistcoat and allowed his eyes to fall behind his sunglasses, looking for breasts beneath her turquoise fleece and settling for her legs, which, if not shapely, were long enough for her to step clean over the fence.

"My name's Siriol," she said. "I'm . . . afraid I have the advantage. I saw you in the Awlman's Arms. You're Oliver, aren't you?"

"I expect," said Oliver.

"I spoke to the barman. I mean, I guessed it had to be you, but he told me you would be coming this way . . . I'm working on a paper about Naomi Chance, you see? The poet."

"Well." He paused, then nodded slowly. "I did think I recognized the book."

"You've read it, of course?"

"I cannot say I have, to be honest."

The girl's face was nearing the colour of the wittan berries. "I have to say," she said. "Please don't think me impertinent, but I really am excited to meet you."

"And why's that, then?"

"Well. You're surely aware that you appear in her work? I mean, her *Drought* collection. That more or less started me writing myself . . . It's one of the formative books in post-pastoral poetry."

"*Post*-pastoral? We in't done yet, girl."

She rummaged in her pockets. "If I could ask you a couple of questions I would be so grateful."

Oliver looked at the sun on the ridge of the hill, at the shadows falling through Hendre Wood: this curious bank where fields were squeezed between shelves of rock and the scrub oaks were red and gold and green where their tops met the angling light. He took the pliers from the box on the quad and turned to the rusty fence around the field. There had been no farmer at Pen-y-Garreg for ten years now, and the gatepost was so soft and riven that he could have prised out most of the staples with his fingers.

"You met in . . . 1976," said the girl. "Is that right?"

Oliver grunted noncommittally.

"And your son. He lives with you?"

"He in there as well, is he?"

"Well. Yes."

"Did." He breathed and pulled back the wire. "University . . . What was your name again? Cereal?"

"Siriol."

"So we're all of us in this book, are we, Siriol?"

"Well." The girl hesitated. "I mean, you are the major figure, really."

"Major figure," said Oliver. "Well!"

The Glanusk burn-marks were rare these days, with most of their gateposts replaced by railway ties, but still you could spot them, here and there, all the way back up to Hundred House. There had been a plan, a hundred, a hundred and fifty years earlier, to build a dam at Aberedw and turn the entire valley into a reservoir. That it had not happened was no thanks to Lord Glanusk, whoever he was, who had bought every farm that might have been flooded with an eye on a profit from the compensation. There were few things, Oliver thought, to be said for farming on shale. One was that you might as well try to dam a sieve. Another was that the ground was so close to worthless that, by and large, you were left well alone. He picked up a flake of stone, which he turned between his fingers then slipped into his pocket for Twm Tobacco. With a nod to the girl he whistled up the dogs and started the quad—pressing through the hole he had made in the fence, rolling over the half-eaten nettles and the thin, bare branches at the head of the fallen oak.

THE HILLS AND the valley were grey with the evening—the sun having gone, the stars having yet to arrive. The yard light was shining down at Cwmpiban. The quad was crossing the Middle Ddole, the grass showing green in the vee of its headlamps, between the shadows of the parting sheep. Its engine was a pair of notes—a deeper drone and a higher whine—which grew among the hedgerows and the contours of the hillside as Etty fetched the empty bucket back from the kennel and Oliver climbed out of the Banky Piece and appeared from the silage and the long-twigged sallies with a dead ewe lolling on the rack behind him: seventy-five pounds' worth of good, healthy animal, as she had been that morning, which was no little money, what with the BSE epidemic and the export restrictions on the beasts.

"I found her by the track," he told her, as the quad fell silent. "She were sclemming, I doubt. That bloody Mervyn . . ."

"It was Mervyn did this, then, was it?" said Etty.

"I shall get him back, don't worry."

"Did you see him, did you?"

"Course I didn't see him."

Etty stopped beside him and leant on her stick, peering at the ear tag and the hole in the skull of the sheep.

"Olly," she said. "Think with your head, would you? That's what it's there for." She looked up into his dim, ruddy face and the bag of flesh hanging under his chin. "It could have been anybody, couldn't it? It could have been the post van. It could have been John. Or Ken. God knows that truck would have taken some stopping."

"Mervyn," said Oliver. "Bound to be."

"Why? You given him a reason, have you?"

"No . . ."

"Well. Do you want to know what I think, do you? I think that sheep's dead because she got out, and I think she got out because the hedge for the Middle Ddole is more glats than growth. If you'd been hedging this afternoon, like we said, not buggering about, then it wouldn't have happened. Simple as that."

"Dank me, I had to go to the tack, didn't I?"

"For eight blasted hours?"

"Have you looked at her, Mam, have you? She's been a goner for six at least!"

Etty sighed and picked up the bucket. "All right, all right," she said. "There is tea in the pot. We'll dump her up the wood in the morning."

For a little while Etty had let herself believe that Cefin's arrival was the change she had hoped for—as if farms still passed inevitably from father to son, as if farming remained an inalienable condition. Once, when she was young herself, a farmer might have been a natural athlete or a brilliant musician; it would have made no difference. He would still have been a farmer. Now the sons with other interests or ambitions would go their own way, and her grandson was no different. He had always had a flair for things like mathematics. She wondered if at least he might phone that day. He sometimes would on a Saturday evening.

"You out tonight, Olly, are you?" she asked as they arrived in the kitchen, where the tap on the Rayburn had run almost dry and the swilling steam clung to her face and hands.

"Not tonight, Mam."

"You want the bath first?"

"No. No, you carry on."

Etty carried the tea tray over to the table, rose the cold-water pail from the sink then went to stand in the hearth's enclosure, between the Rayburn and the old zinc bath. The steam was thick as the mist had been that morning. Even when the water was a reasonable temperature it boiled around her, striped by the light from the joins in the screen, whose top was almost level with her eyes. As she worked her way down the buttons of her cardigan, she watched her son return from the bookshelf, switch off the muted, blinking television, sit at the table and open his waistcoat—although he had stitched another panel in the back. His scalp shone through his trained-back hair. He wiped the condensation from his spectacles and began to turn the pages of Naomi's book, which looked a delicate little thing among his fingers with their great, golden rings.

A minute passed, or two.

He frowned, inhaled and put a hand to his forehead.

As a rule, Etty tried not to look at her naked body. Lowering herself quietly into the bath, she worked the flannel over her hands—their backs brown-speckled, like an egg. She scoured her feet, running the stiff brush under her toenails, but when she came to her slack-skinned arms, the gullies in her sides and her falling breasts, she kept her eyes on her bony knees, which jutted like islands from the gathering soap scum. Unpinning the bun on the back of her head, she unwound its coils to save them from tangling and reached for the shampoo bottle on the rug. The ends aside, she had not cut her hair in thirty years or more. When she brushed it in her bedroom, at her dressing table, it hung almost to the floor. It was white by her face, grey at her shoulders, red where it floated on the surface of the water.

2001

"IT WAS ABOUT 12:30 A.M. on Saturday morning when a giant digger appeared from the range and charged the Army check point, smashing vehicles and scattering protestors and police alike."

"MAFF and the army are standing by to launch a frenzy of killing beyond anything we have seen."

"Every contiguous farm has been classed as a cull zone."

"The minister reacted angrily to claims that farmers were infecting their own flocks so as to claim the compensation."

"Even before the foot-and-mouth crisis the annual income of the Less Favoured Areas fell to their lowest level ever last year, to an average of £2,700. How can anyone survive on such a low figure, let alone raise a family and invest for the future?"

The newspaper, Etty realized, had slipped from her lap and fanned across the hearthrug onto the flagstones. There was a moment in which the rain remained the Wye, the Land

Rover an approaching train; then the gearbox clacked and whined in reverse and the sunlight reverted to the glore of the Rayburn. She had this way of falling asleep. Once or twice she had sat down at two in the afternoon and failed to wake until the clock chimed three, and although now it was eleven at night she cursed herself and her upright chair, which, shaped as it was to her small, narrow body, had left her limbs so rigid that at first she could barely move at all. She eased her head back onto her shoulders until she saw the mistletoe on the beam. She worked each leg, lifting her boots as high as she could manage, and when at last she hauled on the bar of the Rayburn she still stood bowed above the hobs—the shorter hairs around her ears lifting and tabbering on her cheeks.

The rain came searching out of the valley, sending her forwards onto her ash plant, filling her skirt before her like a sail. The security light on the corner of the barn came blindingly alive. She climbed the yard through braiding prills, weaving round the puddles. She knew without looking that Oliver was watching her, hunched by the open door of the shed, where the gutter was flooding, boring a plunge pool in the mud.

"There is no need to come out, Mam," he said.

"It is more business than farming, boy."

"It in't farming, that's for sure."

In spite of the wind, the stench of the yearlings was enough to make Etty's eyes start. They had mexed the shed only four days earlier and already, as she came to the hurdles, her torch found their anxious, confined bodies lifted inches by the morass. If there was a choice then neither of them had thought of it. The last of the money from the Island was gone. The fields were naked, reducing to ruin. The commons had been emptied back in the summer. The tack was a D Zone—an infected area—and with the markets closed, without the Long Field and Rhos Meadow for silage, only the rent from the bungalow left in Molly's will had kept the two of them from bankruptcy.

"Tup get off all right, did he?" she asked.

"Yes, I expect."

"What did Griffin say?"

"Keen he was, if anything. You don't want to think too much on that. He'll keep him safe, don't worry." Oliver's big face hung beneath his rain hat, the stump of a cigarette between his lips, the torchlight seeming to well in his eyes.

There was a jar in the knot of his hand.

"You found the man, then?" Etty asked, more softly.

"I found him."

"Slaughterman, is he?"

"Farmer. Out for Brecon . . . Culled a few days back, his place was."

"How much did he want for that?"

"Grand . . . The credit card's done."

"Call it a fresh start, boy."

"I dunno, Mam . . ."

Besides the sheep, the only sound was the rain in the gutters, its roar on the corrugated roof. Turning to the door, Etty swung her torch from the brake lights of the Land Rover to the glistening ear of the satellite dish on the house. There were headlamps climbing the track to the Welfrey, but only the rain was moving in the yard, so she extracted the jar from Oliver's fingers, took the torch between her teeth and used her knees and her hands to open the lid. He did not speak; he did not stop her. She waited only to touch her chest before she cast the infected rag into the darkness.

THE RAIN WAS fierce on the long, dark windows of the bus station. With the bubble-like lights that ran along the ceiling, Cefin could see little more than a streaming reflection of himself and his notepad, the empty run of plastic seats and the sign for the toilet—although, now and then, a bus arrived and appeared as it blinked, its passengers pouring through the automatic door with a gulp of the cold night air. He brought his head down into his coat, hunching his narrow shoulders, sealing the space between the collar and his itchy woollen hat. Somehow he had not thought beyond this point. There was Adrian, of course, but he had checked his emails back in Dunkirk and knew that his mother was off on a reading; besides, it must have been twelve by now. His sisters would surely be asleep. He searched his mind for some other number, some friendly sofa where he could collapse, but three years lay between them and himself. He couldn't think of anyone at all.

Twenty pixels, he decided. That would do for the left-hand margin, with ten pixels for the top. He scribbled the numbers and considered the paper. With the header symmetrical, he could set the text in a left-hand column and give the bulk of the space to his African photographs, which would weight the page agreeably to the right. He sketched two pictures to the approximate size, then noted down the CSS code in a few, half-intelligible lines. This was the part of design that he loved. The mathematics he could have worked out in his sleep—he had been programming in Maputo for two and a half years, and here for most of a year before that—and while there was a certain music to its patterns, ultimately it was right or wrong. The layout was different. The balance of font and content and whiteness, that was a million different possibilities—or rather the thrill when he got it right.

The rain. Cefin looked again at the windows. He focused his eyes past the scratches in his glasses, past the image of the cleaner who was sweeping the concourse and the droplets running and mingling on the panes, and saw beyond the stands a single streetlamp, orange over a shut-up shop. The rain was pouring from its shivering shade. In the cone of light it was drifting, furious. It did not merely fall but attacked from the side, spun, returned and vanished away into the darkness. Sometimes it did not fall at all, but rose and seemed to collide with the bulb. For several moments he watched it, frozen: that little patch of wildness, alone in the orange-tinged night.

THERE WAS A guelder rose by the looping wall of the abandoned churchyard: a straggling plant maybe seven foot in height, red with berries and thick, turning leaves. Had Martin not bent to put a lead on Cavall, his Labrador, he would never have noticed among its stalks, beneath a railway tie and wrapped in a length of rusting fence, the stone that had intrigued him when he first came to Rhyscog—although, as a bridge, it had been so caked in mud that it might equally have been a slab of concrete. He parted the branches, peered at the visible corner of the stone, then, with a low exclamation, looked past the hurdle where there had been a lychgate at the long-shadowed headstones and the sun in the brilliant clouds.

A tractor was working in the yard at the Funnon—its roar redoubling as it entered the big zinc shed. Loud as Martin called, it was not until Oliver had crossed the muddy slope, deposited a wedge of manure on the mixen, reversed and lowered the tines on his loader that he seemed to notice him, hurrying past the swollen stream, beneath the green-gold leaves of Pentre Wood, dragging his dog and gesturing with his stick.

"Morning, Prof." The cab door opened.

"Oliver!"

"We did think we saw your car last night."

"Last night, yes . . . Oliver, could I borrow you, please?"

Etty was playing Brahms in the parlour—her organ hesitant above the noise of the Ford 4000 and the dozens of sheep that were crowded round the wheel wash at the gate.

"Well," said Oliver. He drummed his rings on the handle of the door. "I cannot see why not. There is bugger all else to do."

Martin thought for a moment that the farmer was being sarcastic, although as he clambered down the metal steps, wincing, closing his right arm slowly at the elbow, he could see no trace of it in his movements. Oliver was not, it was true, a man he would have chosen to sire his only grandson—the news, when it came, had appalled him the more for the strength of his own reaction—but to Martin, at least, he had always been generous, his teasing always shading into deference. He followed him back up the yard—taller-seeming now that Martin himself was beginning to stoop, the black hair sweeping back from his forehead both thick and sparse in a way that reminded him distantly of a warthog. Jealousy, that was a feeling he had identified once the initial shock had abated. Jonathan, whose bitchiness did contain an occasional insight, had suggested that this was some part of Naomi's agenda, and perhaps he was right. Martin had never got far in fathoming his daughter. It was not that Oliver had ever been his type—even at his most regal he was too plainly straight—but, still, he had once been his own discovery, his personal area of expertise.

"Heard from the boy, have you?" Oliver asked.

"I had an email from . . . France." Martin crouched at the guelder rose. "Dunkirk, I believe it was."

"He did write Mother from France."

"There!" he said. "There! Do you see?"

Latin, thought Martin. Latin unquestionably. And if those notches in the near corner were not Ogham, then he would revoke his emeritus status himself. As Oliver returned from the yard with the tractor, roped the long, thin stone to the tines and hoisted it into the open air, the coil of fencing slipped to the ground. The shapes of its mesh were eaten from the grey-green lichen. The stone swung wildly as the tractor pulled forwards. It sank and settled in the darkening mosaic of the leaves by the track.

The letters cut into its upturned surface were crude but decipherable, vertical in the Celtic tradition. That was an *S*, and that a *G*—albeit inscribed back to front.

"SAGROMNI?" said Martin, uncertainly.

"What's that mean, then?" asked Oliver, arriving beside him, muted-seeming, now that Martin came to notice it—his black eyes dull in the shadow of his brow.

"Well, there's clearly more. I'll have to clean off the rest of the lichen and probably make a tracing to read it properly, but, well, it's a name. Sagrom. More of a representative than an actual name, I'd say. It stands for an eminent chief or warrior . . . Where on earth did it come from?"

"Idris found him, on Llanbedr Hill. So, what, it's a gravestone, is it?"

"Well." Martin gave a slight laugh. "In a sense, yes, but it's no ordinary memorial. I mean, these marks here." He ran his fingers up the corner, across a stretch rubbed almost illegible by animals. "These are letters in the Goidelic language. It's an alphabet called Ogham developed in Ireland around 400 A.D., probably because Primitive Irish didn't transcribe well in the Roman system. The letters look a little like runes, you see? Each one is made out of a group of incisions. The stone is bilingual, basically. The Latin, here—you see these letters? They're what you'd call uncial. That's to say, rounded. It's a style that evolved in the Hellenistic East and was first employed in Roman North Africa around 300 A.D. So, the Latin would have been for the benefit of locals, and possibly posterity, and the Ogham would have been for the benefit of Goidelic speakers: the Irish tribes who arrived here in the wake of the Roman withdrawal. Latin inscriptions are not so unusual, of course. There are nearly three thousand British examples, to my knowledge. But Ogham inscriptions—there are fewer than four hundred all told, and the vast majority of those are in Ireland. With the exception of Silchester this must, I think, be the easternmost example, at least in the south. It dates the stone quite precisely, you see, to the fifth or early sixth centuries—right to the dawn of the Christian era."

Oliver growled at one of his sheepdogs, which was harrying Cavall, sniffing her bottom. He glanced at a shower approaching down the valley, darkening the half-bare trees around the stream, obscuring the long-horn cattle at Cwmpiban.

"A gravestone," he repeated. "It bloody would be."

*   *   *

ACROSS THE THREADBARE valley the Funnon was overrun with men, or figures at least—all of them dressed in the same white suits with the hoods pulled up to conceal their faces. They were busy with lorries whose gates already lay open in the mud, unloading rifles from a blacked-out Hilux, plumbing pumps into barrels of disinfectant. Oliver could not believe how quickly this had happened. Not six days had passed since his mother's decision to sacrifice the animals, not twelve hours since he had found a blister on a ewe's tongue, and here, the farm was out of their hands.

The sheep understood; they were clever like that. In spite of the wind and his failing ears, he could hear the two-year-olds in the Banky Piece and the wild, discordant yearlings in the shed. The beasts at the Island were not so smart. They stood around him in the trampled fields, chavelling on a bale of silage. He was almost glad when the lorry arrived, lumbering off the tarmacked lane and bumping towards him down the grass-striped track—the slaughtermen spaced among the clouds on the windscreen.

"Is it just these, is it?" the first of them asked.

Oliver nodded. He weighed the half-full bottle in his hand and dropped his cigarette hissing in a puddle.

"Fifteen?"

"Fifteen."

"I suggest . . ." The man was smoking himself. He waved a tractor onto the verge. "I suggest, Mr. Hamer, that you go in the cottage, or go somewhere else. You really do not want to see this."

For months now there had been saplings on the abandoned hills, rising from the fern, the heather and the feg, with leaves like flags—declaring their species while still not an inch in height. There were wittans and hawthorns, but there were ash trees too, and oaks and hazels. They might have been lurking since the days of the forest, waiting for the sheep at last to depart before, tentatively, they began to re-make the wilderness. The television reported that farming was dying, that it had ceased to be an industry and had become instead a life-support system, in which these Less Favoured Areas were an intolerable expense. For those who were looking for the root of things, well, here it was: these scrawny trees on Llanbedr Hill, riffling as far as Oliver could see, divesting the last of their withered leaves in their first successful autumn for five thousand years.

Somebody had to defend the margins, to keep the past in its place.

The shots from the Island came quickly behind him. The shots from the Funnon rang again from the flank of Cefn Wylfre, as if he were witness to a battle. In the Banky Piece there could not have been more than two score animals left and, as the rifles continued, a wall of men closed round them with sticks, driving them through the gate by the pond until the field contained nothing but their old muck spreader: a roll of wire in its open side. A second string of lorries was stopped along the valley, pressed between the hedgerows, stretching almost from the Pant to the track for Cwmpiban, which appeared to have been blocked by Mervyn's tractor. There were people in the gateways, a couple more crossing a corner of the Long Field, skirting the shaggy, fern-red beasts, heading for the closed-curtained farmhouse.

"You . . . have no ram, Mr. Hamer?" asked the slaughter-man, arriving where Oliver stood.

The killing at the Island, it seemed, had finished.

"No tup, no."

"The records say a Bluefaced Leicester." The man had folded down his hood to reveal a small, balding head, a chin, unshaven, which tapered back into his neck.

Oliver shrugged and offered the whisky.

"I couldn't," he said. "I've not so much as eaten all week."

"We did have a Blueface. A while back now. That'll be him, I expect."

"Records."

"Records."

"Well. All I can say is thank God you've only got the one neighbour."

Oliver did not reply.

A cloud of fieldfares wheeled out of Quebec and settled in the Sideland Field. A hare crossed the lane not twenty feet distant and crept long-legged into the collapsing fern. The men turned back to the holiday cottage, the yellowing larches and the three weepy fields that Oliver had leased almost from the day they were sold, where the others were washing down his quad and the tractor—their cigarettes alone exposed. In the back of the lorry his herd was reduced to a lumpish mass—Charolais cream and Hereford red beneath a polythene sheet.

AT LEAST IN the kitchen Etty had her map, which, for all of its pink expanses, showed every country in the entire world. Since the restrictions closed the little church in Llanbadarn-y-Garreg, where she still made a fist of the occasional services, she had found herself here more often than ever—following the wandering, ripple-fringed coastlines and the mysterious trains of the hills. It was the imagining she liked, the building in her mind, from Cefin's descriptions, of the ruinous fortress on Mozambique Island or the libraries of Timbuktu. The names themselves were laden with images: Xai-xai, Chimanimani, the Skeleton Coast. To think that her grandson had seen these things, had felt the sand of an actual desert, had landed on an island where three thousand people bore the same surname and behaved to one another like members of the same household.

These were the experiences that the labels recorded, although perhaps not even Cefin could have understood them all. They gave the names of places, people and sometimes animals, so that "Elephant" meant a baby walking under its mother, "Ibo" meant yet another unmarked island where the only two cars had somehow collided, and "Cape Town" meant a Christmas spent with Naomi, Adrian and the girls. As the rifles cracked in the hollow of the shed and their female flock became a few keening voices, and then one, and then no more than the rumble of the digger, Etty remained at the larder door, tracing her grandson's slow, northwards progress. "Banjul" was a horde of purple tourists. "Choum" was a train nearly three miles long.

The sheep. There had, in her life, been so many times like this when she had felt herself age, pass from one stage of life to the next, in which her hope, her will, her capacity for joy were minutely, irrevocably less. It was a prickling sensation, like her tissues were crumpling, like her cells were imploding in turn. When she reached the label that read "Dunkirk," which she might almost have seen from her bedroom, she clung to her stick and returned to her chair as if she had made the journey herself.

* * *

WITH THE CLOSING evenings, the yard had long been deserted by the slaughtermen when the security light tripped on the corner of the barn. Oliver did not move at first, although its brightness was plain in the kitchen window—the aerial white beyond the chimney breast, the orchard casting its skeletal shadows. Perhaps, he thought, a fox was looking for a bantam; after all the day's killing it hardly seemed to matter. Perhaps someone had left a phone or a bag, but he had seen no headlamps nor heard an engine, and in the end it was the yelping of the dogs that made him set down his glass of whisky, tear his eyes from the television and haul himself past his sleeping mother, down the hall to the door.

Already the dogs had become sporadic, their calls divided by the silence of the farm. The light, which required little more than the movement of a finger, had switched itself off, and Oliver peered for some moments into the hooded night before he saw a shape just short of the gate—black against the distant redness in the clouds.

"I know what you done," said Mervyn quietly.

"What's that?" said Oliver.

"I seen your tup was gone from the Plock."

"Every fucking creature is gone."

"Not back on the weekend they wasn't. Got him tucked up somewhere nice and safe, have you?"

As Oliver left the bridge for the yard, the light returned suddenly and the two men were facing one another on the tyre-cut slope, between the grey and white cliffs of the barn and the house. There was the carcass of a baler among the blackened nettles by the silage bales. The sallies were yellow round the leaf-strewn pond, whose sluices were rotting and boodged with stones.

"Do you know how long I was breeding them beasts?" Mervyn demanded. "Thirty fucking years! Thirty fucking years, and you—"

"I what?"

"You, you cuckoo bastard!"

Rough as it was, this was Oliver's territory—familiar in its every contour. There was no obstacle within thirty feet. He joined his hands above his swelling chest, pulling the rings from his long, gnarled fingers, his eyes alert to his neighbour's scowl, the spread of his wellies, the set of his monstrous shoulders.

"And even if I had," he said. "Well. Tit for tat, in't it?"

Mervyn inhaled and his big arms lifted.

"You want square, that's fucking square!"

The ancient anger flickered in Oliver's stomach, ignited, whisky-fuelled, and fanned its way along his limbs, easing the daunting pain in his elbow, taking the weight from his heavy leather boots, whose heels rose out of the mud. This was not arm wrestling. He had the height. He had the reach. He charted the lines in his neighbour's cheeks, the riven jowls spilling over his collar, the glint of his eyes in their cavernous sockets, but then again the light went off and he was left in the darkness with the halogen bulb repeating when he blinked—his breath coming quickly in his nose.

Mervyn arrived with astonishing speed. In the instant that the yard reappeared he sent both fists into Oliver's ribcage so that he stumbled, winded, back towards the pond. He followed at a charge, drowning the dogs with a yawl of his own, and while Oliver parried his next with his bicep, the shock of pain that exploded in his elbow made his left arm no better than a shield. With his right he struck out twice, missing with the first but slowing the attack with a blow to his ear that shuddered through the bones to his shoulder. Panting, wheezing, he tried to get the open ground behind him, backing from the sallies through the hoofmarks of the slaughtered sheep—perhaps, in the depths, the hoofmarks of Idris's horse. Thirty-one years he had been waiting for this moment. As Mervyn came again with the light on his head, his face behind his great, balled hands, Oliver remembered something of his training, his movement, stepped as he would have and replied with a jab to his uncovered cheek and another to the beast-like muscles of his neck.

The man, Oliver realized abruptly, was crying. He held his place in the ruts and the leaves—the wildness roaring, possessing his body—but he missed his chance to swing again, while his neighbour hesitated and then fell back, turning a half-circle, unfurling his fingers to cover his eyes. He limped to the silage and leant against the plastic, his shoulders lurching in his ragged tweed jacket, a prill of blood on the side of his head, which joined and parted with the angles of his skull.

"You win," he muttered, when he could speak.

Oliver said nothing.

"You win. I in't got the fight left in me no more."

He looked old, like an old man. The cracks round his eyebrows seemed so deep-cut that their entire structure might just have collapsed. As the two of them stood, the yard fell once more back into darkness—a single lamp high up at the Welfrey, the animal pyres reflected in the clouds—so Oliver waved in the direction of the sensor, holding his left arm as if in a sling, the whisky beginning to gag in his throat.

"I was sorry about old Idris," Mervyn continued. He looked at his knuckles. "Good to me, he was, when I was a little lad—

afore you come along, like. And the man was my uncle. It was a damn shame. The boss was raw cut up about it, he was. We was all of us cut up about it, down at Cwmpiban."

"Aye," said Oliver.

"So." He lifted his face, which was already tightening with the bruising on his scalp. Their eyes met briefly. "You can buy back your fields. I shall be selling them once I has my compensation. They is no use to me no more. I loved my beasts. They was all as kept me going. The kids is gone these ten year now, and they in't coming back, and I cannot blame them. It is just me and old Ruth now, and we is neither of us aiming to start over. So, there you are, boy, you got the Funnon, same as you wanted—ready for your restock . . . Much good may she do you. You and your mother and your dogs."

MARTIN WATCHED FROM his window as Mervyn departed, leaving the fringes of the dazzling light to vanish in the shadows of the lane. Oliver remained among the balding willows, his eyes on the pond, cigarette smoke around his big, bowed head, and when, with the light, he vanished himself, Martin took another sip of his homemade cider and gave a little more wick to the lamp on his desk. *S,* or *Saile:* four straight lines to the right of the corner, the name meaning *willow*— presumably from *salix. A,* or *Ailm:* one short notch through the corner itself, the name, perhaps, meaning *pine.* He knew, of course, that the Ogham on the stone would read much the same as the Latin, but he could hardly pass his findings to his former colleagues without his own interpretation. Besides, with each faint letter he told from his tracing, which lay across the pitted table, one end furling almost to the flagstones, he felt a moment of complete satisfaction—like climbing into a well-aired bed.

The room was warm, sweet-smelling from the levels of steam that lay beneath the stamps on the ceiling. At the Welfrey, whenever possible, Martin tried to live on a traditional diet. In the pot on the chain was a bubbling mash of sliced crab apples and guelder-rose berries, which, his Radnorshire cookbook informed him, would make for a reasonable preserve. His bread he baked weekly in the iron-doored oven. His wimberry tart had been particularly tasty, and his flummery a good deal less revolting than the "sub-gelatinous mass" that the book described.

"SAGRAGNI MAQI CUNOGENI," he read aloud, and the dog looked up from the rug before the fire.

Sagranus. Sagragnus. Again Martin turned to the draughty little window, the dark, empty fields, the few lights buried in the valley, the dimly showing hilltops and the sparks of the animal pyres on Mynydd Epynt. He wondered how different the place would have looked to that eminent warrior as he drank from the *ffynnon* or praised his new God from the old paved road that led over to Painscastle. Then too there would have been pasture by the Edw; there would have been grazing on Cefn Wylfre and the sinuous back of Llanbedr Hill; there would have been the same yew trees in the rounded *llan,* and perhaps an ascetic in a rude little cell with, for neighbours, some forebears of Oliver and Mervyn, battling it out over a couple of acres to bolster their miniature kingdoms.

DURING THE YEARS that he had been away, Cefin had found himself longing for the seasons almost as much as he had longed for these hills. A month or two of feverish rain was no compensation for days that barely altered in length, a climate which knew only shades of heat. One morning, on his twenty-fourth birthday, he had woken in his flat off Avenida Julius Nyerere to a wind on the roof that sounded so much like the winter winds at the Funnon that he could not bear to open his eyes and see his naked body, and the body of Lizha, stretched, sweat-bright, inside the mosquito net.

With the vacuum cleaner weighing from his hand, he leant towards the slit in the gable wall, holding the sill against the rain that howled up the valley and broke on his face, numbing his ears and filling his mouth until his lips were flapping. There had been gales more violent in Cabo Delgado—to have gone outside in some of them would have been almost suicidal—but nothing so raw, so precise as this.

A few more rungs up the aluminium ladder and Cefin came to the eaves of the barn, where he restored his hat to his close-cropped head and, lifting the nozzle, sucked up all the cobwebs he could reach in a clatter of mortar and bits of shale. As a job, of course, it was completely pointless—the spiders were as likely to be carrying the foot-and-mouth virus as the stone itself—but fifteen pounds an hour with neither rent nor supervision was work indeed, even by the standards of the NGOs. He did not hurry as he cleaned the apex of the roof and climbed back down into the empty hayloft, which could not have seen daylight since the year it was built.

"Oh, what shall I do to be saved," he read, "from the sorrows that burden my soul?"

"What's that, love?" asked his grandmother.

"Just something written here, Nana."

"Oh. Yes."

Cefin turned to the chin-high wall and the old woman perched on the granary steps, her coat round her ears and her wellies on the pitching he had washed that morning which still shone dully in the light from the door. She was so small, Etty—no more than bone and sinew and cardigans. It was a wonder she had ever given birth to his father. It was a wonder she continued to battle round this farm—her green eyes peering past red-scribbled lids, her jaw a ledge among the creases of her cheeks and her neck.

The rich fumes of tarmac drifted from the yard.

"Are you not cold, Nana?" he asked.

"Not too bad." She smiled.

"Do you want me to get you a cup of tea?"

"Perhaps in a bit. Tell me a story, how about that?"

"What about?"

"I don't know. Something you've been up to."

"Do you know?" said Cefin. He shuffled the ladder to the left. "Dad has still not asked me anything since I got back. Not one single thing."

His grandmother said nothing.

So he told her about visiting the Querimba Islands—how the palm heads rose from the deep blue water and seemed at first to be suspended in the air, how the tide filled channels through the jungles of the mangroves to beaches carved by outrigger canoes. He described the dhows with their lateen sails, the birds, the fish and the coconut plantations, and how, for all of this plenty, the children were often as naked as babies, with swollen bellies and marimba ribs. He described the music, since she did like her music—the *timbila, xitende,* jazz and *marrabenta*—and he stopped only when the paving machine fell silent outside and one of the contractors called them by name.

OLIVER THREW HIS full weight forwards and crept away from the wind-stripped sycamores with Idris's stone forced flat to his side—its foot cutting open the path behind him, like a plough. The three fingers burned on his one good hand. Every movement he made was a bid to navigate some once-dislocated joint, some once-ruptured tendon, some ancient, indefinable ache. Even at this little altitude the rain was half-frozen; it stung his cheeks and narrowed his eyes. Around him the headstones stood dark above the mud of the church-yard. Beneath him, in the yard, the men were watching from their brooms and tampers. The stable was empty. The beast-house was empty. The shed was so clean, so absolutely spot-less that he would gladly have eaten his dinner off the floor, and still the government woman with her long, probing fin-gernails had insisted that he wash it all again.

"Olly!" called his mother.

"Dad . . ." called his son.

Through the smoke and steam he saw a blue-green car join the vehicles by the pit for the run-off.

"Olly, for God's sake, will you put that thing down?"

Oliver wished with all of his being that Cefin had not come back—not into this—with his easy new confidence, Naomi in his face and the endless tales of his adventures, which fell upon him like the pummelling hail. He rallied his strength and advanced again, but even at his mother's pace the two of them continued to approach. His son shoved his boot like a chock beneath the stone and, with groans and gasps, picked up the foot so its angle rose and came level with the slope. Oliver's feet were slipping; his shoulder felt as if it would at any moment be torn from its socket; and now, on top of everything else, he could not allow the stone to drop. It was the same with the farm. Not that the boy would ever make a farmer—he had known that since Cefin was thirteen years old—but without him here he might have lived with the shame of it. He could have let the whole place go to hell.

"Man up, lad," he growled. "When I was your age I could hoist this bastard over my head!"

"And you did and all, I doubt," said Cefin, through his teeth, "and look at the bloody state of you!"

"You'll be getting no sympathy from me," said Etty. "Neither of you. I'm telling you now."

There was just one slot between the flagstones on the top of the tump that looked wide enough to receive the stone. It was a few inches short of where the altar had stood, among rain-flattened leaves and foot-worn memorials: that one from 1788, that one from forty years before. Stepping over the old foundations, Oliver arrived in the absent church and made his way along the pale line of the aisle. Setting down his end, clenching his hands, Cefin hurried to put his shoulder by his own. It baffled Oliver how this mimmockin boy could have done so much and travelled so far when he, with all of his strength and scale, had only so much as seen the sea twice, and that as a glint through the trees round a motorway. The ice was running down Cefin's glasses. His waterproofs fell from his spindling limbs. He muttered and grimaced, but he held his corner while his grandmother hovered in her dribbling anorak and watched the two of them shove the foot of the stone across the flagstones, into the hole, pause a moment to gather themselves and then, by increments, push it upright.

"Is SHE ALL right?" asked Ada, when Cefin reappeared.

"Cold." He shrugged. "She'll be all right once she's had a lie down."

"They're . . . work clothes," she explained. She plucked at a cable of her roll-neck sweater. "I got away early. I heard you were back. Thought I'd come and say hello."

"You look very smart."

"You look like you've been on bloody hunger strike."

"Honest to God," said Cefin, and dropped into a chair. "There was one time, a month or two back, when I thought I'd imagined supermarkets. I just thought, no. There's a Tesco near my mam's house, you know, so I went in there the other day, just to check. Hell, it was like a palace! I don't know I've ever seen anything so amazing."

"They're after staff in the Spar in Builth. I just saw the advert."

"Well . . . Perhaps not that amazing."

The grandfather clock read half past four, but already it was the edge of night. Flicking on the light, Ada crossed the flagstones in her thick woollen tights to rise a slice of bread for the scraggy old raven whistling and picking at her earring. She watched Cefin dab at his bleeding fingers, wincing as he used the antiseptic. His sun-bleached T-shirt hung from his chest, a dark vee tapering from his colourful necklace. He had given up on his thinning hair and shorn his head back down to the scalp, which was no less brown than his face. He worked with weary, preoccupied movements, his blue eyes pinched behind crooked glasses.

"So," she said, "they've got you cleaning the barn, then, have they?"

"Cleaning bloody everything." He looked up briefly. "Everyone's gone mad round here. This one contractor, he told me I was to hoover the granary. I told him I didn't think the wiring was up to it, and anyway we've only got a broom, so off he goes and the next thing I know the whole barn's rewired and he's waving a brand-new vacuum cleaner under my nose. A nice one too. One of them ones with a face."

"Henry."

"Yeah, except this one's pink. Hetty, it's called. I suppose he figured Nana would prefer it."

"She's so pleased you're back." Ada lowered her voice.

Cefin took a long, slow breath.

"And your dad is . . . I've come by to see them once in a while, you know. You're all they bloody talked about. He missed you. He did. Even if he might have a funny way of showing it."

"Yeah," he said. "He has that."

The machines in the yard were dying with the light. Through the hush of the rain and the popping of the kettle Ada could hear the contractors talking, abusing the weather, discussing plans for the coming weekend. She dropped the teabags into the cups and, when she looked, Cefin was leaning beside her on the Rayburn, lighting a butt that smelt like a joint, which he drew on twice and then passed. He was not tall, Cefin, not like Oliver—only a few inches taller than herself. His face was patterned with the shadows of his glasses and the shadow that parted his forehead. As he fiddled with his lighter and she smoked herself, she felt an urge to embrace him, which caught her so suddenly that she flinched and Maureen flapped on her shoulder.

"Are you lot all right, are you?" he asked.

"Pretty . . . pretty middling, to be honest with you, Cefin.

It's hard enough on us all just now. You cannot move anything. You cannot sell anything. I do try to get back here on the weekends but, you know, we've got Philip, and Dad, and Mam. I don't know . . . I suppose I feel I've got to do something."

"What, though? That's the thing."

Glancing sideways—and it was worse still now that Ada had removed her tall-heeled boots—the first thing Cefin saw was the bloom of her breasts in that improbable sweater, which exposed every curve of her slight, soft belly and the swelling tops of her hips. He looked away quickly to the fading window in its splintering frame, and blew a storm across his pale brown tea. There were letters and newspapers piled on the sideboard. There were cobwebs drooping in the half-lit corners. One of the taps was dripping steadily; it had almost filled the washing-up bowl. He had expected this sort of thing, of course. His grandmother was nearly eighty years old. He had known that the animals were going to be dead, and had heard his father's voice on the phone, and the reality was no more bearable for that. Thank God, he thought, that Ada was here. Even in this extraordinary outfit, with her office smell and expensive hair, she did make him feel like he was sane, after all. Had they been in Africa he might just have said so, but here he could never have been so direct, and besides there were boots on the flagstones in the hall, so instead he gave her a nudge with his elbow and leant to let Maureen hop between their shoulders.

Cefin only glanced at his father as he hobbled through the door and stopped at the table—blocking the light in its conical shade like a piece of the night come inside. It was terrible to see him like this. It must have been days since he had last dyed his hair; a half-inch of grey shone all over his head. His breath was a croak in the depths of his throat. Never in his life had Cefin known him not at least try to impress a young woman—even Ada should have had him preening—and he had not so much as removed his coat, which dribbled from the hem and the cuffs held tight to his belly.

Oliver took his glasses from a pocket of his jacket and sat them painfully over his nose. He steadied himself on the back of a chair, then turned towards the larder door.

"Well, boy," he said, finally. He stood looking down at his mother's map, its obsolete place names and forest of flags. "Are you going to tell me about all this or not?"

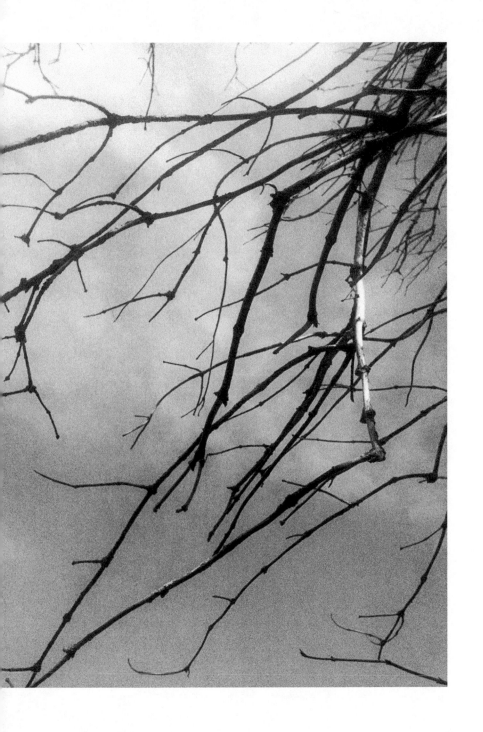

2011

OLIVER DID NOT see the owl return. He looked at the oak tree only as its bare twigs trembled and a few small birds escaped into the sunlight: a siskin, a couple of piefinches. He peered through his new pair of gold-framed sunglasses at the box he had strapped beneath the snow-capped branch, but the owl was keeping her presence to herself so he turned back to Cefin, who was standing beside him, still watching for movement, his fertilizer bags tucked under his arm. They continued to climb through the tracks of animals: the racks of sheep, the arrows of a pheasant, the four, symmetrical toes of a fox. Near the fence for the Far Top Field a mesh of paths revealed every rabbit burrow and daytime squat on the fringes of Turley Wood. He was not such a sly one, the old rabbit. Not like the hare, which Oliver had observed over the years, scouting his territory at a cautious lope before, abruptly, he launched himself sideways—reaching his door in a series of explosions that might have been quite unrelated.

His mobile churred as he came into reception.

"Whazzup (-;" wrote Griffin.

"Whazzup, Meggy?" said Oliver to his dog, which whined and wiggled against his leg.

There were hawthorns here, where the head of the wood dwindled into the fields for the Welfrey, whose cottage Cefin, with his modern views, had stripped back to stone a year or two earlier. Mistletoe, so Oliver had heard, would grow on the hawthorn only in the Wye valley and a few of its tributaries—nowhere else in the world—and while he had hardly checked if this were true he took these green-gold clouds with their pearl-like berries to be a kind of tribute to the place. Reaching his brumhook through the spiny branches, he cut down a sprig, which he tucked like a cigarette behind his ear, then turned from his shadow and the shadow of his son to the blazing light on Llanbedr Hill. The sun had yet to arrive in the Cae Blaidd, and the valley beneath was still half-dark. The wood smoke drifting from the kitchen chimney made pools and levels in the yard; it straggled in the churchyard, round the snow-tipped stone they had stood on the top of the mound. In the Plock the chickens were scratting for grain by the open door of the big new shed. In the Panneys Philip's great Case tractor was driving a canyon through the snowdrifts, delivering silage to the trailing ewes, which the Pant had owned these past three months. He had cut a way to the pond, in passing, smashing open the hole for the circling ducks with a single tap of his loader.

Cefin did something with his own phone, perhaps took a photograph, then sat down on one of the fertilizer bags.

"Right then, Dad," he said.

"I shall see you down the bottom," said Oliver.

"You mind what you wish for." He squinted up at his plastic trousers. "Slip in them and you'll be down before me."

"I am not going sledging, boy. What if one of the neighbours was to see me?"

"What if they saw you chickening out?"

"Yes. Well."

The boy lay the second bag on the snow beside him. "Get on there or I'll give you a shove."

Oliver grunted. He looked at the slope and back at his son in his daft woollen hat with bobbles on the ear-flaps, his hands on the ground as if planning to stand, then he slid the brumhook back into its sheath and lowered himself onto his backside. At once Meg began to lick his face. He grimaced as he kicked and paddled with his hands, his weight coming backwards as he started to slide. Well, that was one good thing for the frame of a giant and a belly that hardly let him lift his knees. The dog sprang wildly down the field behind him, spinning and yelping in alarm. The boy was following, coming headfirst. He dug in a boot to steer for the gate and skirt the frozen wnty tumps, while the dust-like snow boiled into his eyes—momentarily blue and red as the sun set again among the golden larches, lines of light forked out of the hilltop, and he dropped into the previous night.

It brought Etty a warm, enveloping pleasure to think that, after everywhere he had been, Cefin should choose to come and live here. It made her feel as if, after all, she had not lived so little, as if the God to whom she had prayed every night of her life had been listening to her and was listening still. The Welfrey, well, the place might have done for his grandfather's weekends, in the days when he was still able to get up there. It might have done for the boy for a year or two, but it had never been a long-term option. Lamb prices could rally as much as they liked; they could have sold their whole flock at a hundred a head, and sold the chickens, and they would still not have managed the thirty thousand pounds they needed just to put in the electric. And then there was the phone. These computer people, they needed such things. What it was that her grandson actually did remained as mysterious to Etty as ever, for all of the emails she had written with Nancy, for all of the times he had attempted to explain. She was just too old now; that was the size of it. She was content simply that this Internet worked, that his was a respectable job requiring education, that it was something like the future she had wished for.

OLIVER HEARD THE telephone from down on the bridge and he hurried up the side of the slike, swept path, kicking the snow from his insulated gumboots on the wall beside the front door. He had jarred his back on the ruts in the Cae Blaidd, but he was blasted if he would let Cefin see it, and he stood erect as he arrived in the hall, where his mother was approaching with her eyes on her walker and her shoes slow and careful on the carpet. She had, as usual, removed her apron, as if the caller would know or care. At the sudden cold and the outside light she lifted her face to see through her spectacles, nodded to him and waited for her grandson to weight down his bags with a stone on the step, pull off his wellies and help her back into the kitchen.

"Panty," said Oliver, putting the receiver to his good left ear.

"Oh . . ." said Griffin. "I did think I called your landline, boy."

"And I did think you was on holiday."

"Oh, I am, boy, I am . . . Is there a baby, is there?"

"None as I've noticed."

"How's the weather?"

"Bloody starving. Twenty below up Llangodee last night, if you would believe it? Diesel was froze, look. They couldna start the tractor!"

"Never!"

"How's it there?"

"Oh. Hot. Too hot for my liking . . . Afternoon it is, see?"

"Is it, by golly?" Oliver peered through the ice-webbed window, raising his voice against the thundering in the yard.

"Boy get up the fields all right, did he?" Griffin asked.

"That's him coming back now, it is. He's been round Cwmpiban and all. Hell, but that is a machine he's got."

"Heated seat, look. She'll keep you balmy downstairs, I'm telling you now!"

With a clack of the latch on the sitting-room door, Ada appeared on the doormat beside him: her top half, make-up and enough cleavage behind her dangling silver necklaces to swallow a small child; her bottom half, pyjamas and an old pair of tartan slippers. In the middle her belly was a perfect bubble. Since she had that set to her scarlet lips, Oliver passed the phone without another word and set to peeling off levels of plastic—the jeans and jacket he wore underneath as dry as they had been that morning.

In the kitchen Cefin was standing in his socks among a bundle of ash plants, a three-wheeled drinks trolley and a breach of journals from the Ministry of Agriculture.

"Is that Griffin, is it?" asked Etty from the table.

"It is, Mam, yes. Do you want I should help you with that, do you?"

She fiddled with the dial in her ear, so Oliver repeated his question, turning his hands like slices of toast above the hot-plates of the Rayburn.

"Just sharpen up the fire if you would, love, please?"

"Can't I just burn this bloody lot, Dad?" asked Cefin.

"Burn it?" said Oliver. "Bloody antiques them, boy."

It would, it seemed, be another day of waiting. Dropping a few more bruns into the furnace, Oliver looked instinctively at the tall, pale space by the larder door, and then at Idris's grandfather clock, which was once more tocking out the seconds. There had been a time, with the Christmas markets, when his mother could gut and pluck the geese almost as fast he was able to catch them—her fingers sprite among the sharp little pugs, the fern on the floor and the lice in her petticoats. These past two weeks there had always been something getting in the way of them moving out: all of their things to be taken to Erwood, the boiler in the bungalow, the coming of the snow and Griffin jetting off on yet another holiday. And meanwhile Ada was two days due, and four days past the full moon to boot—although you couldn't go listening to that old doddle or you'd be worrying over half of the people on the planet. Had Oliver's word meant a damn with the girl, he would have had her in Hereford a good week since—he couldn't believe anyone required her prognostications all that urgently—but Ada was Ada. She could have gone into labour this very moment, on the phone to her father or back on her webcam, and he would not have moved without her instruction.

The old bunch of mistletoe was so frail and dusty that its few remaining leaves went fluttering to the carpet as Oliver worked the tack out of the beam. There was a pain in his spine as he went to pick them up; he grunted despite himself, but pinned up the new one and took a step back—glancing at his mother, who had, in fairness, stripped the better part of the bird's plump breast.

"There's lovely." She smiled.

"You're not kissing me, I'll tell you that much," said Cefin, who had started work on the bread-and-cheese cupboard.

"Don't be shy, boy. Come along now."

The sun had arrived in the kitchen window; it was working its way down the snow-dressed apple trees, resolving them into molten light. As casually as he could manage, Oliver eased himself into his chair and watched his son kneel to unload the drawers—the window bright on the skin and the stubble of his head. With ink-stained fingers and bitten nails, he piled in a box a nursing qualification from the St. John's Ambulance and a lopsided owl that Oliver had painted at school, an album of earmarks and an ellern whistle that Albert had whittled one winter's evening. Then he found a dog tag: a fibre disk on an old leather bootlace, which Oliver bent to retrieve from the box. He held it at arm's length so he could read the name pressed into its face, then dropped it in a pocket of his jacket.

IT WAS UNUSUAL for the doorbell to ring at the chapel. Nigel did not know many people locally—there were not that many people to know—and its sudden peals made him start and spill redcurrant juice across the slate worktop. Since he was alone in the little galley kitchen, he wiped his hands on the drying-up cloth. He closed the lid of the laptop on the recipe and made his way into the lounge, where Miriam was settled with her first glass of wine and her daily fix of Australian soap operas. Above her a cavity in the upstairs floor allowed a brass chandelier with frilly glass shades to hang all the way from a latticed pine ceiling, which had once been the ceiling of a single room. These features, these intimations of the past; they did bring him pleasure, whatever qualms he had had about retiring to a graveyard. The way that the plaster stopped short of the doors to reveal the original stonework. The way that the windows straddled the floors so that, from the outside, the building might not have changed at all.

He flicked the switch at the end of the bookcase and the lamp shone over its neat lace doily and twice in the double-glazed door to the extension.

"Oh," he said. "Good evening, Mrs. Hamer. Mr. Hamer."

"Good night, Mr. Wilbraham."

The estate agent had warned them that the garden would remain consecrated ground, that they would have to mow around the headstones and admit the occasional visitor. The inconvenience was reflected in the price. In practice, though, the only visitors the graves ever received were this ancient lady and her crag of a son, whom stories followed in such dizzying multitudes that, in Hay or Builth, Nigel had only to mention that he lived in Rhyscog before he was apprised of another. It was said he had pulled up a cattle grid by hand to keep the police from disrupting a fight. It was said he had flattened the face of the butcher everybody called Nosey Powell. He was, supposedly, one of the old type, which made Nigel wonder distantly if the former height of the chapel might have been a matter of necessity. All he could say was that if this vast, grizzled man with his sovereign rings, his garish waistcoat peeping from his coat and a raven on his shoulder like some pagan sentinel had ever been typical, then the valley's population had changed beyond recognition.

"Will you come in?" he asked, since the cold had already

penetrated his cardigan. He could feel the hairs rising on his arms and his chest. "Have a glass of wine."

"No no," said Mrs. Hamer. "You're very kind. We'll just go round the back, if we may?"

"Of course, Mrs. Hamer . . . There's really no need to ask."

"Thank you. Well. We should slip on, then."

"Happy Christmas," he added.

"And to you, Mr. Wilbraham."

Nigel watched them continue along the face of the chapel—their torchlight glancing from the untrodden path, the shadows of the headstones turning beside them, the moon's quieter light on the snow. Mrs. Hamer walked cautiously, planting her sticks, her son not so much holding her arm as taking her entire weight. What was it Bridget had said, at the garage? She'd like a pair of shoes made out of her skin. Nigel did not know much about the woman. She must have been married, to judge by the name. She must have had at least one other child or she would not have come here, every Sunday of the entire year, to that lonely stone tucked against the blank north wall. Whether she actually had been raped as a girl he had no idea, but frankly, in these vigilant hills, he did not think it likely.

He cupped and blew on his smooth, hairy hands, then went to finish the redcurrant jelly before their grandchildren arrived.

IN THE PLOCK the flames boiled into the darkness, acrid with feathers and green-burning paint. The two old mattresses were holding their shapes, but their inwards were open and looked red hot and, as Cefin watched, the bonfire sank beneath them and they folded slowly and merged. The sparks rose high on the pluming heat, out of the moon shadow cast by the chicken shed, drifting only at the height of its roof like stars unfixed from the gaping sky. A few fell again into the fire-coloured snow. Climbing the gate back into the yard, Cefin lugged the diesel drum into the barn and left it by the wooden steps leading to his office. He took the fir he had cut from the Pant plantation and returned across the hard-frozen ruts to the house, which seemed in the moonlight as pale as the tall, sheer fields.

"Tree coming in!" he announced, pushing through the front door, scattering needles on the beige fitted carpet he really would have to pull up. "You all right, are you?"

There was a sign on the door of the sitting room that read A. HAMER: ANIMAL COMMUNICATOR.

"Hmm," said Ada, from his grandmother's chair.

Had Cefin stopped moving he would, he was sure, have been left almost paralysed, as bare as he had felt when they were living at the Welfrey and had climbed onto the great, hunched hill to lie with nothing between themselves and the stars but the tips of their cigarettes. Nine generations of people named Hamer—ten, perhaps at any moment—and now all this was on his shoulders. The house was silent, ancient, leaden. In the kitchen, where he could no longer hear the bonfire, the only sounds were the hiss of the Rayburn, the tick of the remaining grandfather clock and the turning page of Ada's book. He removed his hat, which was rigid with cold, shivered briefly and wiped his misting glasses. He stood the tree in its plastic holder, where the other grandfather clock had stood, and began to untangle the lights in the box— humming to stifle his need for a smoke, or a drink, or anything at all that would share just a bit of the weight.

"Cefin?" said Ada.

"Yeah."

"Would you please sit down?"

"Hang on . . ." He wove the lights round the tree's spreading branches and pushed the plug into the socket for the television. "You don't want the telly on, do you?"

"Sit!" she said.

Cefin perched reluctantly on his father's chair, the heat of the Rayburn ringing from his scalp. The arms of his glasses were still like ice. He picked with his teeth at the skin round a nail while his wife set down her book and stood—one hand supporting the bell of her belly as she waddled towards him over the hearthrug.

"Now then," she said, revolving, lowering herself onto his lap.

She still wore her make-up from the day's consultations. Her unpinned fringe hung into her eyes.

"I was just . . ." he said.

"I know. And there's plenty of time."

"Do you like the tree?"

"I love the tree." She twisted to kiss him, her full bulk pressing on the bones in his thighs.

"I think I'm going to have to move the bathroom. I mean, it's no good downstairs, is it?"

"You'd have thought." Ada remained at her sideways angle. She ran a hand across his chest. "All of them books. You'd have thought one would mention as pregnancy makes you so bloody randy all the time."

Cefin hesitated. "Do you . . . want to go upstairs, do you? I put the new mattress on the bed."

"It's cold upstairs."

Her hand continued to the buttons of his jeans, which she

opened in turn, slipping her fingers into his boxer shorts and stroking the soft skin of his thigh. She held the bar of the Rayburn, got back to her feet and lay in stages on the old rag hearthrug—the coloured lights on her long pale hair and the label protruding from the back of her pyjamas.

"What if it gets things moving?" Cefin asked.

"Then you shall have to drive."

"Well . . . What if they come back?"

"Cefin. They're not coming back tonight." She waited for him to lie down behind her, wriggling pleasurably as he curled to her shape. "Anyway, it's not their house, is it?"

DEATH, ETTY THOUGHT, might look like this: this non-day, this anti-day. For all her decades of Methodism, she had never quite bought the hell of the chapel, nor the tame and sunlit pastures of its heaven. This snowy cast of hills and valley, these snow-cloaked trees with their long black shadows; they seemed altogether more like lifelessness. She heard her son grunt as he picked her up—an arm round her shoulders, another in her knees, as he would lift her into and out of the bath—and arrived on her seat with her two sticks hanging. Thankfully there was warmth in the truck. It dissolved the clouds of her breath on her spectacles. She shivered and buried her hands in her pockets, watching through the arches of the windscreen wipers the high moon over Llanbedr Hill—its face askance, as if its gaze were on some other planet.

Oliver climbed into the driver's seat, put the key in the ignition but left it there.

"Alexander," he said.

Etty felt a tremor in her eyelids.

"Was that him, was it?" He dug in his jacket and held up the dog tag on its broken lace.

"Alexander," she repeated.

"What does that mean?"

"Olly . . ." She winced and turned to look at him: his scarce grey hair left wild by his hat, his face in lines of black and white. "Olly, what can I say? You found that thing, you know the most of it. I . . . It happened. I was ashamed. But you're here. That's all."

The dog stirred briefly by her feet, her tall ears bent on the glove compartment. On the handbrake Maureen was standing in silence, and Etty realized that she could no longer remember if she had always been the same bird or if there had been several, given the same name out of convenience.

"Are you still ashamed, are you?" he asked.

"No, love," she said. She touched his arm. "No."

Beyond the snow on the bonnet and the few tracks striping the rising lane, an upstairs window shone at the Pant and vanished again as its curtains closed on these ghosts of fields, these impressions of hedgerows—these familiar things made dislocate, like themselves. They had, Oliver thought, done everything they could to be rid of the night. They had banished it from the house. They had reduced it to the shadows that fled from the torch or the simple foil for a blackened reflection, covered in the moment it was seen. They had usurped the stars as they had usurped the sidelands, deeming them useless, driving them back into the dwindling hills. He sat with his mother in the cab of the Navara and gradually, as their shoulders subsided, they became to one another again, as they had always been, almost transparent—like the sheer scraps of clouds or the vapour trails where the stars showed so clearly that they might not have been there at all. He knew that the shame had never quite been hers. She knew that he did not really care, not really, not so much as he had ever obliged her to speak. A plane was ploughing its rut through the sky—its three white lights a closer constellation, its blinking red the only colour they could see.

The days, they thought, would be drawing out tomorrow.

ACKNOWLEDGMENTS

I AM HUGELY grateful to everyone who spoke with me when I was working on this book: Finn Beales, Dr. Philip Cleland, Jeff Davies, Toby Eckley, Ieuan and Gwyneth Evans, Chris Havard, Robert and Llinos Jones, Alun Price, Matthew Price, Rose and Elwyn Price, Walter Price, John Pugh, Ernie Roberts and Robert Tyler.

And to everyone who read and commented on its various drafts: Charlotte Ward, Philip Gross, Clare Alexander, Will and Jenny Bullough, Richard Gwyn and Gerard Woodward. And, of course, Max Porter and Daphne Tagg at Granta, and Noah Eaker and Kathy Lord at Random House.

I would also like to thank (the great) Julian Broad, everyone at the *Brecon and Radnor Express*, Trefor Griffiths for the permission to quote W. H. Howse, and Christopher Meredith, whose poem "Borderland" (in the excellent *Air Histories*) was on my mind throughout.

For her work on the tree photographs, and for most other things, my thanks and love to Charlotte, as ever.

ABOUT THE AUTHOR

TOM BULLOUGH grew up on a hill farm in Wales, where he still lives. He has worked as a sawmiller, a music promoter in Zimbabwe, a tractor driver, and a contributor to various titles in the Rough Guides series. At present he is a Visiting Fellow at the University of South Wales. *Addlands* is his fourth novel, the first to be published in the United States.

tombullough.com

ABOUT THE TYPE

This book was set in Baskerville, a typeface designed by John Baskerville (1706–75), an amateur printer and typefounder, and cut for him by John Handy in 1750. The type became popular again when the Lanston Monotype Corporation of London revived the classic roman face in 1923. The Mergenthaler Linotype Company in England and the United States cut a version of Baskerville in 1931, making it one of the most widely used typefaces today.